OP let 10⁴

ICED

CED

RAY SHELL

RANDOM HOUSE
NEW YORK

All rights reserved under International and
Pan-American Copyright Conventions. Published
in the United States by Random House, Inc.,
New York, and simultaneously in Canada by
Random House of Canada Limited, Toronto.

Library of Congress Cataloging-in-Publication Data
Shell, Ray.
Iced/Ray Shell.
p.   cm.
ISBN 0-679-42897-6
1. Narcotic addicts—United States—Fiction.   2. Crack (Drug)—
United States—Fiction.   I. Title.
PS3569.H39295I25   1994
813'.54—dc20   93-44743

Manufactured in the United States of America
98765432
First Edition

Designed by Oksana Kushnir

To all the families who lived in the Louis H. Pink Houses in East New York, Brooklyn, from 1960 to 1970

—love from your paperboy.

Thou shalt neither vex a stranger, nor oppress him:
for ye were strangers in the land of Egypt.

—EXODUS 22:21

And with him are the keys of the invisible. None but he knoweth
them. And he knoweth what is in the land and the sea. Not a leaf
falleth but he knoweth it, not a grain amid the darkness of the
earth, naught of wet or dry but (it is noted) in a clear record.

—SURAH VI VERSE 59

ICED

There ain't no date. . . . .
I don't know what time of day it is.
I don't care.

People call me Cornelius Jr.
That's my name.
I think.
I don't care.

My mother the money woman (she used to be the money
woman, she moved away) gave me that name. Everybody seems
to have a mother.
They curse a lot, they scream a lot, they cry.
I guess it's because they are women.

I used to be somebody . . . . a long time ago.
I don't dream much anymore.
I used to dream in color like the colors of Miami Vice.
I miss that program. When did it go off?
I dream about me. I dream about the shit I used to have.
I USED TO HAVE SHIT!
GOOD SHIT!!!
In fact my shit was very correct, very, very correct as they used to
say back in the day. I don't know what they say now.
I DON'T CARE!!

■

I have to write down what I remember and how I feel before it's
all gone. A little bit goes every day . . . . after I finish pipin'.
I don't want to talk about the pipin' bit yet. That comes later.
When I thought about writing this, I had a very important
reason why I wanted to do it. Wanted to remind myself of what
I was. . . . What I used to be, because I forgot. Soon it's gonna be
gone.

I told you I'm Cornelius. I'm forty-four or forty-five. I had a
birthday a while back.
My mother and sister used to send me cards to remind me that I
made another year (mother-talk).
They don't send me them anymore . . . Maybe they do send
them and I don't get them. Maybe the ghost-people steal
them like they steal all my other shit—like my welfare checks
and bills.
I REMEMBER BILLS!
I REMEMBER RENT!
I'm glad the ghost-people steal the bills.
I call them the ghost-people because I never see them, I only see
what they've done to me.

I live . . . stop. . . . . That word **LIVE** confuses me.
I don't live.
I am alive. I breathe. I don't live.
I remember life. It ain't like this.
It's more like what the TV used to show, not like Cosby, more
like Good Times (remember that show?), we didn't laugh as
much as they do but I had a mother, a father, a brother and a
sister. My mother's name is . . . . Cora. She went away after my
father died. His name is . . . was Cornelius too. I had a brother,
but that was a long time ago, he died too, he died first. He had
a name but it hurts my head when I try to remember it. It began
with an N . . . Nate or Nathan.
I see his face a lot. When the pipe is hot and the smoky
whiteness rushes into my brain, I see his face smiling at me and I

4

laugh. It makes me choke and cough up the goodness and I curse because I'm losin' the goodness and I can't afford to lose the goodness but I still see his face.

NATHAN
He died.
First.

My sister lives down-Brooklyn with her husband, this sucker who don't like me. I used to go down to her place and see her. I would jump the subway-money-thing, catch the train and go down and see her, get some money for the pipe-man and see her, but she told me that her husband didn't want me comin' 'round there.
She would cry every time she saw me. Cry all the time, like a woman. She would take my hand into hers, call me "Junior . . . Junior . . ." like she was trying to wake me up or something. She'd try to feed me. I was never hungry. Not for chicken and rice. Lorraine . . . yeah that's her name. She pays the rent on this place, she must pay it, she or my mother 'cause I don't pay it, and the ghost-people ain't come round to throw me out like they done to some of the other people that used to live 'round here.

You must understand something first.
IT WASN'T ALWAYS LIKE THIS!!!
Things used to be up.
So up.
It's hard for me to tell you how up, specifics escape me.
I see snapshot memories.
My memories used to run across my mind like the movies.
Like a good fast movie. Like The French Connection.
A whole block of memories got smudged or erased when the pipe time came. I don't know how it happened.
Memories that used to hip-hop like angry roaches across my brain movie-style slowed down to comic-strip-frames in a funny paper like Peanuts.

5

Now my memories come in snapshots. One at a time.
I really got to concentrate to focus them in.
Sometimes I feel that I'll just white-out!
There won't be no picture in my mind of anything.
It'll just be white and black interference signals like when the
last picture of TV goes off.

CLICK-SNAP
ME-MOMMIE-DADDY!
Nobody else. Good feeling.
DADDY SMILED THEN!
Didn't march and bark back then. . . .

Fade-fade-focus-click-snap

Nate and me sharing a bed . . . my little brother what's-his-name?

Nappy-head-Nate!

Nathan . . . Nathaniel—yeah Nate!

Skelly-in-the-hallway, handball-in-the-alley Nate.

Maybe I'm just makin' it up.
Maybe it never happened.
There's nothing in this room to tell that there ever was a
NATE.
No picture-letter-card . . . . just a snapshot memory . . .
that keeps crackin' in my head.
I know he died.

Click-click-snap-snap
Lorraine cryin' . . . kicking.
Some people dragging her away from Nate in a box.

Dead-in-his-graduation-suit.
Lorraine screaming . . . beatin' the air . . . screamin' from her guts
like a she-goat was kickin' her in the stomach or somethin'. . . . .
People draggin' her through the church doors.
The people ain't ghosts 'cause I can see them.
I don't want to remember any more right now . . .
I'll get back to it later.
It takes too much concentration.

MARCH 14, 1991 — 3AM

These days (and nights) all I want to do is pipe.

That's all!

My only ambition is to pipe.
Pipin' is my occupation. . . . I will explain later
I am dedicated solely to the whiteness
the goodness pipe brings me.
Symbols are easy. They tell. Quickly.

PIPE = (equals) goodness warmth family cover distance safety one-ness

To be without pipe = (equals) torture confusion coldness hunger

UNTHINKABLE THINGS.

MARCH 22, 1991 — 11PM

There's an old picture of me I keep in an ancient shoebox.
My Holy-Covenant-Memory-Box.
Bits of golden papers, neophyte scribblings, snapshots.

Daddy.
Mama.
Lorraine.
I cut Nate out.
He died.
Certificates. My life.
This is what I keep in a box under my bed wrapped in a woolen
winter coat mama sent me last Christmas (I think).
I look at this picture of me-like-I-usta-be.
I see a dude who looks like he should be president of United
Steel.
This guy is smiling like Al Jarreau . . . .
like he knows something I don't know.
The street-demons that control the pipe-rocks would call this
guy a jerk . . . a sucker . . .

On the street there are only two kinds of people.
Dicks and suckers.
The bigger the dick the deeper the suck.
I hear White boys say of someone they don't like—
"He's such a dick!"
They don't know shit.
Most White people don't.
They wished they could be a real dick.
Come to think of it, the White folk that run the US Gov-ment are
dicks.
In fact:
**THE UNITED STATES GOV-MENT IS THE BIGGEST DICK IN THE
UNIVERSE!!**

They got the whole world sucking.
But they better watch out 'cause the Africans got a real HUGE-
HARD-ON comin' and they're about to fuck ol' Uncle Sam up the
ass without a condom or KY.
They gonna fuck ol' Uncle Sam big-time.

■

This guy in the picture, this Cornelius Jr. is a real wicked dude.
Wicked in the good sense.
Y'know like the homies would call a real brilliant brother "bad"
meaning GREAT, EXCELLENT.
Well, this Cornelius Jr. this me-that-I-usta-be was better than bad,
this me-that-I-usta-be was wicked.

This Cornelius Jr. had it all figured out at fifteen and six months.
He was his mama's joy and his daddy's pride.
Yeah my dad Cornelius Sr. was real proud of me.
I was a true platinum chip off his old diamond block.
I was his Rosetta stone.
Seeing me made anyone understand him and he loved that.
I was accepted into Columbia University at age sixteen.
I was gonna be a lawyer.
I graduated from Franklin K. Lane High School in East New York
at age sixteen entered Columbia and for two whole years my life
was paradise.
I moved out of my daddy's house into an apartment near
Washington Square Park in the Village in Manhattan.
This was 1964.
Washington Square Park was the center of all happenings.

(Excuse me, there's a knock on the door.
I will ignore it.
Probably ghost-people trying to take something away from me.
Probably that freak Linda wanting to suck-my-dick for $10 so she
can pipe!
I need my $10 so I can pipe later.
I just took a hit to put me in a 1964 state of mind.
This shit is so sweet! Like peppermints dipped in honey.
Smoke rushin' my body, feel so warm, so loved. The pipe loves
me! It wants me, like a big-fat-wet-pussy! The pipe sucks me up
as I suck it!
Bliss! Bliss! Heaven! Heaven!)

■

MOTOWN-STAX-BEATLES-ROLLINGSTONES-STAPLESINGERS-
JAMESCLEVELAND-SHIRLEYCAESAR

These were my music Angels.
I played them on my phonograph.
I didn't have no CD or separated stereo shit then, just an old
phonograph player my sister Lorraine and my brother Nate gave
me for a graduation present.
I'd sit in the window of my apartment overlooking Washington
Square Park, the Supremes or the Ronettes singing in the
background, and watch the hippies throwin' frisbees down
below in the park.

". . . . be my baby . . . be my pretty baby. . . ."

Blonde-White-girls in Day-Glo scarves and halter tops would
dance and smile up at me hoping I'd smile back and invite them
up to my room so they could see firsthand if the big-Black-myth
was true.
And "YES" they'd yell as I lifted their thighs high in the air and
shoved my dick as far and as hard as it would go into their
asshole.
And they'd scream "YES."
I never fucked a White girl in the pussy.
My dick is sacred.
My Black dick only fucked Black pussy.

BUT

I'd fuck a White girl or boy (if I was feeling freaky) up their ass in
a minute.
This was a political act to me.
This was my revolutionary statement.

Ferguson (the White boy I roomed with) was a beatnik.
We'd check out the beat clubs that still existed in the Village.
They had been moved lower down to the East Side 'cause folk

*music was comin'. We'd sometimes go to a coffeehouse on
Bleecker St. and catch the no-singin'-mother-fucker Bob Dylan.
I liked his songs though he couldn't sing worth-a-shit!
"The answer my friend is blowin' in the wind. . . ."
(blowin' in the wind my friend blowin'-blowin'-blowin' just like
the goodness from my pipe. I'm blowin' this dick 'n' I don't care
who don't like it.)*

MARCH 27, 1991 — 2PM

*1964–1966—The first free years of my life!
It seems so long ago and so unbelievable that I know that it
couldn't have happened. Maybe I read about it or saw it in a
movie
like Alice's Restaurant
or
Hair
But the reality was better than both of them movies.
Hair the stage play was kind of like it but not really so good.
All I had to do was go to class, work in the record department of
May's department store on 14th St., smoke my reefer, go to clubs
and fuck all the pussy and ass I could get my dick into.*

PERFECTION
*Bliss like this white crystalline wonder
I suck into my brain which torches this memory into action.
I search the floor anxiously
Examining each white ash and lint.
Making sure I drop none of the goodness.*

NATE DIED

*I know he did.
I remember the funeral.
Everybody shocked.*

Everyone crying.
Perfect-Angel-Nate
Nate would stay with me sometimes when daddy got too super-
sonic.
It was said that Ferguson (White-boy-I-roomed-with) was a
junkie.
I didn't know because he never did it in front of me.
He and Nate became fast friends.
Maybe I should have watched my younger brother more
carefully, but I was too busy watching myself. I couldn't take him
everywhere with me. Daddy plastered my soul with guilt.
Mama wreathed my head.
Said I should have watched Nate, should have taken him
with me

BUT

that's why I didn't take him with me.
I didn't want him influenced by the new toys I had found in my
new secret garden. I wasn't going to play snake to his Eve.
I didn't have to.
Ferguson wrapped his white rattle around my brother's black ass
and stung him hard.
Before I could say Smoky Robinson
Nate was a fully-fledged-stealin'-from-daddy-needle-poking-
noddin' **JUNKIE.**

I kicked Ferguson's ass and threw him out of the apartment, but
that didn't help Nate.
Nate was hooked. Hooked hard.
He would disappear for weeks.
I would walk the streets looking for him. I'd wind up in Harlem
on 144th St. in a bombed-out-ghetto-room-with-the-ceiling-half-
blasted-in.
The window nail-boarded shut to keep other junkie demons out.
There Nate would be noddin' or sleepin'.
Piss-shit-stinkin'-dirty-black-from-no-bath-in-a-month.
I would sit there and wait for him to come around.

12

■

IT WASN'T MY FAULT NATE BECAME A JUNKIE!

I say that here and now.
If my mother ever sees this or if anyone reads and knows her,
tell my mama Mrs. Cora Lorraine Washington that
IT WAS NOT MY FAULT THAT NATE BECAME A JUNKIE!!!
Those years 1964–1966 were the only free years of my life.
I had spent all the other years being the perfect son, the perfect
brother, the perfect student, the perfect child.
Cornelius Jr. the perfect!
I should be canonized!
I deserve sainthood at least.
Cornelius Senior was Dr. Terrible.
I feared him more than any hood in the street!
He would kick my ass more thoroughly than any other would-be
Tyson at the time could. He was lethal and sadistic with his shit.
Belt buckles, wire hangers, whips, even heated irons did his
bidding.
I obeyed out of sheer fear.
I craved his approval fiendishly.
His approval, his praise was the rock of my existence.
When his temper cracked the peace of the night sky, we all ran
for cover.
Mama nagged, pleaded, blackmailed us into obedience.
Threatening to feed us to daddy-dragon if we stepped out of
line.
At the end of a day, whenever a key turned in the lock, we knew
it was daddy time. My mind would swim through the day's
events like a drowning man's life flashing before him, searching
every act to see if I was found wanting, if my ass was hanging in
the balance.
I lived like that for sixteen years.
I was smart.
I was brilliant but not for brilliance's sake.
I was not a hood, I was not a thief, I didn't or couldn't run away.
I was not programmed that way.

School was my only way out.
"Education is the key. . . ." mama told me repeatedly.
All day. Every day.
So I learned.
I gobbled up every book, film, newspaper, encyclopedia that
grew out of my school or public library. I devoured information
feverishly, like Dracula, sucking up knowledge so I could pass the
holy SATs and win a salvation-scholarship-prize.
The door to my freedom.
The door to my life.
I succeeded magnificently.
I did realize back then that mama and daddy only wanted the
best for me, and death that owned our neighborhood
frightened them, and that fear of my demise and destruction
fueled their acts of intimidation that kept me and Nate and
Lorraine in line.

BUT

they were doing too excellent a job.
I had to run.
I escaped.
Nate died.
Lorraine got married.
Each in our own way ran from a furnace-love that burned us all
too fiercely.
We were not moths.
Our wings couldn't beat that fast.
Pure love is the essence of positivity.
Pure love is the only love.
Cornelius and Cora loved us paranoidly.

I became a zombie after Nate died.
It was really a case of Night of the Living Dead.
I saw Nate everywhere.
In my closet, under my bed, sitting at my desk, smiling at me
from a calendar.

Nate's face.

Marilyn Monroe's body.

Maybe it would have been easier if Nate had died quickly or we had discovered him dead.

Shot in the arm with the eternal hit that had quickened his spirit and stopped his heart.

A smile on his face, a needle in his vein.

Maybe that would have been easier to take.

It took Nate nearly six months to die.

I found him outside the doorway of the Waverly Theater in the Village, one cold January morning.

I had seen him last at daddy's house.

We had all got together for Christmas dinner.

It was a good time.

I had received fantastic grades that semester, Lorraine was starting a job in Manhattan and Nate had chilled out on the heroin (so we thought).

Cornelius Sr. prayed. Mama sang.

We each said a bible verse and ate.

Stuffed roast turkey, chicken, ham, sweet potatoes, collard greens, potato salad.

A classic down-home feast.

(If I wasn't skying so much from the pipe I'd be hungry just thinking about it. Pipe is my daily bread. Pipe is my shepherd I shall not want.)

Cornelius was not barking. Mama was not nagging.

Being away from them almost made me miss them.

It certainly made it easier to understand them. . . .

BUT

I was so glad that I had another place that I could escape to. Nate was officially livin' at home with Lorraine, mama and daddy, but most times he'd be with me at my apartment or off with some girl or with friends. If you couldn't find him at any of

those places then you knew that he was off somewhere in a nod in junkie-land.
This particular night he said he was going to the movies.
I had some studying to do, so I kissed Lorraine, Cornelius Sr. and mama and hiked up to the subway to get the train back to West 4th St.
Nate took the train with me.
We talked brother talk.
Girls we were dickin'. Guys that we heard wanted to dick our sister.
Cornelius Sr. and mama.
That sort of thing.
Right before I got off, he looked at me with those Bambi eyes of his and asked me to pray for him, which was wild because Nate was always Mr. Super-God, the man who needed no one.
Even as a child Nate played alone and was usually off somewhere wrapped up in his own dimension.
He was almost like a big brother to me.
He thanked me for looking after him and was sorry about all the trouble his jones (as he called it) caused the family.
He said he was starting a methadone treatment in East New York because he wanted to be clean before he started college.
He was due to start at New York University that next September.
He was supposed to have started the previous term but his jones was too strong.

I remember feeling real sad, like swan-song-movie-music was playing in the background, but I shook it off.
It was my stop.
I hugged him, slapped him on the head like I used to do when we were kids, got off the train, turned around and waved at him.
Nate was crying.
He brushed aside the tears and tried to smile as the train pulled out of the station and into the dark-deep-tunnel.

16

I felt kind of scary but I shrugged it off, walked up the stairs and into the cold, juicy, jazzy night that only New York's West Village could deal out in spades.

I walked into Washington Square Park, bought a nickel bag, rolled me a fat joint, smoked in the darkness, as I listened to a would-be Richie Havens strum a guitar in a cracked voice, panhandling for drug money.

Ring! Ring! Ring! Ring!
It was mama-on-the-phone! She sounded wrought, anxious!
Had I seen Nate? Was he stayin' with me?
I told ma I hadn't seen him since Christmas nearly three weeks before.
He was supposed to go with me to this wild New Year's Eve party at La Mama, a freaky-deaky theater place where the actors and actresses walked around naked as a matter of course.
The party was rabid.
It just bit into you and shook your nervous system.

(IT'S FUNNY, all this stuff happened nearly thirty years ago, but pipin' and writin' makes it seem like yesterday. Ask me what happened last week and I'd have to blank ya. Maybe because these are pre-pipe memories, my mind was/is clearer then/now as Judas-according-to-Tim-Rice once said.)

Nate would have loved this party but he never showed up.
I met some freak named Day-Light Moon-Sun.
She sucked my dick as I drank Kool-Aid laced with mescaline, and smoked angel dust.
WILD!

Mama asked me to go up to Harlem and look for Nate and call her if I found anything.
At first I was angry.
I had to go to work in an hour, I had a paper I needed to finish and Nate had promised to cool that drug shit out.

I looked around the local area, came up with zero and went to work.
Later that night after work, I walked up and down the streets of Harlem, into bars, into alleyways, asked people I knew and didn't, stopped and ate some spare ribs on 125th St. and finally about 6am the next day walked out of the West 4th St. subway, cold-tired-hungry-and-angry.
I had spent the entire night walking the streets and had not scored.
I looked across the street and saw this flash of red as I came up the stairs.
It was a hooded, slouched figure, huddled in the doorway of the Waverly Theater, a cinema, right around the corner from my place, frequented by NYU students, art freaks and other assorted weirdos.
I knew it was Nate right away.
I could tell by the way his head hung to the side as he slept.
I ran across the street, my heart pumping like a sledgehammer.
Maybe he had froze to death on his way to see me.
Caught-in-a-nod. He was hard and cold but he was alive.
I could feel his heart beating faintly even though he didn't appear to be breathing. I ran to the pay phone and called 911. The ambulance got there in five minutes. Must not have been much business at 6am in the morning.
The ambulance wanted to go to Kings County Hospital but I insisted they take us to St. Vincent's which was right down the street. When I was sure the doctor was with Nate I called mama.

DADDY LOOKED AT ME LIKE A SNAKE!
I remember that line from some White-boy song.
Soft Cell I think the name of the group was.
Like all this was my fault.
Lorraine tried to take my side. She kept asking me what had happened.
I must have told her ninety-nine times that I didn't know, that I found Nate in the street.

The doctor came out to talk to us.
Strangely enough Nate hadn't overdosed as we thought he had.
There wasn't even fresh heroin in his system.
He was trying to stop.
He was in a coma. It appeared that he might have pneumonia.
Actually they didn't know what was wrong with Nate.
They put him on a life-support system because he was so weak.
He wouldn't have been able to breathe without it.

DADDY LOOKED AT ME LIKE A SNAKE!
"If you had stayed your ass at home, this would never have happened!"
WHAT!!!!
SHOCK!!!!
HORROR!!!!
SHOCK!!!!
The great, the holy, the pure Cornelius Nathaniel Washington Sr. had uttered a profane world!!!!
It wasn't the context of the sentence that the word appeared in that shocked us all so much as the word itself.
ASS
I had never heard that word slide past my daddy's lips!
Behind, butt, rear end. . . .
Anything else but ass!
At first I didn't understand that he was talking to me.
But his knife glare stabbed me to the soul and I knew without a doubt that the ass he was referring to was mine.
He said it again.
"If you had stayed your ass at home, this would never have happened!"

It was always agreed that I would move into Columbia University's dorm when I was accepted into the school.
The dorm was in mid-Manhattan around 90th St.
It was expensive and though I was on full scholarship, it was in a part of the city that I had no affinity with.
After getting the job at May's department store, I met Ferguson,

who also worked there. Ferguson had an apartment near Washington Square Park. He had a cool deal on the place and he needed a roommate, I moved in.

I loved the Village because the people there were different from the dead-headed-tight-assed-nerks that made up most of Columbia University's student world.
At the time all this happened I was thinking about transferring to NYU. I really didn't want to become a lawyer, too much lying, I was becoming more interested in Mass Communications.
I was happy away from home.
I was free.
When the subject came up at home, I argued that living near my campus would be better than commuting back and forth from Manhattan because I'd be closer to my school, closer to my job, it'd be cheaper and safer (mama liked that one) and I could concentrate more on my studies (daddy liked that one).
I knew that daddy had some apprehensions about the idea because it meant that he couldn't monitor my every breath

BUT

Up till now he had kept his reservations to himself.
This was classic Cornelius!
Nate was lying in intensive care on a life-support system in the next room and his being there was my fault because I had moved out of my father's house.

All I wanted was a life!
My own life.
Freedom.
The choice to discover who and what I was.
You can never know what and who you are, living in your parents' house.
Everything in that house is a reflection of their choices.
Down to the color of the toilet paper in the bathroom.
I left home to explore these choices.

I didn't leave home to make my brother into a junkie and die in St. Vincent's Hospital from a weird and strange disease that had no name in 1966.

I believe now that my brother was in the hospital suffering from what we now call AIDS.
Yeah, they say it takes eight years to incubate and all that shit, but the truth is they don't know how quick or how long it takes to get AIDS.
All I know is that my brother Nathaniel had been messin' with needles for at least two and a half years before he died—it could have been longer.
He probably used other people's works at first.

During the six months that he stayed in the coma, every disease known to man and some not known ravaged his young body.
After about four and a half months Nate became unrecognizable.
Scaly, dry, dark patches would appear on his skin.
The doctor said they were bed sores;

BUT

then the sores started growing a gray-black-furry-mossy-kind-of-shit that appeared in Nate's nose and throat as well.
Fungus they called it.
Some nights I'd sit by his bed looking at this creature that used to be my brother and I'd hear his strained, rattling, hoarse breathing. Sometimes he'd break out into a coughing fit.
I'd have to hold him down, take the mask off his nose and try to clean his throat of the growing-mossy-fungus that was clogging his windpipe.
I wanted Nate to die.

I couldn't bear watching him suffer like that.
The doctors assured us that being unconscious made it easier for him but it was hell on us.

21

Mama had our minister come by the hospital to pray for Nate
but it did no good.
No miracle came.
The brother I knew was dead already.
The doctors didn't know what was wrong with him so they
couldn't treat it.
It was a no-win situation.
We all suffered.
I couldn't study.
I couldn't work.
We lived six months at that hospital.

After daddy stopped blaming me for Nate's circumstances, he
started blaming mama, then finally himself.
I don't know which was worse.
It knifed me up to see my father, that once proud paragon of
discipline, humbled to a whimpering, frightened dwarf of
himself feverishly imploring his God to save his son and offering
his own life so that his youngest could live again.
I remember the last night of Nate's life.
Dad was crying and praying and shivering over Nate's bed.
Mama and Lorraine had gone home.
It was just the men-folk of the family.
Nate, silent-cold-furry, like some sleeping wolf-man.
Daddy, pleading-sobbing-praying.
Me, watching.
A silent witness.
Mute from too many prayers, too many denials.
I watched my father's shoulders shake and heard this moan that
oozed up from the pit of his stomach like bile.
I pulled daddy away from the bed.
He turned on me not understanding at first.
Sorrow had weakened him.
He collapsed into my arms crying and babbling incoherently.
I realized then that I loved this stranger in my arms, that I had
always loved him.

I forgave Cornelius Nathaniel Washington Sr. for everything right
then, and decided that I had to do something.
I had to end this.
There's only so much suffering anyone should be made to
endure.

SECRETS

*My secrets are sinister
my secrets are full of guilt
I try to ice-pack them far away
under the section of my life called HURTS.
My secrets hurt me . . . . . .
and as much as I try to skateboard away from them
on a cloud of goodness
they creep up on me
in the darkness of a day
or night
my secrets wear Converse sneakers
fuck Filas
I never hear them coming. . . .*

*I gently led my weakened father to a chair near to Nate's
bedside.
I took the other chair.
We sat there silently like two new lovers who had only just
realized that there was a thing called love between them.
We sat staring at the prone figure in front of us.
Straining to hear his breathing.
Wishing that we couldn't.
Afraid of the thought that was snaking around us . . . . .
that was coiling around our hearts . . . . .
binding our minds into one.
We said nothing.
My father took my hand.*

It shook in my own like a small sparrow that was wounded and
couldn't fly and didn't want to be released.
This was our transfiguration.
I became the father.
My father became the son.

TEARS

I had cried so many in the days and months before that surely
my well must have run dry, surely my soul must be parched,
cracked, thirsty. . . .

BUT

TEARS
FRESHLY FLOWED
tearing down my eyes
rivuleting into my mouth
down my chin
I got up, lifted my father from his chair.
"Go home daddy."
I knew that he knew
I knew that he was afraid
I knew that he wanted me to do it
because he couldn't.

Daddy walked over to the bed, kissed Nate on the forehead and
made the sign of the cross over him.
A protection.
A benediction.
Daddy walked past me never looking back.
Walked out the door.
I was alone
with Nate.

I knew that if I thought about it too much I'd run out of the
room and catch my father up.
But the thought of more coming days like this, more pain like
this, more tears like this, set my mind, steadied my heart.

■

There was a confusion of wires and tubes that connected Nate to the various machines that pushed life into and through his body.

I didn't know enough about any of them to know which one was the right one.

I looked for the fabled plug that I could pull that would stop my brother's life factory.

There were about three or four and I couldn't be sure which one was the one.

Fuck it!

There was a pillow under Nate's head.

I pulled it carefully out from under him.

Nate moaned softly.

His eyes opened and for a moment I thought he was looking at me.

CHRIST!!!!

I was no Judas.

I was no Cain killing this helpless Abel.

I could hear the Nate I knew laughing and joking like as before, back in the day.

He had a way of saying "Go-'head-boy!" that was so "on," so "there."

This was the spear I needed.

"Go-'head-boy!"

I did.

Slowly I pressed the pillow down upon Nate's face, gently like a white cotton ball that you gingerly press against a painful pus-filled-pimple that you know has to be burst but are afraid will hurt a lot.

I pressed the pillow down upon my brother's face.

"Go-'head-boy!"

I could feel the imprint of his face through the pillow and I worried that I was hurting him.

■

"Go-'head-boy!"
Nate's arms began flailing wildly and his legs started jerking and kicking. I almost stopped because I was afraid a nurse or orderly would hear and come running into the room and catch me in the act.

"Go-'head-boy!"
Strangely enough, Nate's flailing arms grabbed 'round the pillow and his hands grabbed at mine—not pulling them apart and off but pressing mine down against his face as if he was helping me.
He was helping me.

"Go-'head-boy!"
I knew it was over.
Nate was gone.
The body stiffened then stopped.
The hands pressing against mine relaxed.
I held the pillow down against his face just a bit longer to make sure.
I got the pillow back under his head and was holding his hands when the nurse rushed in.
She saw me holding Nate's hands.
I wasn't crying then but she understood I needed to be alone.
If she suspected anything she never let on.
Never.

I stayed there holding Nate's hands.
Thinking about what had happened, what had led us to this moment.
All the millions of moments we had shared since my memory began.
Drinking in this face before me, trying to superimpose the face I remembered against the alien face before me.

The nurse must have called my family, because by the time the sun had come up they were there.

My father led me away from the bed, walked me to the hallway,
bought me a cup of hot chocolate, hugged me against his
breast.
I cried then.
I cried like a child.
A tired hurt child.
Mother was silent. Spent.
Lorraine took it the hardest. She became hysterical.

The following days were worse. The funeral worst of all.
I told you about that already.
Lorraine had to be carried out.

The long drive down to North Carolina, to Grandma's old house
and the family burial ground, was brutal.

MARCH 27, 1991 — 11:30PM

You must understand something.
I was not some fifteen- or sixteen-year-old street kid who picked
up the pipe, trying to be "bad" or looking for some new thrill.
I was forty years old when I started pipin'.
It came as a dead end to a long highway of events.
Events that chipped and cracked away at the foundation of
what I called my life.

People see me sitting on the stoop of my building and I know
what they're thinking.
"Dirty . . . stinkin' . . . crack-head"
I can see it in their eyes.
Especially mothers' eyes.
Eyes prayin'
that they never have to see
their child
sittin' as I am,
in my place.

MARCH 29, 1991 — 11PM

Had this terrifyingly horrible dream this afternoon . . . surprised
me.
I don't dream that much anymore since the pipe became my
daily companion.
I'm not smoking as much these days.
It's gettin' expensive.
The end of the month is comin' . . . I'm runnin' out of
money . . . cut down . . . economize.
I cut down my smoking . . . I am more clear . . . I remember my
dreams . . . catch my thoughts more easily which most times isn't
such a great thing . . .

Had this horrible dream.
This evil dream.
I am convinced that evil is the shit of creation . . .
It was about Lorraine, my sister.
In the dream, it seemed that Lorraine was sitting on the top of
this gigantic nest . . . it seemed like it was about twenty-five or
thirty feet high.
Lorraine was glued to it . . . couldn't get away.
The nest was made of bones . . . white bleached bones.
This huge mounded-bone-nest
. . . at the top sat Lorraine smiling . . . a demented Mona Lisa.
I tried to climb the nest of bones to reach and free her.
The higher I climbed the higher . . . faster the nest grew.
Lorraine smiled like she was enjoying it.
Suddenly Lorraine started grunting like she was trying to pass
some great turd that was stuck inside of her . . . grunts grew
louder . . . sharper . . . turned into screams . . .
Lorraine fought to free herself from the bony nest.
I tried to reach Lorraine.
She screamed clawing at the air above her . . . trying to free
herself from the nest.
Some huge white mess bustin' out from under her. . . .

It stunk.
I thought it was the white bony nest growing again underneath
Lorraine . . . the stinkin' white mass explodin' outta Lorraine's ass
was alive.
It stunk like shit from a dead man's stomach.
Lorraine screamed . . . fightin' . . . clutchin' the air. . . .
Her struggle threw the nest off balance toppling Lorraine, flyin'
her headfirst into a shallow ditch filled with white
earthworms . . .

BUT

the fall didn't free Lorraine from the nest . . . from the stinkin'-
white-oozing-something that was escapin' from her ass.
The white-oozing-something was a head . . . a huge white
head. . . .
Fully grown . . . this was no infant.
More and more of the head oozed out . . . lifted itself up . . . I
could read the features . . . they were mine . . . my head . . . my
face. . . .
Lorraine screamed white blood from her mouth and nose.
The stinkin' white me emerged from her ass full-grown. . . .
A naked-stinkin'-white-giant . . . horrible.
Poor terrified Lorraine tried to crawl away from the nest in
vain . . . the white-me-monster pulled her back, eating her, head-
first . . . white blood gushed from each terrible bite . . . finishing
her off.
The last leg emerged from what was left of Lorraine's backside.
Horrible.
Gigantic white-me-monster looked down on tiny-me.
Couldn't have recognized me as itself because it started chasing
me.
Stinkin'-gigantic-white-me-monster with the big foot was about
to squash me . . .
I woke up.
Sweating.
Mama usta interpret my dreams.

I'd be afraid to tell her about this one.
Don't even want to think about what it must mean.
I do depend on Lorraine too much.
I drain her time and energy.
The dream might have something to do with what Lorraine told
me the last time I saw her.

Thought she'd never leave . . . shouldda been happy to see
her . . .
I was at first.
I hadn't seen her since last September when she and her dick-less
husband drove me to North Carolina to see mama . . . thought
she came to see me to give . . . some money.
She fuckin' wanted to know about what happened in North
Carolina.
Why mama don't wanna talk about it.
That was after she screamed at me about the lack of furniture in
the house. She went from room to room shaking her
head . . . moaning about mama's beautiful furniture.
She started crying . . . I hate it when Lorraine cries.
"You gotta get yourself together Junior . . ." she said staring at
the space where mama's three-piece suite used to sit proudly like
a sentry on display.
"I'm having a baby Junior . . . . do you hear me? . . . I said I'm
having a baby!!!"
She didn't act like she was happy about having a baby, she was
crying and carrying on.
"I've put in for a transfer at my job . . . I don't want to have my
baby grow up in this wicked city. . . ." She looked at me hard when
she said this like it was my fault that the city was so wicked.
"You gotta get yourself together Junior . . . . me and Kenneth will
not be around to help you no more . . ." All I could think of to say
was to ask her when all this would be happening.
She didn't know exactly. She thought it would take months. She
wants to be moved and settled before the baby is due which is
late October, early November . . . years away from now . . . . eight

*months . . . years away . . . bags of time to get myself
together. . . . . .*
*Lorraine started crying some more . . . walked back and forth
through the apartment sniffling, wringing her hands like some
Lady Macbeth rubbing away blood . . . don't know what she's
crying about.*
I'm the one who should be crying!
She's got big butt Kenneth!
Who I got!?!
*Don't even want to think about it . . . I won't think about it, it's
such a long-way-away. . . . .*
*A lot can happen in eight months . . . could clean myself up in
eight months. . . .*
I could. . . .
Will I?????????
Who knows.
*I tried to make more small talk with Lorraine about the
baby.*
*I tried congratulating her, she just sucked her teeth, looked at
me hard, kissed me real quick, grabbed her pocketbook . . . left.
Just like that . . . didn't even leave me any money!
Ain't seen me in six months, she acts like that.
I don't know what's wrong with the girl.*

*I gotta go to the Centa-Renta now—the Pepsi clock across the
street is screaming at me, it's time to run rocks.
I gotta run rocks tonight so I can get my daily portion.
I've had enough clarity and enough dreams for one day.*

APRIL 1, 1991 — 2PM

*Find it hard to pick up the pen today.
Confession is good for the soul . . . at what price?
Wish I could write to God . . . I don't know if I believe in God
anymore.*

If I did I wouldn't have allowed all this shit to happen to me.
Wouldda cried out to him long ago.
I cry to the pipe.
Thoughts of God threaten me . . . make me feel even more
unworthy.
I need someone else to review me before I can stand in the
majesty of pure holiness.
Maybe I do still believe in God.
I can't face him.
I need someone like Nate I can describe these events
to . . . . someone I can lead by the hand through my garden of
sins . . . make them understand that this wasn't all my
fault . . . that it wasn't always like this . . .

Wish I had a twin brother who I could share these dark secrets with.
Someone just like me . . . not afflicted like me. A twin-me-like-
I-usta-be . . .
I wish he was at the door now . . . I'd let him in . . . we'd sit on the
floor, I'd slowly explain all this darkness to him.
He'd be the pure self that I once was.
The star I'll never get to be.
The brother Lorraine once had.
I miss the me-I-usta-be . . . . . he was a great guy.
He listened.
Calmly . . .
He'd be shocked 'cause he wouldn't know about any of this
murkiness. This murkiness would be alien to him like it once was
for me.
He'd listen, understand . . . I could write to him the parts I
couldn't speak, I wouldn't care if he read it because I know he'd
understand.
He wouldn't judge.

I don't really know why I'm writing this . . . who I'm writing
for . . . myself . . . the world?? . . .
For now I'll write to you . . . my earlier self . . . my twin . . . my
brother. . . .

The white paper.
The white spaces stretch before me endless.
I fill it and presto—I'm not alone.
A word . . . a thought lives with me . . . comforts me . . . challenges
me . . . worries me and fills a need like the goodness does.
So yes I will continue talking to you, I will continue to tell you
my secrets and I won't lie.
I lie daily so I won't lie to you.
". . . . don't dream it . . . be it. . . ." Rocky-horror-shit but true . . . for
once.
Think it and make it so Cornelius. . . . . .
I need you Cornelius. . . . .
I need you my perfect self. . . .
I need you my innocent self. . . .
I can't go on if you don't sit with me and guide my hand.
I need you. . . .

APRIL 17, 1991 — 5PM

I haven't written for a while.
I've been away.
Bingin'.
I usually do it about once a month.
Usually at the beginning of the month after I've received my
check.
The last week of the month is so hateful.
It's the time when I have almost no money.
I feel bad because I can't get high unless I go terrorizing.
Terrorizing is what I call the bandit or criminal activities that I do
to get money for food or mostly for pipin'—when I don't have
any more check-money or Lorraine-money, or mama-money.

More secrets
Sometimes when I think about the things I've done to get my
pipe money I laugh.

I'm usually laughing while the goodness is rushing into my head and the sounds crack off in my brain.

DOOOOOOOOOEEEEEEEEEEEEEEEEEEEE . . . .
DOOOOOOOOOEEEEEEEEEEEEEEEEEEEE . . . .

The world spins
turns upside down
the dooooooooooooeeeeeeeeeeeeee starts
and I'm laughing at what I did to get back to the goodness.

Not being a natural thug, violence comes hard to me.

SO

I try to avoid personal confrontation or acts of physical violence.
I try.
But sometimes, mostly in winter
when I've become sick to the back teeth of begging
and it's so cold
that all you want to do is get the money quick and get inside
out of the cold
I have threatened to cut a few people.
I was only trying to scare them.
Usually some old White lady or man or some nerdy-looking-
White-male student-type.
I avoid young White women out of gratitude to Pia, a young
White woman who was my friend.
She helped me a lot during my middle-passage years, the years
after I got out of the army.
I'll tell you more about Pia later.
But I don't do young White women because I owe Pia.

I don't do Black people young or old male or female for two
reasons:

1. It would not be politically correct.
   I could never agree with Black-on-Black crime
   it's a form of cowardice.

Hurt those like you because they're easier to get next to.
Kill those like you because their lives are cheaper.
You serve less time for killing a Black.
Kill off the competition.
You become top dog of the heap.
Still answerin' to the White man.
Still his lackey.
Still his house nigger or should I say
his 'hood nigger.
There are those who would say that what I do to myself is a crime.
But it's my choice.
I do it to myself.
I try not to hurt anyone else.
I try.

2. All Black people are **CRAZY!!!!**
They're fucking out of their minds.
I'd be their victim before I could say "boo."
Even if I picked on an old Black lady, she'd probably be packin'
an Uzi or a brick and shoot the shit out of me or knock me to kingdom come.
The young "Yo-Yo" boys and girls are all gangsta-mad and would rearrange my anatomy after my first glance.
They do it all the time anyway without provocation heaven forbid I provoke them!
And perhaps
I am a coward too.

APRIL 17, 1991 — 9PM

On the train coming back from Lorraine's

I usta love the subway when I was a kid . . . usta cost ten cents.
Me, Lorraine 'n' Nate would ride the subway every Saturday
afternoon downtown to Hoyt and Schermerhorn St.
Our church was in downtown Brooklyn . . . Saturday afternoon was
Youth Choir rehearsal.
We couldn't sing but we went anyway.
It made daddy happy. It gave mama some peace.
Riding the subway back in those days usta be an adventure.
All kinds of people getting in and out at the different stops.
Complete strangers talking to each other.
The subway was a great place to meet folk.
There was always one drunk who would fall over every time the
train lurched to a stop and everybody in the car would scream
with laughter.
Even the nuns.
Nowadays nobody talks.
Riding the subway is a living-torture-nightmare.
You take your life in your hands.
Nobody bothers me though . . . I am an essential part of the
nightmare.
Makes me laugh.
People are so scared.
Too terrified to make eye contact.
Don't brush up against nobody, God forbid step on someone's
shoes, you might get the shit shot outta you. . . .

BUT

nobody troubles me.
I always get a seat.
I am given a wide berth.
I am always reminded of what I am whenever I ride the subway.
People see me coming, they back off like I'm Dracula or
something.

I must look fierce . . . I don't know . . . I don't have a mirror.
I jimmied the mirrored door to my medicine cabinet and sold it
for $5 a while back.
I don't see myself on a daily basis.
I can't look that bad.
I know I don't stink . . . that much. . . .
I know my clothes are shitty and I'm skinnier than Spike Lee
which makes me laugh because I usta be big!
Almost six feet tall.
I was never body-beautiful but I could turn heads if I wore shorts
or a swimsuit.
Tongues would hang.
Fuckable . . . that's what Quandza used to call me. (I'll tell you
about Quandza later.) Good and fuckable. . . .
Now the only ladies that approach me are other pipe-fiends and
church ladies trying to save my soul.
I should eat more but I ain't never hungry.
I eat rocks.
They eat me.
Alive.
I can feel myself wastin' away . . . bit by bit . . . like my mind.
My mind usta be a jewel.
Now it's mostly glass like my pipe.
Like my pipe it's full of smoke.
I decided that I had to start fanning my mind.
That's why I'm writin' this to blow away the mists.
I'm glad I started writin'.
It forces me to think.
It occupies my time.
It makes the wait until the next hit bearable.
It's made me think about people that I've hypnotized myself to
forget.
Memories of people that I thought I had captured in my own
Pandora's box have now flown the coop. They're bearin' down
on me, draggin' new crazies into my circle of guilt.
It's weird.
I start thinkin' about writin' about someone, next day when I'm

37

out beggin' for pipe money, someone will walk up to me, put
something in my white cup. They'll be a dead ringer for the
person I was thinkin' about writin' about.
Like this red-haired girl sittin' across from me.
Redheads make me nervous and jumpy.
I couldn't remember why until I thought back to last night,
thought about Pia and what happened to her.
But I wasn't ready to write about Pia last night so I pushed
thoughts of her, the twins, Dukey, far back into the shadows of
memory. Then who should get on at the last stop but this Pia-
look-alike-red-haired-White-chick!
If she don't get off soon I'm gonna move to another car.

The train is stopping.
She's gettin' off.
Good.
I ain't ready to talk about Pia yet.

This goofy-snagga-toothed-hippy-haired old guy just got on
wearing a Hair T-shirt.
I ain't seen a Hair T-shirt in eons.
Hair takes me back to the day.
The good old days . . .
". . . my body is walkin' in space . . ."
I always wanted to be in Hair . . .
Get up on stage and take all my clothes off.
Get paid for it.
Musta been big fun.
I saw Hair.
In 1969.
I went with Quandza, this light-skinned-big-hipped-chick who
introduced me to Boston, my dream city.
Quandza took me to see Hair. I loved it.
I danced on stage at the end.
Shared a joint with a hippied Black girl whose gigantic tits were
the only things she had on.

*Yeah, good old Quandza . . . . good old Boston . . . I'll tell you
about Boston . . .*

*I was pipin' last night.
I started thinkin' about Michael Jackson's face.
This song popped into my head . . . this song from Hair . . . now
this hippy guy walks in wearing this Hair T-shirt . . . true
synchronicity . . . I was pipin' last night, was thinkin' about
Michael Jackson's face and this song popped into my head,
". . . trippin' from mainline to mainline . . ." I kept seein' the trip
which is now Michael's face . . . trippin' from shade to shade. . . .
". . . trippin' from mainline to mainline . . ."
I waited all day to get torched.
I'm tryin' to build a will.
I wait.
The reward for waiting is realization of the most virgin . . . most
perfect . . . most sacred . . . first, fuckin' hit!
I take into my mouth my guilty glass dick whose heated shaft
leads to the belled pussy at the end, whose aluminum pussy
hairs hold whiteness of mind, body—soul's salvation . . . I don't
give a fuck! . . . I love to suck!
The whiteness chills me . . .
The goodness soothes me with electric heat pins . . . sometimes it
hurts.
Not as much as daylit reality.
Reality fuckin' hurts.
The only way to survive reality is to ghost-shadow.
The really really rich and the really really poor share only this
magical gift. They are the dons of ghost-shadow.
The really really poor own nothing else except the gift of the
Holy Ghost.
The really really rich own everything.
The extents of their treasures are shadows to them . . . figures on
a computer screen . . . they've never seen all of it . . . they couldn't
touch all of it . . . they've inherited, bought shadows.
They survive.*

Magnificently.
The really really poor, we too survive . . . dreadfully.
The working rats.
The middle cats are highly visible.
They cannot ghost-shadow.
Everybody sees them.
All the time . . . crowded trains, planes, buses, crowded highways
and city streets.
They are everywhere.
Buying.
Paying.
The highly visible working rats and middle cats survive, barely.
They are killed, robbed, sued, accidented, taxed, raped in their
fire to become really really rich top dogs . . .
You never see the really really poor people . . . you see evidence
of their work. Read in the papers, see on the news . . . horror of
their lives . . . yes there are millions of us hanging around, lying
around, dying in the streets. No one acknowledges us . . . nobody
sees us . . . or someone would do something about us. Ghost-
shadow—the new urban-guerrilla warfare
disguise . . . . invisibility . . .
Yes you definitely see evidence of the ghost super-rich.
America!!
The living testimony.
Its plundering imperialism . . .
You never see the really really rich . . . . you see them on TV, in
the movies, in newspapers.
They never visit the ghetto. There are no really really rich Black
people but Michael Jackson is workin' on it which is why I
mentioned him earlier. I was torched last night thinkin' about all
this shit, through the white haze of the high I had a vision of
Michael Jackson.
White-face-and-all.
The fire of the whiteness anoints my mind elevating me to
prophet of the pipe.
An Elijah of the smoke.

I do have visions.
Big-time.
Last night while contemplating ghost-shadow, feeling sad at the realization that there are no really really rich Black people, Michael Jackson came to me in a vision.
I laughed.
Michael was crying.
He was dressed in money.
Millions and billions. . . .
His face was broken . . . I was lying on the floor on my back. . . . I saw him on my ceiling above me . . . he didn't dance . . . he didn't squeal . . . Michael cried.
I hollered!
It was too funny . . . which is why I love to pipe . . . everything becomes too funny . . . I have to laugh . . . I have to.
It's the only way I can stomach what I've allowed myself to become.
I've had to do a lot of weird shit just to be able to pipe.
Shameful, hateful, hurtful deeds that I've tried to erase from the videocassette of this life make me laugh . . .
As I remember things I have done to get piped, all I can do is laugh.
I've sold my dick for the pipe—which makes me laugh because there was a day when I would have given my dick away to anyone who could make it feel good.
Maybe that's the key.
It's in the feelin' . . .
Those that paid me to suck on my dick musta got a good feelin' from it or they would never have parted from their money.
Yeah! I loved the feelin' of their warm wet mouths on my dick. . . . .

BUT

that's not what I was thinkin' about.
My mind wasn't in it.
I was thinkin' about who I could go to and get some more rock
for the pipe now that I had money again.
The memory of those dismal souls (degenerates—daddy
wouldda called them) gaggin' heatedly on my dick as they
jerked themselves off, kneelin' before me after parting with as
much as seventy-five dollars, makes me laugh!
I laugh because I couldda-been-a-rich-man.
There are a lot of suckers in the world—each payin' hard coin
for a suck of good feelin'.
I laugh and laugh . . .
My voice laughs back at me like a lost echo in this busy,
crowded canyon of a city.
I laugh and see that me and the jerk kneelin' in front of me are
one.

SUCKERS . . . . . .

I laugh as I remember a job I had once when I first started pipin'.
I worked as a waiter for a hotel on 48th St.
I don't remember the name of the place.
At first it was a great job. Every day I had tips (money that the
customers left me because they liked my service or the jokes I
told them as I served them their creamed-chipped-chicken-on-
rice) which meant that every night I could go straight to the
pipe-man and get a daily ration of goodness.
I would work from 3pm to 11pm, get home at 12 midnight, be
up smoking all night, then it would be time to go to work again.
It was alright when I was on a four-day work schedule . . . after I
worked my four days I could collapse. Sleep away the next two
to three days.

BUT

When business picked up I was put on a six-day schedule. . . . .
I CRACKED UP!!
I DIDN'T EAT!!!
I COULDN'T SLEEP!!!

BECAUSE . . .

The pipe is a grim-hard-taskmaster. It demands total devotion and attention from its slaves. The pipe replaces the natural need and hunger for food and sleep with a mega-lust-thirst for the milky-weighed-sweetness that emanates from its sticky chalky orifices.

If the pipe is a callous spider weaving white smoky webs among the sinuous branches of my brain, then my soul is the juicy fat fly, ensnared, hypnotized, willingly-waiting to be devoured . . . . . . bit . . . by . . . bit . . .

No love is deeper . . . or stronger . . .

No pussy tighter or wetter . . .

No money is enough . . .

I COULDN'T SLEEP . . .

Sleep deprivation sucks.

I started hallucinating after working five days in a row and not sleeping at night.

Smoking all night.

Big-time hallucinations!

I would be ladling chicken-noodle soup into a bowl and the noodles would turn into forty-skinny-white-Diana-Rosses-snake-dancing-out-of-the-ladle-shimmying-into-the-soul-bowl-screeching-"Stop in the name of love"-loudly!!!

Of course I dropped the ladle and the bowl, howling with terrified mirth!

A White Jewish lady with blue-gray hair sat down at one of my booths.

She was wearing one of those blue-gray-fox-wraps that have fox or chinchilla heads with teeth on one end and claws and feet at the other end.

This lady gave me her wrap and asked me to hang it up.

I know that she must have handed it to me but it seemed to me that the blue-gray-beady-eyed-fox-thing jumped out of her hands snarling and barking at me.

I wrestled the chinchilla-fox-thingy to the floor screaming like a

43

deranged Cherokee, trying my level best to stomp the beady-
eyed-teeth-baring-fiend to death!!!
The blue-gray-Jewish-lady was mortified.
She sued.
Of course I was fired!
That was back in the mid-eighties . . . I think . . .
It had to be around that time because that was the time when I
was doing all those weird jobs.
Money to live (I told myself).
I didn't acknowledge my addiction.
Pipin' was a pastime for me.
I hadn't taken it up as a full-time occupation.
I wasn't in love.
I was infatuated.
I was having an affair.
We hadn't gotten married.

I've been a kitchen porter, a telephone sales operator, an
insurance salesman (that lasted two days), a coat-check boy, etc.—
easy jobs, pseudo-respectable jobs that would last a few weeks,
maybe a month.
Back then I would try to just smoke at weekends . . .

BUT

more and more frequently I'd get lost in the weekend, emerging
into view on Tuesday afternoon, realizing I had missed a day and
a half of work and another job would be lost.
And I would never understand how I had let it happen again.
I'd rage against myself.
Tearing at myself, then becoming low as the truth of my actions
raised its sheepish head, and I'd get so low that I'd have to get
high, and the viciousness would start again.

I'm lost now AND it'd take too much energy to get found.
I know . . . I've tried.

Maybe not hard enough . . . but I'm a success.
A successful addict.
Allegianced and married to a rock-of-these-ages.
A true and literal slave.
One time last year or the year before—I didn't have any money
and I hadn't been hired as a regular rock-runner at the Centa-
Renta—I sold myself to a dealer for six rocks.
His price was a week for each rock.
He owned me for six weeks.
Where he went, I went.
He kept me high but I had to work for it.
Clean his house. Cook his food. Wash his clothes. Wash his car.
Do his errands. Amuse his girlfriend, which was the worst.
His girlfriend, I think she called herself Rubber, was a bit of an
S&M freak.
She pitied me, she said, and every night would instruct me in her
brand of drug therapy, which consisted of her beating my bare
ass with a cat-o'-nine-tails for five full minutes before I could
smoke each rock.
I let her do it too. Hell I had no choice. I was a slave.
She told me that if I associated pain with smoking, I'd stop.
She was wrong.
I kept smoking and she kept beating my ass.
Hard . . . I bled.
Rubber was a freak.
She would beat my ass and finger-fuck herself at the same
time.
I was glad when my six weeks was up and her boyfriend set me
free.

I remember all these things as I sit on the train comin' back from
Lorraine's house.
I told you before I was bingin' and I had spent all my money, so I
went to Lorraine's to get some more.
Her husband Kenneth wasn't there.
She gave me some money.

A pipe-man on her block knows me. Of course I went to see him
and bought.
I sit on the train laughing as I write and remember.
I am so bold.
I light my pipe in full view of passengers.
This nerdy-looking Black boy reading Essence nearly pisses his
pants as he watches me.
I laugh!
I see his thoughts flying across his forehead like subtitles in a
foreign film.
"Help!!!! . . . . . I'm sittin' next to a crack-head! What's he gonna
do???!!!"

Lorraine had asked me the same thing
"Whatcha gonna do with yourself? . . . You're killin' yourself . . . Is
that what you want?"
I looked at her.
My little sister.
My sweet little sister, now a married-lady-with-a-baby-on-the-
way.
I put my hand on her stomach and smiled a Michael Jackson
smile.
Effective.
Empty.
Reassuringly useless.
Lorraine sighs and gives me twenty-five dollars.
Says it's the last time.
Says Kenneth doesn't want me comin' 'round anymore.
Says mama is worried about me.
My daddy Cornelius Sr. doesn't worry about anyone.
He doesn't have to.
He's dead.
He died about two years after Nate died.
Daddy never got over Nate.
He never said this but I think that daddy felt that his God had
failed him or left him.

Anyway, after Nate's funeral, daddy stopped going to church.
Six months later he stopped going to work.
Then he stopped getting up.
Just stayed in his room.
In bed.
Mama bringing in his meals.
Didn't want to see anyone.
Stopped talking.
Then one Tuesday evening, he just stopped.
Dead.
Heart failure the doctor said.
Another funeral.
Another crack in my family fabric.
Fuck! Not just a crack . . . a whole fuckin' tear.
A-ripped-asunder-holy-temple-veil.
The End.
Brother-Father-Husband.
My mother moved to North Carolina.
Lorraine got married.
I found the pipe.

I am supposed to be telling you about bingin' and about being at the crack-houses and I will.
I know I'm wandering but I can only catch my thoughts as they come to me.

APRIL 18, 1991—MIDNIGHT

There's about three main houses or spots that I know about in this neighborhood.
There's probably more.
Secretive places that only those-in-the-know use.
Most times I enjoy smoking in the privacy of my apartment.
When I first started smoking in '85 or '86 I smoked alone inside, because I didn't want no one to know what was up with me.

My denial days.
Virgin smokes they were.
The first hit.
The best.
Now I smoke anywhere.
I don't give a shit.
My favorite spot to smoke in is the Centa-Renta.
I call it that.
In my boyhood days it used to be called the Community Center.
We'd go there after school to play pool or dominoes . . . to
study . . . to play skelly or cards . . . to hang out and sneak feelies
and kisses with the girlies behind the curtains on stage where on
Saturdays magic shows and movies would unfold as we
ooooohed and aaaaahed in the auditorium that doubled as a
basketball or handball or volleyball court during the week.
When we got older, we'd sneak cigarettes and reefer and wine
and pussy and dick in the toilets.
The Community Center is dead now.
Shut and derelict.
Killed to death by the demon Reagan's Federal-Urban-Welfare-
War.
The US Government will have a lot to answer for on the day of
judgment.

It's all about bingin' spots now.
The Community Center closed in 1983.
The building was reclaimed by the Solo-Peppermint-Kings (a
posse of dealers and pipers) one cold winter's night in 1985.
Legend has it that Tee-Rhone, one of the Solo-Peppermint-
Kings, after being thrown out of his home by his mumsy when
she discovered his nocturnal activities, broke into the Center and
made it his new home.
He had a pipe-warming-party that night and a spot was born.
The Centa-Renta is always aflame.
24–7 as the song says.
Weekends are its busiest times.

You can buy and do there.

The Centa-Renta has lots of space with lots of places to go to smoke in private or share with friends or a honey-bunny, and for the most part it's kinda clean.

There are no-go areas there, like the toilets where the Vampire-Zombies hang out.

I call them Vampire-Zombies because their brains have been zapped by too much of everything.

You will always smell a Vampire-Zombie before you see one.

Weeks of caked up shit clog up their assholes.

Literally.

They don't care about toilet paper.

Piss is the only liquid that's been near their clothes and skin in months.

I don't blame the pipe because hey! I pipe and I'm clean.

Kinda . . .

(My mother wouldn't agree but she's in North Carolina.)

They are usually homeless.

They're fierce-looking. Dirty-dusted-gray-looking.

Their brains are marshmallows.

They are truly the dangerous ones.

They will do anything to get piped.

ANYTHING!!!!!!!

Shoot, stab, bite, gross-you-out, until you give them some money just to get away from you.

I am not one of the Vampire-Zombies.

Not yet.

That's why I'm trying to write down this shit.

To keep my brain cells dancing.

To keep a flow-going-you-know.

Centa-Renta is my favorite spot because it's part of my-story.

A part of me.

I spent many happy hours as a boy in this place . . .

. . . Wondering what kind of life lay ahead of me.

Sometimes when I walk in here and I'm racked by guilt crazies
and I haven't been purged from my despair by Mother Pipe, I
may sit in a corner and cry dark-secret-tears.
Nostalgia tears.
I-couldda-shouldda-wouldda-been-tears.
NO! I AM NOT PROUD OF MY SITUATION!!!!
I accept it . . .
I don't think I can change my situation this late in my life . . .
I am forty-four or forty-five years old. . . . . . .
The spark is dead . . .
The tires are shredded . . .
The well is . . . well . . . gone . . .
I accept it.
After pipe-time, all is forgotten and forgiven in the sight and
sound of a doooooooooeeeeeee-baaabeeeeeeeee-head-rush.

Sexpo's is the spot I go to when I'm short of cash and sharin' is
the order of the day.
I also go there when I'm in the mood for love and my body
needs a little female-tongue.
Sexpo's used to be a Jamaican shebeen. A shebeen is a sort of
erotic-exotic after-hours place, where you can buy and eat the
best food yo'-mama-never-cooked, you can listen to reggae
and soul and funk music, drink beer and wine and spirits, smoke
reefer, rap to whoever you wanted to, or whoever would listen,
relax and while away the night until the sun arises bringin' in
that Monday-morning-feelin'.
Sexpo's was only open on weekends, though you could buy
reefer thru the peephole-in-the-door—24–7.
Sexpo's wasn't too far from Euclid Avenue train station. People
came from everywhere to hang there.
Even White people.
You had to walk down an alleyway, then down some steps that
reeked of piss that led to the speakeasy-type doorway where
some eyes would scope you out to see if you were cool enough
to gain entrance.

Once inside . . . Hey! It's your party! You-could-die-if-you-want-to!

A few did.

Reefer wars in the late '70s and early '80s laid claim to many a young man and a few ladies too.

As the price of reefer rose and the price of cocaine fell, knives and machetes were replaced by Magnums and Uzis. Hippies were replaced by zombies, as determined drug barons dueled to control their drug-hold in the 'hood.

Back in the day these battles were fought behind closed doors in spots like Sexpo's. They hadn't taken it to the streets yet.

As long as the niggers were killing each other, the police let the party run on, but after a White girl from Boston was killed in a drug-war cross fire, the original Sexpo's was raided, trashed and bolted.

The new Sexpo's resurrected only two summers ago.

Dark, damp and cold in the winter, with trash-can fires to heat and illume myself and others like me, lounging on cardboard couches sucking.

Dark, dusty and hot in the summer; sunbeams slanting through bashed, broken boards. Sparks from candles and lighters and matches like darting fireflies illume our fevered-sweating-faces as we sit bug-eyed, sucking.

Sexpo's is for couples.

The deal being, two can suck as cheaply as one.

Double-suck-Sexpo's.

We take turns at the top.

Top being the pipe.

If you ain't at the top then you do the bottom suck.

It's part of the deal.

If the honey I'm with is at the top then I'm at her bottom sucking her pussy dry as she sucks manna from mama-pipe's-titties.

If I'm at the top. . . . . . .

then baby . . . bay-bee . . . bay-bee . . . my dick is getting wet and

the pipe is getting wet and I'm comin' and comin' and goin' and
comin' and the dooooeeee is doing meeee . . . . . dooooiiiing
meeeee . . . . bay-beeeee . . . . . please pleeeeease . . . .
pleeeeeease meeeee. . . . .
There's nothing in the whole entire other world or this world
like it. . . . . . .
I could die.
Right there.
In a double-suck-symphony.

I've saved the worst spot for the last.
This spot has no name.
This spot shames me.
It really isn't a spot.
It's Eric's apartment.
I only go there when I'm desperate and low.
This spot scratches off the scabs of my guilt.
I don't even want to write about it. . . .

BUT

I promised myself that here on these pages I would not lie.
I would pour out my soul . . .
like oil . . .
on the altar of these pages.
Truth hurts. . . . . . .

APRIL 19, 1991—7:30 AM

I haven't smoked in two days.
I'm trying to practice a bit of self-control.
I'm trying.
It's hard to justify spending what little money I have left, since
I've only come off a binge two days ago. . . . . .
I still haven't told you about bingin'.
I will.

I'm working on it.

It's too early for this writing shit.

But I've gotta do something.

Gotta fill my time.

I spent the entire night playing yo-yo games.

"Shall I . . . shall I not . . . get a hit? . . . no! Get a hit? . . . get a hit? . . . no . . . no . . . no!!!!???? . . . . . No."

I almost burnt up the ten dollars I got left from Lorraine so I wouldn't have any money.

But that would've made things worse . . .

'Cause sooner or later I will go out that door and find a spot and a glass dick that's got the goody-goody-feelin' so I can suck again.

It's only a matter of time.

If I don't have any money then it's terrorizing or worse—Eric's spot.

I hate that fuckin' cunt Eric!!!!

I was about to tell you about Eric's spot the last time I wrote but I couldn't.

Every time I think about Eric I get a bad, bad case of the guilt crazies.

I call them the guilt crazies because anytime I think about something that I've done in my life that was really low, I start to feel guilty.

The overwhelming depth of the guilt drives me crazy.

CRAZY.

I physically hurt.

My heart pounding.

My head bursting, threatening to open itself.

I got dents in my forehead from banging my head against the wall, trying to hurt the guilt.

If I can hurt the guilt then maybe the crazies'll stop hurting me.

There are several wide-screen events in my life that bring the guilt crazies roaring in like wounded-bleeding-ravenous-lions, livid and jumpy, ready to tear my chicken-fried psyche to itsy-bitsy-pieces.

The guilt crazies.
Man they get me whenever I think of Nate and what I did to
him. . . . . . .
Whenever I think of Pia and what I did to her. . . . .
Whenever I think of Eric and what I let him do to me. . . . . . .
I've told you about Nate.
I will tell you about Pia.
I'm about to tell you about Eric.
The only thing that keeps the guilt crazies at bay is the blessed
pipe.
The pipe of peace.
It nourishes and quiets my soul like sprinkled holy water on a
fresh garden of white daisies.
I gotta get some more rock. But not now.
Eric first.

I first met Eric Meyers sometime during the winter of 1989.
I can't remember exactly.
I hadn't been smoking long, but it was starting to get regular
and that was worrying me.
I couldn't understand what was propelling me toward what I
thought then was my doom.
It was after my first binge.
I was horrified at the amount of time and money I had spent
torchin' my brain.
I decided I needed help.
I NEVER WANTED TO BE AN ADDICT!!!
I didn't want to become a dirty-stinkin'-Vampire-Zombie.
I went to the medical building on Crescent St.
They referred me to Eric Meyers—a substance-abuse therapist.
When I heard the name Eric Meyers I thought he'd be this White
Jew-boy, which was cool with me because me and Jews have
always been cool.
When I walked into Eric Meyers's office, I was shook to find out
that he was this Black man.
He was about thirty-seven, 5'9", powerfully built.

I sat down and started talking to him.
That first day after I left Eric I was so happy.
I thought I had found salvation.
I knew I was going to be alright.
I had an affinity with Eric, he kinda reminded me of Nate.
I started going to his sessions.
At first there were about four people in the group, then as I got more confident and open, I joined a group of fifteen or twenty. We'd sit and talk about ourselves and why we smoked or snorted or shot up.
We tried to analyze our problems, tried to help each other find solutions and draw strength from our answers.
We made support tapes that we took away and played in the early, quiet hours when your body and mind wanted to stray and your soul was so scared it would be lost again.
After six months of nearly daily sessions, I was almost clean.
I still had the occasional hit now and then, but it was nowhere near the amount I was hitting before the sessions and nothing like my batting average now.
I'm crying as I write this.
Crying. . . . . .
Crying angry-couldda-shouldda-wouldda-if-only-tears. . . . . .
A few months was all I needed to skate away to a new life.
I look around this bare, dingy, gloomy place that is home to me and cry.
There was still a fire inside me then. . . .
I couldda-shouldda-wouldda-been a king . . . not a penniless-pauper, morphed to a mistress that doesn't give two shits about me.
IF ONLY. . . . . .

Me and Eric got tight. Real tight.
He gave me his phone number and address and told me any-time I got anxious to call him.
The night I did finally call Eric I wasn't particularly anxious but I was lonely.

The pipe had filled a huge crack in my life, now that I was trying to do without it, I could look at and around myself and see what I didn't have.

I didn't really have family.

I had no girl, and no real friends.

So I called Eric.

I just wanted to talk and be with someone.

I called Eric and he told me to come over.

He didn't live too far from me.

He had an apartment in Cypress Hills project quite close to the project I lived in.

Eric had a nice place, a big powerful stereo, a VCR, television, furniture.

He had a home.

Looking at his place made me want those things again.

I sat down and we started talking.

He fixed me a drink, vodka and orange juice I think, then he went into his bedroom and changed out of his jeans into some running shorts.

When Eric came out of the bedroom he was bare-chested. The running shorts showed off what was the biggest dick I had ever seen on any man, boy, dog or horse.

It was shocking.

I couldn't keep my eyes off it.

I knew that he knew I was staring at it but I couldn't help it.

Eric sat down in front of me in this fur armchair, slowly opening and closing his thighs which made his dick seem like it was breathing.

I was fascinatedly freaked.

He offered me some reefer!

CONFUSION—BIG TIME!!!

Here was my drug therapist offering me drugs!!!!

Eric said that I was stronger.

He told me that marijuana wouldn't hurt me, that I should think of it as a social smoke, and that pipin' was an antisocial smoke.

Eric put on some music and rolled a joint.

He started smoking.

I trusted Eric.

He was helping me and I liked him so I took the joint.

We smoked about three more.

Everything was delicious, I felt normal. I felt like I was sharing something . . . life maybe. I felt like I was living.

Eric smiled at me.

I could see from the snaky hugeness crowded into his shorts that I was turning him on.

It was obscene.

Embarrassing.

Terrific.

Still smiling, Eric lowered his shorts and let the monster loose.

It stood up unheld like a cobra ready to dance.

I should have left then but I couldn't move.

I wanted to tear my eyes away, punch Eric in the face and run out of the door.

But I just sat there staring at the thing.

It wasn't even a dick anymore. It was alive.

It spoke to me.

"You like me?"

Its voice was thick and heavy.

"You want to smoke me?"

I opened my mouth to curse it but my throat felt constricted . . . tight.

"That's right . . . open your mouth . . . wide . . ."

I never saw it move but suddenly it was standing right in front of me.

The dick-monster was in my face. Staring at me.

"Open your mouth . . . wider . . ."

I opened my mouth to scream—I know I did but no sound came out.

My mouth was stretched open to my nose by a thick-beefy-hardness.

The monster was in my mouth.

I grabbed it to push it away from me.

I've got big hands and I couldn't even get my hands around it.
My throat was hurting.
The monster was sliding in and out of my mouth slowly getting faster.
From another dimension and time I could hear Eric moaning.
Someone was playing music . . . I wondered why.
The monster was in my mouth sucking my breath away.
"Come up for air."
I heard Eric say this. Eric had to have said this because the monster was in my mouth riding my throat like a Derby winner.
My mind was crushed pebbles on a sand bank. There to be seen but mostly invisible.
Dazed and confused as the song says.
Eric pulled something from the shelf, lit it up, inhaled and blew it in my face.
I recognized the sweetness.
MY DRUG THERAPIST WAS PIPIN'!!!!
This time I did scream.
I jumped up.
Found my feet.
Flew out of the door into the night. Still screaming.
Crying lava-hot-tears . . . cry baby.
Eric was Judas, Dracula, Satan.
All things evil.
I stayed inside my apartment for a week.
Vomiting . . . crying. . . .
Wallowing luxuriously in a crater of self-pity.
I finally went outside and called my mother collect.
I cried when I heard my mother's voice.
I begged her to send me some money so I could come to her.
I told her I needed to see her. I needed to be with her.
Mama was calming, reassuring.
She told me to pull myself together and go home.
She would call Lorraine.
Lorraine would take care of things.

I said good-bye and hung up the phone.
I walked around and around my project before going inside my
building and up to my apartment.
I remember wishing that I had a radio so that I could hear some
music, but I had sold my stereo months before when I was out of
money and the pipe was calling me.
The pipe was calling me again.
The pipe talks to me. Like the voice of God.
Like God talked to Moses and Abraham and Jesus and
Mohammed and all the prophets of old.
The pipe talks to me. . . .
That's why I didn't want to be alone.
That's why I wanted to be with my mama.
That's why I wanted a radio. . . .
To block out the voice of the pipe.

Lorraine finally came. She paced around the kitchen nervously.
Hands shaking.
"Mama can't afford a round-trip ticket for you, but she wants to
see you . . .
She's worried about you . . . She told me not to give you
cash . . . She wanted me to go to Penn Station and buy the ticket
for you but I don't have time to do all that Junior . . . You're a
grown man . . . some things you should be able to do
yourself . . ."
Lorraine was turning more and more into daddy the older
she got.
She laid a hundred dollars on the table.
"This is enough for you to get a one-way ticket to Wilson . . . Get
yourself a few clothes . . . I know you don't have many and I don't
want mama to see you like this."
I could never talk when Lorraine was with me.
I would look at her and guilt would rise like hives blistering
my skin.
I was her older brother.
I should be taking care of her.

"Junior . . . Please don't smoke this up . . . go and stay with mama, she might be able to straighten you out . . . but it's up to you . . . If you smoke this up then I'll know that you don't care nothing about us . . . I'll know that I don't have any brother . . . This is your mama's money . . . If you smoke it up remember you're smoking your mama. . . ."

I wanted to tell her that I had already stopped smoking.

She had said during the last six months that I had changed and was almost like my old self, but I didn't want to tell anyone that I had stopped until I had. To tell Lorraine about my six months of therapy meant that I would have to tell her about Eric.

I didn't even want to think about Eric, I certainly couldn't talk about him.

I said nothing.

Lorraine walked about the apartment, wiping dust here, washing a spot there. There wasn't much to wipe or wash.

The apartment is virtually empty except for an old couch in the living room, a bed I found in a dump and the old kitchen table that mama left me when she moved south.

Lorraine took her coat, kissed me on the forehead and left.

I left the money on the table.

I couldn't look at it.

I wanted to run after Lorraine and make her take it back.

I was afraid to be alone with the money.

Right then was when I needed Eric.

Right then was when I needed somebody stronger than me to talk me through the coming quicksand hours.

If I hadn't sold my tape recorder I would have played one of my support tapes to give me strength.

The pipe was laughing at me.

Laughing because I had run from it to get help and the help I had run to had smiled me right back into its grip.

I was about to go berserk when I just stopped.

I remembered what the money was for.

I knew what I had to do.

I laughed, it was so simple.

I would take the money, get the subway to Penn Station, get on
a train and go see my mama.
Tonight.
Fuck clothes! I'd buy some when I got there.
Mama would be so happy to see me. I would be safe there.
I became excited.
I had nothing to pack really.
I ran to the bathroom, washed my face, my body, rearranged my
clothes, stuffed what few underclothes and other clothes I had
into a shopping bag, grabbed the cash off the table, stuffed it
into my shoe, left a light on, locked up the apartment and ran
out of the building.
I felt like I was leaving Alcatraz.
I walked the twelve blocks to Euclid Avenue, got the A train and
was on my way to Penn Station.

APRIL 19, 1991—5PM

I had to stop writing.
I was tired which was a good sign.
I slept for about seven hours and woke up hungry, another great
sign.
My appetite is back for a while.
Don't worry I'm not about to wander.
I'll finish my piece about Eric.

The train ride was forever.
I wanted it to get me to Penn Station before the pipe started
shouting at me.
I knew that it would be shouting at me real soon.
I hadn't had a smoke for about two weeks.
As long as I was doing the sessions I was alright.
I could call up Eric and he'd pull me through but I hadn't talked
to Eric since the night of the snake and I certainly wasn't about
to call him again.
NOT EVER!

At Washington and Clinton this couple got on the train.
They were very young, very intense.
They sat right opposite me.
I took one look at them and I knew.
They were pipe kids.
These kids were amped. To the max.
Eyes bugging out.
Jaws locked tight . . . Teeth almost clinched.
Primed and hyped big-time. These kids had just piped.
I could almost smell the smoke on them.
They didn't talk to each other, they just stared straight ahead,
sometimes looking at their clothes, picking at imaginary lint,
seriously examining the speck closely, then flinging it away.
A pipe ritual.
First paranoia.
You always checked your clothes while pipin' to make sure you
hadn't dropped any on yourself.
You couldn't let the tiniest piece of rock escape.
It had to be smoked . . . all of it.
Just once they looked at me then burst out laughing.
"Cornelius!"
I jerked my head around. I thought someone had called me.
"Cornelius! What are you doing . . . What the fuck are you
doing . . . you got a hundred dollars in your pocket . . . Do you
know how big a rock you can get for $100!!?? . . . You don't have
to do it all yourself . . . you can sell most of it . . . Yeah! you could
do quiet deals in your apartment . . . just you and a couple of
hit-heads you know . . . Look at those kids in front of you . . . they
are hyped!!! . . . look at their eyes!!! . . . Cornelius the pipe is
sweet today! . . . you been missing some prime hits! . . . You
should talk to those kids . . . they could tell you where to go . . ."
The pipe was shouting.
Strong.
And it made so much sense.
Pipe was so persuasive.

So truthful.
So practical.
Pipe knew me.
Pipe didn't lie to me.
I got off the train.
For about five minutes I thought about throwing myself under
the next one.
To be done with it.
I was tired of fighting and running.
I couldn't stop the pipe-talk.
I didn't want to.

I was at Hoyt and Schermerhorn, not too far from Lorraine's
place.
I ran up the subway steps.
Ran to Lorraine's apartment and stabbed the buzzer.
No answer.
I buzzed and buzzed again.
No answer.
Lorraine's front door was eight feet of solid oak.
I thought about taking the money and sliding it under the door
but I knew that would be stupid, I'd be giving it away.
I screamed and cursed and kicked the door, still killing the
buzzer, still getting no answer.
I called up to her window.
"Lorraaaaainnne!!!!! . . . . . Loorrrraaaaainnnne!!!!. . . . .
Loorrrrrraaaaainnne!!!"
A window opened.
"Motherfucka stop that yellin' or I'll put a cap up yo' ass!!!"
It wasn't Lorraine.
I don't even know who said it, I didn't look back, I was already
walking away from the building.
I was fucked.
Truly fucked.
Tired of being tired.
Tired of trying to be strong.

I walked aimlessly around the block not knowing or caring
where I was going.
Then the laughter started.
I thought at first that it was me laughing but it wasn't me.
I was too fucked.
Evil, satanic laughter bounced off the buildings around me and
slapped me about the head.
It was the pipe laughing at me.
Laughing a hangman's noose around my neck.
Laughing a leash around my feet.
Laughing like a fisherman, pulling in one that thought it had
got away.
I was standing in front of the spot of the pipe-man who lived in
Lorraine's neighborhood.
I rang the bell.
Of course the door buzzed open.
I went inside.
The rest is his-story as opposed to my-story.

The mama-money lasted maybe two days.
I smoked and smoked and smoked and smoked. . . . . .
Crying-smoking-crying-smoking-laughing-smoking. . . . . .
Guilt-smoke this was.
Binge-time.
This is the binge.
Smoking until there is nothing left.
Nothing in your pocket.
Nothing in your mind.
Oblivion.
Resolution . . . at least until the next time.

By the end of the week I was a shaking-shivering-wired-mess-of-
serrated-nerves.
I went to see Eric.
I had to.
He was the only person I knew who would be happy to see me.

I had been living inside my head for the past week.
I had to hear a voice.
A voice that wasn't the pipe.
A human voice talking to me.
A human voice that wasn't laughing or shouting or cursing at me.
"Get out the street! You dirty-stinkin'-fuckin'-shit-ass-crack-head!!!"
I had to feel arms around me.
I had to be touched.
No matter what it cost me.
I had never binged like that before.
I had smoked myself into a glacier state.
I needed warmth.
I was iced.
I was afraid.
I had never gone this far before.
I felt like I was being jet-propelled through a slow-motion film.
Cars, buildings, people, crawling like slime as I whizzed through them.
I was moving faster than I could think.
I was beyond thought.
Certainly beyond speech.
I didn't even know I was at Eric's spot until he opened the door.
He looked at my bugged eyes and knew.
I said nothing. I couldn't.
Eric took me inside.
He put me fully clothed into a hot bath.
I lay in the hot water, teeth chattering, staring bug-eyed straight ahead.
Drowning in paranoia.
Scared of the water, scared of Eric, scared to be alive.
Eric took a washrag and squeezed the hot water onto my forehead.
Over and over again.
Baptizing my mind. Melting my anxiety. Warming my soul.

At that moment Eric became the sun.
I was Pluto, the darkest, coldest, most distant of all worlds and
the sun had found me.
The sun was drawing me closer to its fiery rays.
Warming me.
Melting the iceberg coffin I had welded myself into.
I was sweating.
The sun burnt off my shirt, consumed my pants and underwear
in the fire of its nuclear rays.
I floated in this volcanic lake, the sun's rays like tentacles
touching every part of my body.
Caressing my chest, my stomach, my ass, my thighs, my legs, my
feet, encircling my dick, warming me, raising me, hardening me,
blessing me . . . saving me.
I floated above the bathtub like an astronaut spacewalking.
I looked down upon my naked body lying in the water.
I saw Eric washing and kissing my body.
I watched him pulling the foreskin of my dick back and forth
and back and forth on its hardened shaft.
Faster and faster. I watched Eric pump my dick like an anxious
adolescent impatiently pumping a soda from a fountain.
The foam in the pit of my stomach rising . . . rising. . . . .
Nearly at the eve of explosion.
Eric stopped suddenly.
My body jerked involuntarily from the sudden shock of release.
I opened my eyes angrily, ready to curse his tease.
Eric wasn't there.
I stepped out of the tub walking uncertainly into the bedroom.
Eric stood at the table.
Pipe in hand. Flame at its base.
"He's got everything you need here!"
Pipe-talk pushed me closer to Eric.
He kept his back to me, knowing my approach.
"You could live right here. Eric loves you!"
I smiled at this knowledge. Placed my hands on Eric's shoulders,
turned him around to face me.

Eric smiled but did not offer me the pipe.
I knew what he wanted.
I knew what I wanted.
I reached for the pipe.
He smiled, pulling it away from me.
"Play the game."
The master instructed me.
I followed Eric around the bed.
Sat down when he sat down.
Stretched and lay down at his side.
I reached over to him to grab the pipe. Surely now he must
know that I was in obeisance.
Surely now I must be rewarded.
Eric smiled an even thinner smile and held the pipe over his
head.
I turned onto my stomach.
Quicker than a smile Eric was on me; straddling me like a round
pony.
He laughed. I followed laughing along.
"I want to go deep-sea diving . . . will you take me down into your
diving bell . . . ?"
Eric whispered this question hotly into my ears. I didn't rightly
know what he meant.
His yard-long dick rubbed stiffly along the rift in the small of my
back.
He lit the pipe and inhaled two quick hits.
The room reeked of peppermint.
"I want to go diving!" His voice more insistent.
"Give me a hit and we'll go diving."
I laughed expectantly and reached for the pipe.
"No!"
Eric snatched the pipe away.
"Promise first!"
Breath harsh against my ear, dick rubbing like sandpaper against
my back.
"Promise him! Promise him anything! Paradise lives in his hand!"

A voice at my ear. A voice at my brain.

Both menacingly insistent.

My desire for the pipe, stronger than my fear of the dick, pushed me.

"I . . . promise . . ."

A hand wet with oil of some kind found its way into the crack of my ass.

Two adventurous fingers pushed rudely up into my virgin anus.

Pain stiffened me.

The pipe was at my lips.

"You promised!"

Eric's voice was of a demon. I said nothing.

My mind or some part of my mind screamed like a maniac.

"No! . . . No! . . . No! . . . No! . . ."

Over and over again.

I was the sea Eric wanted to dive into. My waves rolled away.

INSIDE ME. . . .

Before I could think-scream-protest . . . Eric was inside me.

Huge-lightning and thunder together . . . tearing through me. . . .

PRIMAL PAIN

I know I musta bled.

I hope he was wearing a condom.

The pipe was in my mouth.

It was lit.

The smoke hurried into my lungs gasping for escape.

And for that moment it didn't matter I was committing a venal sin. . . . .

Being debased.

Subverted.

For a moment I was transported . . . but only for a moment.

The pipe is very cruel in the time it takes with you.

Its power truly momentary; three minutes max.

Which is why you always want more . . . and more . . . and more. . . .

I came down crashing as Eric came crashing down into me.
I tried to throw him off, it only lodged him deeper inside me.
Again he thrust the pipe in my mouth lighting it.
Fucking me with the pipe; fucking me with his dick.
I was truly double-fucked.
Again and again, faster and faster, in and out of my ass, my
mouth, my ass . . . ass . . . my . . . mouth, then a sonic rush to my
head and a pulsating pressure inside me near my stomach.
Eric moaned and moaned, pushed in farther and farther,
grabbed me around the head moaning and crying. I sucked on
the pipe bewildered.
Trying to change the channel.
Trying to smoke away the nightmare.
I forgot who I was.
Maybe I was really a woman.
I prayed I was.

Eric finally pulled out of me.
I didn't care.
I didn't note it.
I had the pipe.
I smoked to forget. To block out shame.
I got off the bed.
My knees buckled.
I took a hit to block out the pain.
Something felt torn inside me.
I was bleeding.
I took the pipe into the bathroom as I tried to wash away as
much of the nastiness—
bloodandsemenandoilandshameandpainandmeandEric—as I
could.
I hit again.
I came back into the bedroom. Eric was still in bed. He didn't
look at me.
He said nothing.
I found my wet clothes. I kept smoking.

Clothed, I went to the front door. Eric got up. At the door he gave me a big stuffed bag of white rock. I said nothing. Not even thank you.
Still smoking. Found my path home.
Sat in my tub and smoked and smoked and smoked and smoked and smoked and smoked. . . .
Binge!
Binge!
Oblivion!

That's how it is with Eric and me. I don't go to his sessions anymore.
I never call him. . . .

BUT

when the need arises and I have no money . . . or I don't want to spend it . . . or I am low . . . I will find myself at Eric's door and we repeat those sordid, silent motions.
He gets what he wants.
I get what I want.
That's the deal.
I lie to myself.
I tell myself that it doesn't matter.
I don't know who I hate more.
Myself or Eric.

APRIL 22, 1991—3 PM

You now know what bingin' is.
I have smoked away thousands of dollars.
I have given away thousands of dollars in the pipe's name.
One time I got back some money from an accident claim.
I had fallen down on the ice in front of my building and broken my ankle.
The city was supposed to put down some sand and had not. I

sued, Lorraine helped me fill out the papers for the claim—it was
she who pushed me to file for it.
I was so happy when I won my case. I was awarded three
thousand dollars.
I had so many things that I wanted to do with the money.
I made lists of things that I wanted to buy for my apartment.
Furniture and stereo equipment . . . home things. Ordinary things
that added up to life.
A toaster and an ironing board. Sheets and pillowcases. Toilet
paper, light bulbs.
Take-for-granted things.
I was gonna give my mama a thousand dollars just for her
trouble all these years, and Lorraine a thousand for helping me
file for the money.
As it happened the check arrived when Lorraine was away in
North Carolina with Kenneth visiting his parents, since it was so
close to where mama was they were going to stop and see her
also.
I was alone.
There I was in the house with a check for three thousand dollars. I
had no papers, no identification so I couldn't cash the check. I did
have a savings and checking account years ago but it was so long since
I'd used it, it was probably closed. All my important papers had
been taken from me for safekeeping by Lorraine. Not wanting to
think about the money, I took the check and put it inside the
ancient shoebox with the picture of me-like-I-usta-be.
Outta-sight outta-mind.

A week passed.
I was running out of money.
I was determined I wasn't going to touch up the check.
I had been good I hadn't spent any money on smoke.
I had smoked of course. . . .

■

BUT

to pay for my habit I had gotten a job at the Centa-Renta.
The Solo-Peppermint-Kings who ran the Centa-Renta were
childhood friends of mine and gave me a job working the
customers that came in to buy.

A house may have many dealers selling in it depending on how
big a house it is and its volume of business. Most times the
dealers themselves never sell directly to the hitters, so they
employ runners, addicts like myself, who bring the money to
them; we get the rock from them and take it back to the
customers. In return for this service the runners get free hits or
money if they're shrewd.

I could tell a hitter that it will cost him, say, twenty-five dollars
and a piece (of rock) for my trouble and I'd go to a dealer I knew
who'd sell it to me for, let's say, twenty or even fifteen dollars. I
could even do a deal with a dealer; every five bags I sold for him
I get one free.

If you work it right you can run and smoke and make rocks pay
for themselves; but the nature and the power of the pipe
dictates a situation where things hardly ever work out right,
especially for the addict.

Most successful dealers **NEVER** pipe.

They only **SUPPLY**.

That's their power.

Their main object is **MONEY**.

Most runners are addicts whose only object is the pipe. Money is
only important as the material that grants us the object. The
pipe.

Addicts never kill simply for money. They kill or rob or hurt to
get money or something that can translate into money because
that's what the dealers want in exchange for drugs.

If you have no money and you don't want to terrorize you can
trade off possessions of value for hits. That's why I have no
furniture or clothes. I've traded or sold them for pipe-money.

Anyway to keep from touching up the check, I got a job running
rock in the Centa-Renta. Things were great for a day or two.

I was high, I was happy.
Word got round that I had rock so some hitters I knew started coming by touching on me for a hit. When you have rock you are in a powerful position.
It's like a gangster with an Uzi. You've got mucho juice.
An addict with rock is an emperor. He can demand payment from other addicts in any form imaginable. You can punish people who wronged you in the past by humiliating them or even worse force them to humiliate themselves in public just for a hit.
I've made two fifty-year-old men, married with families, suck-each-other-off in the main room of the Centa-Renta in front of other hitters (we laughed!) simply because one of them had stuck me up with a knife and thieved my rock a few months earlier. They couldn't hurt me because I was protected. While you are working for a dealer you're under his protection, so if anybody fucks with his rocks they get burnt. Literally and/or figuratively.
Fire-fire or gun-fire.
Both do major damage.
I once made this girl (who I liked but who had blown me off when I had nothing) squat, shit and eat her own shit before I gave her a piece of rock.
And she did it too.
In front of people.
We laughed.
There is no dignity in pipin'.

I loved being a runner.
The power I felt was intoxicating.
I had forgotten what self-esteem felt like.
I looked at what I was doing and I said to myself:
"Hell! I can be a dealer! This shit is easy! I got money . . . I'll just buy a hundred dollars' worth of rock and sell it! I won't smoke it I promise!"
I only had one problem.
Dealers don't take checks.

At least not from addicts.

There was a dealer in the Centa-Renta named Spartacus. I had known Spartacus since the third grade when I used to help him with his homework—sometimes he'd help me out with a piece of rock when I was low. He was also one of the dealers I was runnin' for and one of the few I halfway trusted. I thought that if I showed Spartacus the check to let him know that I was good for money, he'd front me a hundred dollars' worth of rock.

As you can imagine this "business" idea came to me while I was kite-flying with the pipe.

I went home and took the check from its hiding place and put it in my shoe.

I went back to the Centa-Renta. I found Spartacus in his "office," a back corner of what used to be the stage area of the Community Center. I showed him the check and told him what I wanted.

At first he said nothing. He just looked at me. Then he reached into his pocket and gave me five ten-cent bags (fifty dollars' worth of rock). He said he couldn't front me any more just then 'cause he had to sell the rest to get his "buy" (money to buy a quantity of rock) money. He told me to go home, put the check in a safe place, not to tell anyone what we were doing and that he'd come to see me later that night. He also said for me to make sure I was alone when he got there.

Man! I felt like a midget with a twelve-foot dick!

I walked home tall and proud for the first time in many-a-year! I said to myself, "Hell! This shit is easy! I shouldda started dealing ages ago! No more jerk days for me!"

I felt so good that I promptly forgot what I had promised myself. The pipe started talking. We decided that a celebratory smoke was a must.

On the way home I saw this honey-bunny named Lee-Ann, a girl from the 'hood who was a major-league hitter and still had some looks left. I invited her up for a double S (smoke and suck); of course she accepted my invitation. By the time I kicked Lee-Ann's ass out two hours later, we had smoked up nearly three of

*the ten-cent bags. I kicked her out because she was doing more
smoking than sucking and that wasn't the deal.*

*Lee-Ann stood outside my door for nearly half an hour
screaming and banging before she went away. I sat inside
listening to her as I smoked away the rest of the bag.*

Of course I was laughing.

*I thought that Spartacus wasn't going to show because it had
got so late and he hadn't come yet.*

*Finally, about five in the morning, just as I had lit up the last of
the five bags, there was a knock at my door. I was wired and
bugged and had forgotten that I was even expecting Spartacus. I
crouched down on the floor in a Kamikaze-paranoid fear. No
one ever came knocking on my door at five in the morning!*

"Cornelius!? . . . Cornelius!!!! . . . ."

*Someone was urgently whispering my name through the look-
out hole under the knocker. I crept closer to the door.*

"Cornelius!!!! Open the mothafuckin' door!!! . . . it's Spartacus!!!"

I laughed! Spartacus???! What the fuck was a Spartacus??!!

I laughed some more.

Then I remembered.

Spartacus the rock.

I opened the door.

*There stood Spartacus with some young dude I had never seen
before. The young dude was carrying a golf-club case.*

*They both pushed past me before I could fathom if I should let
them in or not.*

Spartacus smiled and came off all friendly.

He apologized for the lateness of the hour.

He said he needed me to do him a huge favor.

I laughed! Me do him a favor!!!

*He said he hadn't been able to bring me the other five bags I
wanted because he had run out of stuff before he had made
enough "buy" money, and he didn't have enough "buy" money to
get a new stash.*

He said he wanted me to loan him a thousand dollars.

I laughed. I told him I didn't have a thousand dollars.
Spartacus came over to me and took me into the kitchen; he
said in a real low voice that if I signed my check over to him, he
would go to his bank in the morning, cash the check for me,
bring me back one thousand nine hundred dollars, then he
would bring one thousand dollars plus thirty percent interest
tomorrow night after he had finished selling. He cajoled and
smiled warmly, telling me that I could trust him and that we
were boys from way back and how I'd be really helping him out;
and maybe I should have said yes but bells started ringing in my
head and I saw Lorraine's face and mama's eyes.
I told Spartacus that I had arranged for my sister to cash the
check for me when she returned to the city. He asked me when
she was coming back. I told him that I didn't know.
Spartacus turned his back on me as if he was thinking. He turned
around and asked me again to help him; telling me that since he
had trusted me with those five bags I should be willing to trust
him as well.
My mind was racing. I had to get out of what was becoming a
very sticky situation. I didn't know the guy in the other room. I
didn't think Spartacus would hurt me, but you could never tell
with dealers especially when money was the object.
Well . . . he said if I couldn't or wouldn't help him then he had no
choice but to take back the bags he had fronted me.
My heart, my mouth, my head, my ass fell onto the floor and
crashed through to the cement landing in the basement six
floors below.
I just looked at Spartacus.
I felt like a blind worm who had just been snatched up by an
eagle.
"What-the-fuck-is-he-going-to-do-with-me?" thoughts ran
through my brain like murky diarrhea.
I heard myself telling Spartacus that I had smoked them.
Spartacus smiled.
He held out his hand. His money hand.
I shook my head.

Spartacus walked back to the living room.

I stayed where I was.

My mind was trying to make some connections but the pipe short-circuited my thoughts; making them blink in my head like year-old Christmas-tree lights.

I heard Spartacus talking to his partner whose name I can't remember.

"Cornelius . . . come in here man . . ."

I tried to read his voice. It sounded amiable. It sounded reasonable so I went back into the living room. Spartacus was standing in the middle of the room facing me. Next to him stood what's-his-name, brandishing a ferociously-evil-looking submachine gun.

Spartacus looked at me . . . came over to me, hugged me, kissed me on the forehead like a father; he even had tears in his eyes. He told me that what's-his-name was his dealer and needed his money and that he wasn't leaving the place until he got his money. Spartacus said that he had done all he could for me and that he was gonna leave the apartment and perhaps me and what's-his-name could come to some arrangement. And then before I could scream "Spartacus!!!" loud enough for the whole galaxy to hear, he walked out closing the door quietly after him.

Well there we were.

Me and what's-his-name.

I didn't laugh.

I was wired. I was bugged.

I was very paranoid and I was scared shitless!

I pissed my pants.

What's-his-name took the butt of his gun and cracked me in the mouth with the other end; knocking me down, busting my lip and knocking out my two front teeth. Before I could get up, he spiked me in the back, bashed me against my ribs, whacked me in the face again; then while I lay there on my back bleeding but too fucked and scared to cry, he put the barrel of the machine gun in my mouth and told me what I was going to do. I was to get the check, sign it over to Samuel Jude Avery (Spartacus's real

name) and if he had to tell me again, he would shoot me in the mouth then push my body out the window.
He asked me if I understood.
I blinked.
He let me up.
What's-his-name walked behind me with the machine-gun snout poking me in the back.
I thought about jumping out the window so I wouldn't have to give up the check but we were only six floors up and with my luck I'd probably survive but be paralyzed forever.
I got the check.
I signed it.
What's-his-name took the check then bashed me in the side of the head with the gun, knocking me out.
I woke up hours later.
Pain crisscrossed my body like ice-skaters on Benzedrine.
It sounded like it was raining outside but I couldn't see because the blood had caked my eyes shut. I peeled off the dried blood and tried to get up. My left eye caught a glint of white off to my side.
There were five small but tightly stuffed ten-cent bags lying there on the carpetless floor.
My heart started beating.
I hurried to the front door and locked it. Snatched the bags to my chest, ran quietly to the bathroom clutching my pipe and my nirvana; locked the door and smoked and smoked. I didn't even bother to wipe off the blood. I smoked myself silly.

I still go to the Centa-Renta. I still see Spartacus. I even still run for him from time to time. We never talk about what happened and I never saw what's-his-name again. Lorraine came home and asked me if I had received the check. I lied. I told her no. She wrote the City many, many letters. She told me the City had written her back saying that I had received the check. I told her that perhaps someone had broken into my mailbox and stolen it. Then one night she came over to my house crying. She didn't say anything. She opened her purse and fished out a faded rust-

splattered piece of paper. She cried some more then ran out of
the apartment. I sat in my chair puzzled. I almost laughed. I
picked up the faded browned paper. It was my check. Canceled.
My three-thousand-dollar check signed in ink in my handwriting.
Countersigned by Samuel Jude Avery in ink and splattered with
my blood. Blood money. I always wondered how he explained
the blood to his bank.

Lorraine didn't come to see me again for months.

MAY 3, 1991—11:30PM

On the train coming back from Lorraine's

Today is Lorraine's birthday.
She had a party and invited me over on condition that I didn't
embarrass her.
I couldn't be fucked up.
For the last few days I've taken it easy, which was hard 'cause I
have money.
The weird thing is I feel great.
The party is still going on but I left early.
Lorraine has a great job in the city; she is a head secretary for a
large and important stocks and securities firm. She had a lot of
her co-workers from her office at the party.
Since I am her older (and only living) brother she introduced me
to all of them.
Most of them are White.
Her husband Kenneth is one of those middle-class, wanna-be,
upwardly-mobile niggers and when I showed up at the front
door for the party he nearly had a stroke. I wonder why Lorraine
hadn't told him I was coming.
Now I have no problem with trying to get ahead.
In my day I was the most upwardly-mobile Black man New York
had ever produced. I was on my way to the top space-shuttle style.
But I hate it when these niggers act like they've seen the light

and in seeing the light they think they've got to get whiter than the light.

I guess I should be the last person on earth to pontificate on Black consciousness especially as the state I'm in could be looked on as the antithesis of anything positive about the Black race.

BUT

HEY!

White people have committed the most heinous crimes against Black people, Jewish people, Arab people, themselves, Indian, Asian people, generally everybody, and they still run the world! So I can say what I fuckin' think and I don't give two shits who don't like it!

Just because I'm a crack-head doesn't mean I don't have an opinion on things.

You'd be surprised and shocked; some crack-heads run this country.

There are crack-heads running your churches, your schools, your buses, and flying your jets!

Crack-heads are everywhere!

It's just that these "important" crack-heads have the money to make their addiction palatable to themselves (like billionaire alcoholics and coke-heads) and can afford to dress and disguise their condition.

They are what I call functioning addicts; which is what I am. Which is what Eric is, and look what he does for a living.

I was having a great time at the party.

I came early and borrowed some of Kenneth's clothes so I wouldn't look out of place and embarrass Lorraine.

I had saved some money and got myself a haircut and bought Lorraine a card and a box of candy.

She invited me to the party weeks ago and sent me notes reminding me.

Lorraine is trying to rehabilitate me.

I love Lorraine.

She thinks that all I have to do is be around the right kind of
people and I'll click my heels and be back home and out of my
Ozzy-drug-world.
Lorraine wants her big brother back.
I love Lorraine.
Her baby is due in about six months and she wants her baby to
have a family.
It's hard having a crack-head as a family member.
We are not dependable.
We cannot and do not offer support. Not even to our own
children.
We take.
Often.
We are not there for you.
We are not there for ourselves.
We are there only for the pipe.
Anything or anyone that gets in the way of our getting to the
pipe becomes the enemy.

Lorraine has some nice friends; she also has some asshole
friends.
There was this fifty-five-year-old White office manager guy who
arrived armed with two dozen roses and a magnum of
champagne. Lorraine doesn't drink. He popped it open anyway
and became the instant life of the party. "Talkin' loud an' sayin'
nothin' " as the song says. He's one of those people who would
ask you where you got your suit so that he could brag on his and
tell you that it's an Armani or a Hermès. He'd ask you what you
did for a living so he could, with fire in his eyes, reveal to you
how many thousands of dollars he made last year. I wondered
why he even bothered to come to this party. People like him
usually don't like Black people, but my sister is a gem, everybody
loves her, even assholes.
Anyway this jerk worked the party like Madonna—humbling
everybody, feeling magnificent in his superiority. He finally
worked his way 'round to me. He took one look at my borrowed

clothes and praised me for my style and inquired where I had purchased such tasteful threads. I took a sip of the champagne and told him that I had found them in the street.

He laughed loudly, slapped me on the back and proclaimed me a miracle. He then launched into a five-minute monologue on the joys of owning a 26-carat jeweled-rock Cartier watch. I don't own a watch so he couldn't ask about mine—instead he asked what I did for a living. I took another sip of champagne and told him I was a professional crack-addict. He was sipping on his champagne as I revealed this. He duly choked, spluttered, his glasses fell off.

He retrieved them laughing loudly, slapped me on the back again and waved Kenneth over. Laughing uproariously, he imparted to Kenneth the information I had imparted to him,

then nearly killed himself laughing some more.

Kenneth was not amused.

He looked at me like I was a maggot that had crawled out of the roast pork on the dinner table.

Kenneth marched me into the bedroom and told me that I was embarrassing him and that I should leave before I ruined the evening. I told him that he had no right to be embarrassed—it wasn't his party, and that I would leave when I was good and ready.

And I wasn't ready to leave, I was having a great time!

There were a few Black girls there but most were White-with-big-big-hair secretary-types. One matronly woman with a Phyllis Diller hairdo was holding forth on the blessings of gentrification. She and her roommate (probably her lover), another matronly Black woman, had bought a brownstone, about two miles away in mid-Brooklyn, for a song a few years back. They had done it up beautifully and now it was worth a half-million dollars but because of the recession they were finding it impossible to sell. They were surrounded by a quartet of multicultural-upwardly-mobilers tut-tutting and clicking their commiserations. "What an awful bore this recession is!" they said. How dare it impede their God-given American right to make as much money as they could get away with. Then the Black

*matronly type launched into how the recession was responsible
for the rise in crime; and that how, as a Black woman, she was
ashamed of her people for being responsible for most of it; and
that she thought that it was the duty of our Black leaders to
apologize to our fellow White Americans for the actions of these
deranged criminals, and to assure them that the greater majority
of Blacks were God-fearing-decent-human-beings.
I told her she was crazy and bugged!
Everything stopped. Forks stopped in midair.
All eyes turned to me.
I asked her:
"Has any White man in the US Government ever apologized for
slavery? Has the US Government ever made any kind of
restitution or even an offer of restitution for the billions and
billions of dollars that our ancestors lost as a result of being torn
from our original land?"
I said:
"The Government is finally giving some land back to the
American Indians, as they damn well should, but what has the
Black man been given back, except welfare, affirmative action
programs, housing that packs us in like cattle and so-called
equal-opportunity programs that were unequal from the word
go!"
Well bay-bee! It was too quiet, you couldda heard a roach fart!
Lorraine smiled at me. There was a kind of proud look in her
eyes.
This emboldened me. I continued.
I said:
"Crime and other negative acts committed by so-called Black
criminals are the unconscious reactions of a people cruelly
disenfranchised, for centuries, by a self-righteously-evil-hostile-
host-nation.
Mr. Laughing-loudly-White-man broke in indignantly:
"What about the other immigrants that came to America and
were also persecuted, but through hard work and education
were able to prosper and give something back to this country!"
Heads swung to me like spectators at a tennis match. I took a sip*

of champagne and surveyed the pond of expectant faces looking at me as if I were some Malcolm X come again. Some horrified, some bemused, others quietly affirming . . . "Go-'head-boy! Git 'im."

I did.

Taking another sip of champagne I continued:

"Black people never came to this country as immigrants. We never came. We were forcibly stolen, raped, chained against our will and dropped into this foreign land. Purposely separated from tribe-fellows of the same language so that we couldn't communicate and come together for our common good which would have meant death to our imprisoners. Centuries later we still can't communicate with each other and come together for our own common good. Black people have never got over slavery. White people don't want us to, it wouldn't be in their best interest for us to do so. Even without education for our masses, which we had to march and fight to get, the few of us that have escaped and made something of our lives have excelled magnificently. We dominate American culture. We are American music, sports, entertainment, science, literature—you name it we've done it. You better thank God for our 'small' criminal element. If every Black person in this country suddenly got conscious and did the right thing, shit, we'd take over, you guys wouldn't be able to stand it; and you know this, which is why you make a concerted effort to keep us down." I drank some more champagne—I wasn't finished yet.

I looked ahead to the kitchen doorway where Lorraine was standing with Kenneth. Lorraine was crying softly, pride-tears, Even Kenneth was looking at me like I was a new being. The matronly Black woman rose up and offered me her hand, wanting to make my acquaintance. I actually felt good. I smiled to myself, maybe there was life beyond the pipe.

"But what about those dirty, stinking drug addicts that're bringing this city down! I don't care what you say! Slavery's got nothing to do with what they're doing! It's a disgrace and there's no excuse for it! Somebody should douse them all down with gasoline and throw a match!" Mr. Laughing-White-wonder wasn't laughing. He was sweating and bug-eyed behind his steamed glasses.

I turned on him, mouth ready to justify my existence, my right to live. Lorraine's eyes caught mine just as I was about to attack. Her eyes were apprehensive. She imperceptibly shook her head. No. My sister knew me.

She knew I was about to jump out of my disguise, and reveal my true identity, with all its scary-media-misconceptionalized-luggage, to all and sundry present. I had already told Mr. Laughing-loudly-White-man that I was a crack-addict and he had laughingly blown it off—if Lorraine hadn't stopped me I would have not only told him again that I was a crack-addict, I would also have told him how I became one.

BUT

nothing I could have told that man would have justified my life to him and others like him. I would have only wrecked my sister's birthday party and perhaps harmed her budding career; a career she wanted and, with a baby on the way, desperately needed. The idiots there among her co-workers and superiors would have known the dish about her elder brother and judged her in my light. They would have decided that she must be cut from the same cloth.

Only then did I realize how much my family had suffered because of me and my life. I was truly the black-sheep-in-the-closet-nightmare-relative-that-no-one-outside-the-family-ever-needed-to-know-about. I understood why Kenneth didn't want me around. I felt for them. I felt for myself. I, as the English say, lowered the tone. I looked at Mr. Laughing-loudly-White-man, shook my head and said nothing.

Conversation started again, tentatively.

I went over to Kenneth and asked him for the light cloth coat he had loaned me. Even though it's May, it is kinda chilly.

Kenneth hugged me!

For the first time since he'd known me, he showed me some
brotherly warmth.
I almost cried.
"You've got too much going on inside that brain of yours to be
destroying yourself like you are . . . we gotta talk." Kenneth shook
my hand firmly and helped me on with his coat.
Lorraine gave me a bear hug and a big kiss. She held me at arm's
length, shook her head and said "Thank you." She smiled me an
I-love-you smile.
I went over to Mr. Laughing-loudly-White-man, shook his hand,
bid the other guests adieu and walked outside into the chilly-
trying-to-be-warm New York spring night.

That's why I'm on the train, on my way home, rather than at the party.
If I hadda stayed and said my piece I would have truly turned
Lorraine's party out. There would have been a revolution in that
room. Mr. Laughing-loudly-White-man's view of what should be
done to drug addicts and criminals is not an original idea. It's an
opinion held by a lot of people, Black and White; and perhaps
it's a valid point.

BUT

Burning up all the addicts and dealers will not stop the problem.
The Black dealers and addicts are low men on the drug totem
pole. The real power brokers are White Government boys who
allow the drugs to be imported into the country. The Black
dealers are only modern-day slave overseers working for the
White slave masters. The Black ghetto has replaced the Southern
plantation and we, the inhabitants of the ghetto, are now
chained to drugs, to welfare, to hopelessness, to crime. That
environment, and products of that environment, are created and
manipulated by the White boys in power.
It is a Black and White thing!
No! Fuck that!
It is a poor thing!
It is a have-not thing!

The poor are the niggers of the world.
The only blame I put on my brothers and sisters who are dealing
and criming is their inability to see that they are being
marionetted by the White boys.
These aren't things I read or heard about. These are things I
know.
I too am a marionette.
My tragedy is that I know I am—I've always known.
It wasn't a Black man that introduced me to cocaine or the pipe.
At the time I was introduced to the Big C, most Black people
couldn't afford the drug. It wasn't in the 'hood. Reefer ruled the
roost, then came heroin, then came the big C. At least that's the
way it came down in my 'hood.
I can't speak about anyone else's experience except my own.
The White boy that hooked me had only one object in mind.
Money.
He knew that if he hooked me and others like me, we would
become a source of eternal money for him.
The US Government could knock out drugs in six months if it
wanted to.
It could get rid of all the crime associated with it, if it wanted to.
It will do something about it soon.
Those young Black turks who are busy terrorizing the 'hoods are
doing too excellent a job. As per usual White folks don't care
about what happens to Black folks as long as it happens in Black
neighborhoods. If the Blacks tear up and burn down their
ghettos, the White property developers will happily pick up the
pieces for next-to-no-money, gentrify or reclaim the area and
sell it to other White folks, or better yet upwardly-mobile-Blacks-
Jap-Asians-Chinese, for megabucks. The ones who lose out in
this deal, as per usual, are the poor. Too poor to capitalize on
this American dream, they are moved out and rehoused in
another ghetto further outside the mainstream.

BUT

When the violence overspills into the White neighborhoods, as is happening now, and spilling into the schools, as is happening now, alarm bells start ringing in the Government White boys' heads because the niggers are messin'
with the bigger bucks.
Big Business.
Commerce can't commence in instability. Instability scares Big Business away; and before the White boys watch their bucks flee out of the urban cities which have become drug war grounds, they will truly change the picture.
The US Government will before long legalize drugs. It will set up drug stores or bureaus where registered addicts can get the drug they want as well as the education and therapy they sorely need. The Government will legislate an arms control law. It will lock up the drug barons and confiscate their cash, arms and drugs because it will be in the interest of the US Government to do so. None of this crazy-druggy-crimey-violent-bullshit will go away until the US Government does all of the above and more.
The crime and guns and death and devastation associated with drugs are all money-related.
*People will pay **BIG BUCKS** to get what someone says they can't have—i.e., drugs.*

BUT

*When the Government legalizes drugs and controls its sale it will automatically take the money objectives (the cost of smuggling, the cost of drug-processing, the cost of hush and protection from Government authorities etc.) out of the picture, and the crazy shit will stop. Young, Black drug turks **will** have to go back to school and learn how to do something else. Their careers will be over because there won't be any more money to be made out of the drug trade.*
As it happened with Prohibition and alcohol, so it will happen to drugs.

■

Tonight is a breakthrough of sorts for me.

For the first time in years I think I might have a reason for stoppin' this shit and cleanin' up my life. Watching those people at Lorraine's party react to the-me-in-disguise, the newish clothes, a haircut, lucid, gave me a sense of real power. They were listening to me as if I were important.

IT FELT GOOD

I think I can do something in this life before it's all over but I don't know what. Perhaps if there wasn't a recession and jobs weren't scarce, I'd clean up and get one.

Hell! All I need are my two front teeth and I could be Jesse Jackson!

I do know that the hardest thing for me or any addict is to develop the will to change. It's all in the mind.

I do have good days. Days when the desperation isn't as fierce and the pipe talks with a softer tone. And for some reason, warmer weather is easier on me. The sun enables me to have some faith if only I can stay awake during the day to appreciate it.

Something is stirring inside me.

Perhaps I may be alright.

Perhaps there is such a thing as hope.

I do need to tell you about how I started on the pipe before I tell you about Pia. My mother has disowned me because of the Pia incident and that's probably the biggest guilt crazy I carry around my neck right now; probably bigger than the Eric shit. How I began to pipe belongs to the my-story portion of my life that I call my middle passage years, the years right after Nate died.

There was a time when the boundaries of my actions were well and truly circumscribed. This was my circle of life, which excluded specific things that I didn't do.

Now I'll do anything depending on my need to pipe.

People who meet me in the street these days, old neighbors who

*knew me as a boy, look right through me, never seeing the
golden-wonder of promise I once was.*
I've changed.
*I've swum through rough-lightning-flashed-muddy-waters to get
to the other side of my youth through my middle passage years.
Someone told me . . . I think it was some history teacher
somewhere . . . that captive Africans had to cross the middle
passage of the Atlantic Ocean in order to enter America. It was
said to be the most treacherous part of the journey from
Africa . . . many of the captives died . . . it musta been some rough
trip . . . I have to say amen, because my own middle years, my
middle passage, are the hardest times of my life . . . I'm still going
through them. Hoping one day I'll emerge on the other side
ready to enter the wisdom of my twilight years . . . somewhere
between now and then I've got to prepare a life for myself . . . a
life without the pipe.*
I don't know if I can.

I can't write any more now.
I'm tired.
I want to sleep.
That's a good sign.

MAY 20, 1991 — 3:35PM

*Before I start telling you about my middle passage years I gotta
bring you up to date with what's been happenin' since I last
wrote.*
*Lorraine came up to see me about a week after her birthday
party. She was really excited.*
Her job is transferring her to San Francisco.
They're gonna give her a raise and a house.
*At first she wasn't gonna take it because of Kenneth's job, but
the deal is too good to let it pass. Kenneth's all for it.*
He'll find something out there.

I prayed against this happening ever since Lorraine told me. . . .
I was selfish. . . .
Selfish prayers don't get answered. . . .
So it's happening.
They are leaving to bring the baby up in the sun.
Lorraine will be bringing my rent book and my other important papers out to me before she leaves. . . .
I'll have to start paying my own rent. The thought of responsibility scares the shit out of me. I don't trust myself enough to have to take care of myself . . . Not yet.
It's something I'm gonna have to come to terms with because I'll be alone here; except for close neighbors who I've known all my life.
I could give my rent book to one of them and get the welfare ghosts to send my rent money to them so they could pay it for me like Lorraine used to.
Maybe I could get the welfare ghosts to send it straight to the housing people, I don't know if they do that.
I'll have to find out. I'd rather they send the money to someone I know . . . someone I trust.
But could I trust them?
Would they just take my money and not pay my rent!!!??
The thought of being homeless is just too awful to contemplate.
A true road to Vampire-Zombie-Land.

Lorraine's not due to leave the city until August.
I've got a little time to think things out and plan.
Plan. . . .
That's a fucking laugh!
I haven't had a plan for my life since God knows when.
But I'm gonna haffta do something.
Maybe I should get some roommates. This place is too big for one person.
Suddenly I'm full of maybeeeeeeees. . . .
maybeee I should get a roommate
maybeee I should get a lover

maybeee I should get married
maybeee I should give up the pipe
maybeeeeee
maybeeeeee
I'm sick to death of maybeeeeees!!!!
Truth is. . . .
I really don't want to do anything.
I should stop writing about this Lorraine shit because it's making me low.
Reeeeeaaaalllll low!
I've got a couple of bits of rock left but that's for later on tonight.
I just got some money about five days ago.
I'm trying to be scientific with my smoking.
I'm buying enough for a daily smoke but only at certain times.
I'm trying to make my stash last until the next money time.
My money comes on the 1st and the 15th of the month . . . I need more money.
Maybe I should get a job.
But everyone says there aren't any, so why should I bother to look?
I know that I was really feeling high after Lorraine's party . . . feeling like I had it within me to clean up and change direction but I was counting on Lorraine being around to help me make the change . . . but now . . . maybe I should go with her. . . . .
That wouldn't be a good idea.
She's got a baby coming and she doesn't need any dead weight around her neck.
Lorraine's going away is truly gonna push some change buttons within me.
I know my life is supposed to be up to me. . . . . . .

BUT

I don't know. . . . . . .
I
don't
know. . . . . . .
The only thing I've been doing with any kind of regularity
outside of pipin' is writing this diary.
I don't even know why I do it anymore.
Me and the pipe.
Me and the paper.
Two Ps in a pod.
or
a pipe.
I look at the lines on this blank white paper and I sigh. . . . .
Maybe the filled lines give me a sense of living . . . of working.
If I've written a few lines of thoughts and feelings then maybe I
am alive
and . . . and. . . . .
I don't fuckin' know!!!!!!??????
The guilt crazies are standin' around in the corner watchin' me
and waitin' for a signal to move on me . . . The more I write the
lower I'm getting.
I WISH LORRAINE DIDN'T HAVE A FUCKIN' JOB!!!!
WHY DOES SHE HAVE TO LEAVE????!!!
DOESN'T SHE KNOW I NEED HER!!!!????
DOESN'T SHE FUCKIN' KNOW!!!!????
I really don't know what I'm going to do.
I wish I was about twenty years younger.
It's laughable that at forty-three years of age, I have no future.
Not even a hint of one.
I need a smoke.
I used to say that I need something but I now know what I need.
I need a smoke.
But I'll have to wait.
I've got to develop a will.
That's the only way I'm gonna live.

If I don't get a will together . . . .
I'm gonna die.
I'll keep writing.
It'll pass the time.
When darkness comes . . . every night the same . . . I light my candle
to heat my goodness . . . then my first hit . . . not till then. . . .

The middle passage years. . . .
Nate died.
Then daddy died.
We buried daddy next to Nate in a family plot in North Carolina.
After burying daddy, mama decided that she was gonna stay in
North Carolina.
The old apartment held too many ghost-memories for her.
Mama really loved daddy.
It's strange.
I never saw them kiss or hug but I could always sense a closeness
between the two of them.
It was like mama was daddy's better self. . . .
I don't mean better . . . gentler . . . calmer.
Mama's eyes were permanently misty after daddy died.
I'd walk into her room to bring her a cup of coffee and I'd catch
her crying.
She'd try to smile and wipe her eyes as if she had a bit of lint
caught there.
But I knew her heart was breaking.
If mama hadn't moved, she would've died.
I do believe that people can die of a broken heart.
Some things are too big to bounce back from.
This home we had in East New York was too full of horror-story-
memories so mama stayed in North Carolina.

Me and Lorraine stayed together in New York.
That was the strangest.
Lorraine was seventeen.
She had graduated from high school that past June.

We had all gone to the graduation.
It was daddy's last public appearance.
He died the week after.
Mama had petitioned the Housing Authority for a change of
apartment shortly after Nate died.
Mama thought that if we all moved to a new place it might give
the family a new lease on life.
She was hoping a change would kick up daddy's spirits, but
daddy died before the authorization to move came through . . . It
came two days later . . . I remember the day it came.
Mama opened it and started laughing like a mad woman.
I rushed outta my room to see what was up.
She laughed and laughed then started tearing at the walls as if
trying to scratch the paint off. I grabbed her and sat her down in
the living room.
Then the dam burst.
Mama, who had held herself together all through the Nate
ordeal and daddy, now totally unraveled. She cried and
moaned, cried some more then laughed. It was clear that there
was nothing I could do to comfort her. I left the apartment and
went over to the Community Center. I was glad Lorraine wasn't
there to see mama like that.

Moving day was the same week as daddy's funeral. I called the
Housing Authority and told them that we would be moving as
soon as we returned from North Carolina. They were kind,
helpful and understanding.
I drove Lorraine and myself down, along with mama's things, in
the green '63 Pontiac that daddy had bought and taught me to
drive in. Mama rode in the hearse with daddy's body.
There wasn't much of a funeral.
Daddy didn't have much family left.
Both parents gone and a sister we couldn't find.
We had the service and on the way back to Grandma's house
mama told me that she was staying in North Carolina and for me
to look after Lorraine.

Grandma's house would be her new home.
Grandma (mama's mother) had died years before when we were
children, but it had always been called Grandma's house.
At first Lorraine wanted to stay with mama—she didn't think
mama should be alone. But mama persuaded Lorraine that she
would have more opportunities in New York City and, especially
since she was due to start a business course at NYU in
September, it would be better for Lorraine to stay in NY.
I think that mama wanted to grieve alone.
Mama needed to let go and release all the repressed anger and
pain that she had held on to during those hard three years.
We had a last family dinner.
Mama prayed over us and anointed us, gave us a thousand
dollars, kissed us both and waved us on our way.
I drove back to New York in a daze.
We didn't talk, me and Lorraine.
We were each buried in our own thoughts.
We got through the next few weeks somehow.
Packing up the old apartment, moving into the new one.
It wasn't too hard.
We moved from the 3rd floor up to the 6th floor.
The apartment I'm living in now.
It has three bedrooms.
Lorraine had one, I had one and we used the other for a study.

Being alone with Lorraine showed me how little I knew her and
how mature and strong she had become.
She was no longer nervous little Lorraine.
I couldn't stand to spend much time in East New York.
It depressed me.
I really missed my apartment in the Village.
Of course by this time I had been kicked out of Columbia. I had
missed so much work when Nate was sick and I had never made
it up.
May's department store rehired me and gave me a full-time
position.

I found excuses to stay in Manhattan as much as possible.
I was drifting.
I was kinda seeing this girl, this medical student named
Quandza . . . a Black girl.
A high-yellow girl.
Quandza had come into May's one sunny afternoon early in July.
She paid for her things at my register.
Quandza had gorgeous blue eyes and a big ass. She struck up a
conversation with me as I rang up her stuff. She was kinda
interesting. It was almost closing, she invited me for a drink and waited
for me as I counted up my till.
We went to a little club in the Village.
I think it was the Bon Soir.
Quandza talked a lot, which was great because there wasn't
much talk in me at the time.
I was empty.
Dry.
Arid.
Quandza invited me home that night.
I went.
Not so much because I wanted to fuck her, but it meant that I
wouldn't have to go back to Brooklyn.
I wouldn't have to sit with Lorraine at a table built for five that
now sat two.
I just didn't feel like pretending that I was happy and that things
were getting brighter and better, trying to raise Lorraine's
spirits, so I stayed with Quandza.
I fucked her and fucked her all night; it wasn't even an erotic
thing, more like therapy. I used her body like troubled minds use
a psychiatrist. I cried as I fucked her. I literally fucked away my
guilt about Nate . . . the hurt and anger of daddy's escape now
that we needed him most and my confusion at mama's
abandonment of me and Lorraine. I fucked Quandza hard and
good. Afterwards, Quandza was lustrously breathless, she
claimed she loved me but I knew she was lying. She loved the
fuck. That's what she loved.

But she was company, so I hung out with her for a while.
She also liked to get high and kept the best reefer, so she was a
big plus all around.
Quandza was the one who first took me to Boston.
We had been seeing each other for about three weeks.
Lorraine was really happy that I was out and about.
Her and mama wanted me to go back to school, I said I wasn't
ready yet, but I was working and seeing this babe so they were
happy.
I was normal.
Anyway, Quandza was a Gladys Knight freak and she heard that
Gladys was performing at this club in Boston and she wanted me
to go up there with her for the weekend.
I wasn't that hot to go.
I had heard that Boston was real cold and real racist.
Two of my least favorite things.
But Lorraine thought that it shouldn't be too cold in July and
that it would be good for me to get away from New York City.
Quandza begged me, plus she was paying for it, round-trip. I got
time off from work and I went. . . .
We flew.
Eastern Airlines.
Quick trip too. A half hour max.
I hate flying.
Too much tension.
Too many scared people.
Everybody's so peachy nice to each other when they fly; as if
their being nice will earn them brownie points with the great
Sky God and he won't crash their asses out of the air.
I was glad when we landed.

It was a magical weekend.
I fell in love.
Not with Quandza.
Boston . . . B . . . B . . . B . . . Boston. . . .
I loved Boston.

So many people from everywhere . . . so many colors . . . so many sounds.
A whole rainbow colony of newness.
I didn't want to leave.
Quandza had some girlfriends who were students at Boston University—they had an apartment so we stayed with them. One of them tried to fuck me but Quandza caught wind of it and promptly cussed the girl out. She was cute this girl.

We saw Gladys Knight at the Sugar Shack—this was a wild, wild Black club. It was full of P and Ps . . . pimps and prostitutes. Gladys Knight was ethereally magnificent . . . while she was singin' I decided that I was gonna move up to Boston as soon as possible. I decided right there in the Sugar Shack that this was the place where I wanted to go back to school.

Quandza got mad at me during the weekend because I spent most of Saturday walking through the South End.
Alone.
There was just too much to see and smell and taste and hold.
I was greedy . . . I wanted to experience this beauty alone.
Graphic artists and musicians.
Street performers.
The most prettiest people I had ever seen anywhere.
Men and women.
Even the White people were pretty.
An absence of tension.
I didn't have to keep looking over my shoulder.
I felt like I could walk any way I wanted to.
I didn't have to profile.
I didn't have to act Blacker than Black.
I didn't have to have an attitude . . . at least not a belligerent one.
I could just be.
I loved it.
I could forget.

Sorrow and pain took a backseat to joy and discovery that weekend.
I didn't think about Nate or daddy or mama.
Not once.
I loved it.

MAY 21, 1991 — 2AM

Another fuckin' tangent!
I can't find my rock!
I know I didn't smoke it!
I have been waitin' all day for my first hit and I can't find my shit!
Nobody's been here so it can't be stolen.
My first thought was to go out and buy some more but I squashed that.
I've got to build a will.
I promised myself that I would only buy enough for five hits daily.
I can get five hits for about fifteen to twenty-five dollars.
I'm really fucked off!
I can't write no more.
I'll try to sleep.
No hits tonight.
No flights.
No trances.
No perks.
I didn't even scrape the do-do from my pipe and smoke that because I knew if I started then I'd want to go out and buy.
Maybe I should feel triumphant that I didn't give in and cop but I'm just fucked off that I was a good scout all day and at my appointed deliverance time I couldn't partake.
I know it's in the house somewhere.
I'll look for it tomorrow.
I'm fucked off.
Royally.

MAY 21, 1991 — 2:38PM

The sun is shining on my head.
I've moved the only chair in my room close to the window and
the sun is shining on my head, warming what will probably be
my bald spot.
I can see the Pepsi clock from here. It sings time digits. I wish it
had an alarm or chimes like Big Ben.
I went to sleep anxiously last night.
I slept fitfully.
I woke up high. I had been dreaming of hits. I often do but these
hits were different. These hits were alive. Breathing hits. In the
dream I was sitting in this room, as I do, looking out the window. I
remember it snowing and snow looking like fluffy chips of
goodness all flyin' around outside. I remembered pushing my tongue
against the windowpane . . . then I heard these voices—voices
screamin' out my name. It wasn't just one voice, more like a chorus.
They sounded like a chorus of Alvin and the Chipmunks—or when
you speed a record up, a Michael Jackson record—real high and
freaky. I remember runnin' round the apartment, buggin', tryin' to
figure out where these screechy scary voices were comin' from. It
wasn't like they were in another room because I heard them
everywhere I went . . . I heard them real close like they were in my
back pocket, which is where they were, I stuck my hand in my
pocket and pulled out my stash of hits. Inside the plastic bag the
rocks were alive . . . they were living heads . . . no bodies . . . just
heads, perfect miniature Mount Rushmores of living crack. They
were all the same person. Pia. . . . ten hits of Pia . . . some were
cryin' . . . some were laughin', but they were all screamin' my name.
It freaked me so bad that I ran to the bathroom to flush the bag
down the toilet . . . but I couldn't . . . yeah they were heads of Pia,
but they were still rocks . . . crusty white rocks with Pia faces . . . I put
them into my pipe one by one and smoked them . . . I'll never forget
the horror screams as each tiny face blackened, liquefied, then
curdled into the smoke that bled into my lungs . . . I smoked Pia and
it was good . . . the best . . . in my dream the hits were so potent,

they set my head spinning off its axis like a world gone hyper. . . . .
My head spun around and around my neck like a satellite
deployed in space; then spun off my neck and crashed into the
ceiling.
Blood and brains spattered everywhere.
That's what woke me up.
The crash.
And I was high.
Deliciously high. . . .
I drank some water and sat, as I am, in the sunshine.
Sometimes I don't know if writing this down is such a great idea.
It makes me remember things I would rather not.
Like Pia, and I know why I keep thinking about her so much. It's
because I'm gonna haffta soon tell you what happened between
me and her, but I ain't gonna tell you now.
Everything in its time.
I still haven't found my rock, but it's daytime and I'm not supposed
to think about it, so I'll write about Boston instead. . . . .

After I got back to New York City with Quandza, I immediately
set about trying to move my life from New York to Boston.
I called the Boston Tourist Guide and got a listing of all the
schools in Boston.
I applied to three small colleges in the area. I wasn't interested
in any of the big schools because I wasn't interested in going to
school really, I just wanted to be in Boston. I had enough credits
for a couple of schools but they weren't offering any financial
aid so I decided I would just get to Boston, get a job, then get
myself in school.
I felt kinda guilty about leaving Lorraine alone, but Lorraine
wasn't bothered.
I think Lorraine was excited about the prospect of having her
own apartment and living her life exactly as she pleased without
having anyone, including me, looking over her shoulder.
I knew exactly how she felt.
Freedom is positive.

A pungent positive.

Freedom is singular.

Addictive.

Lorraine had tasted freedom briefly, after mama had moved to North Carolina, during my escapades in Manhattan and Boston.

Freedom tasted good to Lorraine.

She wanted a whole bellyful.

Lorraine was glad I was going to Boston.

Mama wasn't so sure it was the right idea.

She lamented the breaking up of the family. From one solid rock, crushed by death and circumstances into three splintered pieces.

Solo.

Independent.

That us three hadn't clustered into a smaller but stronger rock-family worried her, but she understood our need for independence because she needed it too.

Freedom.

Cornelius Sr. had ruled us all with such an iron hand, had sealed the loose ends of our individual spirits with the adhesive of his personality, that none of us knew what our own true feelings about anything were.

This was especially true for mama who had for years submerged, even redesigned her entire persona to fit in and complement Cornelius Sr.'s desires and demands.

This is what marriage meant to mama.

BUT

The King was dead.

Long live the Queen.

And the Princess.

And the Prince.

Mama didn't like my going to Boston but she understood it.

I went.

Trees . . . flowers . . . swans and rowboats growing in the gardens . . . hippies throwing frisbees, sucking on reefer-joints in

the Commons . . . students marching and protesting
everything . . . music everywhere . . . sunshine just like today's
crashing around this enchanted B-town-place, frame the first
memories of my earliest moments in Boston.
I didn't fly.
I took the Greyhound so I could get a good close look at this
New England.
I arrived in Boston the last weekend in August 1969.
I got a room at the YMCA not too far from the South End.
I spent the first few weeks just walking around.
I hitched and walked everywhere.
I was ready for everything and anything.
Mainly.
I was ready to heal.
I forgot about going to school and just dove into the transient
gypsy life of the young people that flowered everywhere in
Boston like fragrant poppies.
I hung out in Harvard Square. I visited jazz clubs in Boylston St.,
Palls Mall and the Jazz Workshop. I attended free dance and
drama classes at the Elma Lewis School of Fine Arts; Elma Lewis
was this eccentric Black dance-diva from the 50s who felt that
art was every Black person's given heritage.
It was a rich, thick, herby cake I was eating.
I was full.
I was happy; perhaps for the first time in my life.
Happy just to be.
The thing I loved most about Boston . . . the place crammed
full . . . Black folk from every state you could name. These Black
folks weren't looting, rioting, killing or generally makin' fools of
themselves like a lot of Black people are prone to do.
No.
These young Black people were all students.
Attending colleges and universities like it was their right.
Like they were supposed to be there.
I learnt how to be Black in Boston.
I had enough teachers.

There in blue-skied-college-towned-Boston were Black people from every state in the Union.

Geeky-looking Blacks from Ohio, shrunken-malnutritioned-looking-Blacks from Arkansas, snappy-big-boned-beat-your-assers from Mississippi, stuck-up-bourgeois-White-ti-fied-Blacks from Washington, D.C., gorgeous-exotic-spicy-Creoles from New Orleans, cerebral-sexy-mellow-Blacks from Georgia, pouting-pretty-ambitious-Blacks from Texas, stylishly-cool-Crayola-colored-Blacks from Connecticut, beach-crazed-baring-chestied-Blacks from Rhode Island, the coolest, the sexiest, the even-more-down-than-NYC-Blacks from Philadelphia.

Can't name them all. They came from everywhere . . . Bean-towned-Boston played hostess to all of them.

Blacks from Boston were a law unto themselves.

Honest-down . . . some of the prettiest people I have ever seen anywhere.

Even the men were pretty.

A touch too country about a few things but you couldn't read Black Boston.

White Boston was another thing entirely, but I ain't writing about them. Whoever had it going on in their own personal hamlets across the country, when they moved to Boston they brought it with them. Boston benefited or suffered depending on what was brought.

I loved the South End where the YMCA I lived in was.

It reminded me of the Village. It was full of artsy shops, a plethora. Psychedelic bars. Full of professional alcoholics hosted by music. I would walk down the steps of the gray-stoned building, turn to the right or left and within a half hour would be in the middle of a cinematographic adventure. People would just come up to me and talk to me. I guess it was because I was new.

Guys that lived in the YMCA were either students or transient working men on a schedule.

I didn't get to meet many of them.

I did meet Mercedes.

Mercedes was a relic.
He was about forty when I met him.
Mercedes had been living at the YMCA before I moved in. I had
never seen him. By this time my mama-money had run out. I had
taken various jobs to pay my rent. When I met Mercedes I was
working at Carvel's, an icecream parlor on Boylston St.
In fact I met Mercedes at Carvel's.
Mercedes.
This thinnish, bearded, Amiri-Baraka-looking poet-
philosopher . . . shouldda wrote his beliefs down in a book. It
wouldda sold millions. Mercedes truly had the answer to the
world's problems, it seemed to me he did, while sucking joints in
his room at the YMCA. Mercedes's room.
A revelation in itself.
Mercedes was a media freak.
He had up-to-the-second state-of-the-art stereo, radio, four
televisions, a film projector, a slide projector, maps, graphs, an
arsenal of books and information crammed inside this tiny-boxy
room that he had lived in for seven years.
It was smaller than my room at the Hotel Operatic.

Mercedes had some wild ideas.
He proclaimed one warmish day that people talked too much.
He had just passed me the joint.
I pulled on it.
He said, "The whole world should shut up for five years . . .
talking and things that talk, plays, movies, radio, records and
especially TVs should be banned, people should be forced by law to
read . . ."
I choked, spluttering the reefer.
Mercedes had all kinds of ill ideas.
He thought that the world's governments should admit that
they don't know what the fuck they're doing, give all the
inhabitants of the world each $250,000, declare a world holiday
for the next seven years while the nations' leaders stopped
warring and planned for the world's future for the next
fourteen years.

"People work too much and too hard for nothing . . . that's why
everybody's crazy . . . they work too hard, even if it's nothin' but
thievin', killin', or nothin' at all . . . they do it too hard an' ain't
got shit to show for it!"
Mercedes would then take off the cool green half-shades he
always wore, even at night in the darkness, stare ahead as if
tuning his subject in clearer.
"If the whole world worked hard together for seven years then took
seven years off planning what to do for the next fourteen
years . . . we'd all be saner . . ."
It sounded like stew to me but when Mercedes explained it . . .
it kinda made sense.

Mercedes was into jazz.
He'd take me with him to see Thelonious Monk or Sun Ra at the
Jazz Workshop or Palls Mall.
Mercedes was a daddy to me in my first years in Boston.
He schooled me mucho.
Mercedes was into Malcolm X. He admired Martin Luther King.
He thought Martin was more the soldier-king, even though
Mercedes thought he was fighting a useless battle.
"Things were better before integration . . . at least we had our
own shit! . . . we had Black-owned funeral parlors an' shit . . . and
then we marched an' shit, an' tore up an' shit, so the White folks
finally say . . . OK niggers, we goin' to let you in, and
bang . . . niggers rush into the White. . . . fast. . . . an' our
shit . . . our 'hood shit dies . . . the Orientals own us now . . ."
Mercedes was a separatist.
He believed that Black youth needed to know more about their
own culture before tainting themselves with too much up-close-
exposure with White culture.
"Black folks don't know shit about themselves . . . all they know is
what they see on TV and they ain't no real Black folks on TV at
least nobody I know . . . I don't know no Julias . . ."
"Julia" was a TV nurse, played by Ms. Gorgeous Diahann Carroll. It
was the middle-class forerunner of The Cosby Show.
Mercedes felt that young Blacks who mixed with young Whites

were in danger of cultural poisoning, that without guidance
they would end up politically White-washed.
I tried to assure Mercedes that the Black students I mixed with
were actually learning something about themselves by being
away from home.
These students were getting primed and quality guidance from
the Black instructors, professors, older Black students and Black
activists of the day. Blacks like Angela Davis, Bobby Seale, Huey
Newton as well as Malcolm X and Dr. Martin Luther King.
I argued that by living among the Whites perhaps now we could
understand them and not fear them, and perhaps they in turn
could learn about us and maybe together we could discover
some common ground.
Mercedes would listen to me calmly, light another joint, sigh,
then laugh.
Mercedes was good for my political head.

The summer flew past dissolving into fall.
Technicolor Boston fall.
The students came back chastened after Nixon's firing squad
dealt death to the children of Kent State—sending a message to
Black activists everywhere.
"We've killed our own and we'll kill you too, so cool down. Now!"
They did.
Politics, real political activity went underground and stayed
there; like a groundhog waiting for the sun of dissatisfaction to
show its face and cast its simmering shadow against society's
sidewalk. That sun is on the rise. The streets will awaken soon.

Quandza, the girl who introduced me to Boston, would travel
up from New York from time to time. Through her I met lots
of different females, friends of hers or friends of her friends. I
was always happy to see Quandza. I think she was puzzled and
frustrated that I didn't push the boundaries of our relationship
further. I really liked her and we spent some wondrous times
together, but Boston was mine and I didn't want to tie myself

down to anything that would intrude upon the freedom that my new world had bequeathed me. For that reason I didn't cultivate lasting relationships with anyone for a while.

By the summer of '71 I was beginning to run out of money again so I started looking for another job.
The Boston Phoenix, a hippy-dippie-newspaper-cum-art-music-politico-guide, was my bible.
I scoured their want ads looking for work.
New England Merchants Bank was hiring night clerks.
I didn't really like the idea of working nights but I thought it might be a good idea because if I did finally get into school I'd have my days free.
I filled in the application, went to the interview and was hired.
I immediately hated the job.
It was boringly banal.
I had to sit at a desk from 11pm to 7am and categorize checks.
American Express checks, BankAmericard checks, that kind of bullshit.
It was weird working at night.
There was only two Black people working the night shift; myself and a plumpish but cute-ish woman of thirty-nine named Maggie Ames.
Maggie was one of my Boston casualties.
There's a bevy of ladies in my life. . . .
Standing in a bunch. . . .
Carrying huge loads of baggage. . . .
Fighting each other to get to the front. . . .
Of the revenge line.
At the front of this line stands Maggie.
I had put all my memories of Maggie outside my experience of Boston because I had well and truly fucked up her life.
Wow!
Another low-life chapter in my book of crimes.
I'd really like to skip the Maggie section but the picture wouldn't be complete without her frame.

I didn't even want to get involved with Maggie.
I thought she was too old for me.
She was almost old enough to be a KIND OF MOTHER to me; in fact that's how our relationship started.
My first week at Merchants started on a Friday which meant that I had no money until the following Friday.
I had waited until I was truly out of money before I looked for a job and when I got the job at Merchants I had only enough money to pay my rent at the YMCA, and a bit left over for food. I didn't even have enough for carfare or lunch. I didn't mind the carfare bit because I walked or hitched everywhere, and Merchants Bank wasn't too far from where I was living; about a forty-minute walk.
I always took an hour's nap during my lunch break which came around 3am, so I wasn't bothered about eating lunch, however when work was over at seven in the morning I was always starving. I guess Maggie noticed that I never ate anything so one day near to the end of my first week at the bank, she brought me a fried chicken sandwich and a piece of home-made vanilla cream cake. I didn't want to take it because I could see already by the way she was always looking at me that Maggie was interested in me and I didn't want to get involved.
I wasn't ready for a relationship yet.

BUT

Maggie was very persuasive and very funny.
She had a way of putting things that made me laugh and laugh.
She called our manager Ms. Thing even though he was this fifty-year-old Jewish man.
After that first time, Maggie brought me lunch every day.
When I asked her why she was being so nice to me she laughed that turbocharged laugh of hers and said that she had spoken to my mama and promised her that she would keep meat on my bones, then she laughed again.

*Soon I wasn't sleeping during my lunch breaks but would be up
laughin' and shootin' the shit with Maggie.*

*Maggie had a laugh that could bang the universe into existence.
It started out as a low bubble then ballooned and ballooned
into a high, hard bellow that would float above everything in its
wake.*

You could always tell a Maggie laugh.

I became glad to know Maggie.

She was a friend.

Maggie loved a party.

Maggie loved to eat.

*I can remember huge breakfasts at Ken's on Boylston Street
after work.*

*We would punch out, Maggie would make a phone call and she
and I would wind up at Ken's eating till I thought I'd burst.
Pancakes drenched in sweet butter with maple syrup . . . and lean
smoked fried bacon . . . and hash brown potatoes and eggs;
topped off with hot steaming cups of hot chocolate—Maggie
hated coffee.*

This was almost a daily ritual.

*One day though, after Maggie made her daily call, she came out
of the phone booth looking worried. She said she had to go
straight home.*

*She never explained, not even later that night, and I forgot
about it until the morning after a late-night party that Maggie
had taken me to. The party had been explicitly toxic.*

*Maggie drank like a back-slidden wino but she abhorred drugs.
After the party Maggie was so tight she could barely walk.
I put her into a cab but before I could tell the cab where she
lived she was fast asleep. I couldn't take her home with me
because women weren't allowed to sleep over at the YMCA. I
was kinda happy about that in this instance. I jumped into the
cab with Maggie and rode with her into Roxbury where she
lived in a brownstone walk-up, not far from Dudley Station.
I hadn't spent too much time in Boston's official ghetto so it was
an experience going there.*

It wasn't as beat up as a lot of New York's ghetto areas, but you immediately knew that this was where the poor people lived. The cab stopped in front of her building. I paid the driver and tried to pull Maggie out. I had succeeded in getting Maggie's limp body out of the cab and was trying to maneuver her into a more manageable position when someone tapped me on the shoulder. I turned suddenly nearly dropping Maggie. Standing on the curb looking very concerned and worried was the most exquisitely beautiful child–woman I had ever seen. She looked like that girl from The Cosby Show when she was in that movie Angel Heart. My heart stopped. "What's wrong with my mother!!!???" The child–woman had asked this again before I realized that I was stupidly staring mouth-wide-open-at-her. Even though it was about 9:30 in the morning and I had been up all that night dancing and drinking, I felt electrically thrilled at this vision of great beauty before me. "What's wrong with my mother??!!!" she asked again. "Your mother?" I stupidly repeated. "Is she drunk?" Her voice was warm caramel over freezing cold vanilla ice cream.

MAY 23, 1991 — 5:34AM

I've been up all night.
I found my rock last night.
I tore the place apart looking for it.
Not that there's a lot here to tear apart.
It has been a few days since I last smoked.
Not because I had given up.
I just couldn't find my shit and it was bugging me out.
Making me really para.

*I was beginning to think that some ghost-people had come back
and were trying to bug me out.*
*At first I thought I'd see how long I could go without it but then
the principle of the thing began to raise its ugly head.*
I am an addict.
An addict smokes.
That's what I am.
That's what I do.
Fuck it!!!
When the day comes and I kick, well so be it!
But until that day comes I smoke on. . . . .
It's my fuckin' right and I don't give a shit who don't like it!
*I raged and stomped around the house like a Hitler until I found
my shit.*
I tore all the dirty linen off my bed.
I emptied all the drawers in the kitchen onto the floor.
I opened all the medicine vials in the drug cabinet.
*I threw over my solitary couch and tore off the lining,
unearthing errant quarters, nickels, pennies and dimes.*
Spare change.
Money that had been eaten up by this ancient couch.
I was glad to find some money.
Money is always handy.
In any form.
*I finally found my rock among the things in my box that I keep
under my bed.*
The box with the picture of me-like-I-usta-be.
*I don't remember putting the rock in the box but I musta done it
—it was there.*
*I remember being in the middle of a smoke when someone
knocked on the door startlin' me.*
*It freaked me because nobody ever knocks on my door except
Lorraine and that freak Linda when she wants some pipe and Mr.
Green—a neighbor downstairs who I've known since I was a boy.
Mr. Green sometimes knocks on the door every other week to
see how I am.*

I think mama asked him to keep an eye on me.
Make sure I don't kick the bucket or something.
Anyway, I ran to the door and looked through the peephole
and saw some official-looking White people.
It freaked me.
I didn't know who they were.
I ran around looking for a place to hide my shit.
Then I figured I wouldn't open the door.
I figured if I didn't open the door they'd go away, but then I
heard them talking about me.
As if their eyes were walking around the apartment and could
see everything I was doing.
I musta run to the bed, pulled out the box and dropped my shit
inside.
I musta done it real fast because I don't remember doing it.
All I remember is the old people's voices echoing around the
apartment.
"Mr. Washington? Are you there Mr. Washington?"
They stood outside the fuckin' door calling "Mr. Washington . . ."
I was wondering how they knew my name.
"Mr. Washington are you there?!!"
And they kept whisperin'!
I wanted to open the door and scream at their ugly wrinkled
fuckin' faces!!!!
"No I ain't fuckin' here! Can't you see I ain't fuckin' here!!!"
Finally after ten forevers they went away to another apartment.
They were Jehovah's Witnesses.
And I shouldn't cuss Jehovah's Witnesses because they're God-
Folk and you gotta be careful how you treat or think of God-
Folk because they can get in your chest and under your skin.
They can give you enemas through your brain and make you
wonder how you got here in the first place. I know because
daddy and mama was God-Folk and they were masters of the
thing.
Even after the wrinkled White people left my floor, I could still
hear them whispering about me; telling each other secrets

about me that I didn't even know about. I stood at my window for hours looking to see them come out the building. Then I thought that maybe they went out of the back and I wanted to go outside and make sure they were gone but I could still hear their voices so I knew they were around and sure enough they finally came out the building and walked toward the skelly-park and the monkey-bar-park where Lorraine used to fall off the monkey bars and knock out her front teeth and daddy would yell at me because I was the oldest and I should have been watching Lorraine more carefully daddy would yell, and they were still talking about me. The old wrinkled White fucks were still talking about me. They were pointing claw-fingers at my window and threatening my life. If I had a gun I wouldda shot them! Fuckin' gossipin' wrinkled farts!!! And I'm cussin' them not their God!!!

I gotta get some sleep.
I been hittin' all night and I'm para-para-para.
I keep seein' tigers in my hallway. . . .
I see people two blocks away outside my window and I can read their lips and I know they're talkin' about me like them wrinkled old White folks. I sit naked in the dark and try to squeeze myself thru the tiny crack of light under my front door. . . . .
I almost made it last night but I had clothes on. . . . . .
I'm tired but my brain is on fire. . . . .

MAY 23, 1991 — 9:30PM

The whole day is gone.
I didn't wake up until a half hour ago.
I'm fuckin' pissed.
It's 9:30 and I should be at the Centa-Renta stocking up for my run.
I can't even get a wake-up hit now, 'cause I blasted myself sideways last night.

I'm too greedy.
I don't really have time to write this shit right now but I need to.
I'm supposed to be building a will.
Instead I'm bingin' every time an opportunity presents itself.
No control.
No focus.
Cornelius you gotta do better.

I did wake up hungry which is a good sign, so I opened a can of tomato soup and ate that with some bread and cheese I bought two weeks ago.
It was still good.
It hadn't turned green yet.
Last night's hits were the best.
Ever.
I hadn't smoked in days and the first hit after not having any in a while is like a virgin hit again.
It's like a first orgasm.
I spent the entire night trying to get a hit like the first one.
OK.
Yeah. . . . OK.
I'll get back to Boston.

The beautiful child–woman turned out to be Maggie's daughter.
She helped me carry Maggie upstairs and put her in bed.
I started to leave and the girl asked me if I wanted a drink.
I said no.
Not because I wasn't thirsty but I didn't think it would be right for me to be in Maggie's house and she not know about it.
Maggie was upstairs in bed—out like an empty Bic lighter.
I left.
Went home to sleep.
It was Sunday so I didn't see Maggie until Monday night at work.
We didn't talk about Saturday night and she didn't bring up the subject of her daughter so I didn't either.

116

I was sick of working nights.

It wasn't too bad during the week, but Friday nights were the worst.

There were lots of jammin' events at different schools that I wanted to go to and a lot of these happened on Friday nights.

I decided I'd have to find a day job.

Fuck school for now.

But I wouldn't quit Merchants until I had another job.

I remember one time Mercedes told me about a lunatic rave that happened downstairs at this club called Pericles. This jam happened on Saturday nights and was supposed to be a major drug event. I promised him that I would be there.

Maggie was beginning to get clingy.

She had my whole week mapped out for me and would tell me on Monday night what we were doing on Saturday night. And since I had nothing better to do, I always went along with it; but this Saturday I wanted to go to Pericles and told her so. . . .

"Great," Maggie said, "I'll go with you!"

I didn't want to tell her that I wanted to go alone or with someone nearer my age so I didn't say anything.

That Saturday night rolled in like a fog.

I was already zippered by the time I was to meet Maggie at the bus stop on the corner of Massachusetts Ave. and Boylston St. We walked over to Pericles, which was downstairs in the basement.

The scene was eclectic.

Multicolored hippies, soul divas in Angela Davis drag, Hendrix clones, gays, straights, bi's, everything and everybody. My pulse raced as I walked about this neon Hades. Janis Joplin screamed into a mix of Crosby Stills Nash & Young with Motown and Stax there cooling for good measure, and when the temperature got chilly James Brown was blasted in to give the dance floor a hot shakedown.

The place was molten.

Maggie clung to me.

I think she was scared.

We drank cup after cup of Kool-Aid which was in this water-fountain cooler.

I didn't want Maggie to know that I smoked, so I would periodically go off for a piss and bum a joint from whoever it was that had one.

It was at one of these share-rees that I met Dalek Dali, the owner of the place and a record producer who also owned a recording studio upstairs. He was this cool-middle-Eastern-looking White boy about twenty-nine years old. Dalek had this ascetic-looking face. He actually looked like one of Christ's disciples that you see in paintings. We started talking and I happened to mention that I was a law-school dropout. This seemed to intrigue him, he gave me his card and told me to call him the next day. I put his card in my pocket and went to find Maggie. She was on the dance floor shaking several tail feathers with this eight-foot-tall Egyptian-looking dude complete with Pharaonic headdress. Maggie blew me a kiss so I went scopin' the party. I ran into Mercedes and we proceeded to get majorally fucked up. I was so high.

Visually this place was a mind-fuck.

There was this black-lit European and African art with psychedelic projections on sheets and canvases that changed color, subverting the actuality of the party into the synthetic-cartoonishness of the techno-pop-props; transforming this seedy basement into the only Alice-in-Wonderland-Oz-heaven.

Maggie came back to me, eyes popping, laughing like a hyena on speed.

She handed me a cup of Kool-Aid as she downed a cup herself, then started screaming and running around the basement beating at her back as if possessed.

She would run, then stop, scream, beat at her back, laugh, then start running around the place again. I caught up with her, then tried to find out what was up. When Maggie's face turned into Betty Boop then into Road Runner, I knew what was wrong with both of us. The Kool-Aid we had been downing at every opportunity was laced with acid, and we were tripping our tits off. I started laughing at the realization, as Maggie laughed, then started screaming about there being eagles on her back and she had to get them off.

Before Maggie could run off again, I grabbed her and told her that the eagles had flown away. That seemed to pacify her.

I knew I had to get her and me out of this place to somewhere safe before who-knows-what happened.

The acid was kicking our ass.

Space-age monsters and demons descended the stairs of hell as we tried climbing up into the dark night. Right as we got to the top near the exit door, Maggie let loose a banshee yell and fell backward down the stairs.

Thank God there was a crowd of angels below who caught her in their wings and flew us up and out of the cave into the night.

Yellow cabs were levitating in the air singin' "Purple Haze," snortin' fire through their grilled teeth. I signaled one as if lassoing a horse. One cab snorted then stopped. Inside was a White-alien-Dracula. I opened the door and pushed Maggie, who was now cooing like a pigeon, into the backseat.

Talk about a magic-carpet-ride—the drive back to Maggie's place was ferocious.

We flew through rainforests and Irish deserts before entering the wild-wild Congo-land that was Dudley Station full of tribal pimps and flamingo-plumed goddesses in twelve-inch stiletto pumps. We arrived at Maggie's house.

Finally.

She was busy singing the theme from The Mickey Mouse Club. Fervently chanting the names of the hallowed mouseketeers . . . Donny . . . Bobby . . . Annette. . . .

I paid Dracula, got the keys from Maggie after chasing her around the block dodging the snakes and werewolves.

At last I caught up with her, pushed her up the stairs and into her apartment.

The gorgeous angel–child wasn't there. Thank God. Maggie

would have been mortified if her daughter had seen her in that condition.

I sat her down in front of the television and turned it on, which was a mistake.

She screamed and stood up on the couch crying that the little Indian people were coming out of the TV with hatchets. I looked and saw it too, so I looked away and switched off the set. I found the refrigerator in the Antarctic kitchen and fed Maggie and myself glasses of milk, desperately hoping that it would neutralize the acid demons raging in our brains.

I put some music on.

Some nice cool jazz.

Miles Davis I think it was; it seemed to calm Maggie down.

I led her like a child through the garden of her apartment into the swamp-hot bedroom and tried to make her lay down.

She giggled and started kissing me; taking my tongue and sucking on it like licorice, running hands over my chest and stomach, then laughing like some nine-year-old who had seen her daddy naked in the bath.

I kissed her back.

Soon we were laying on a yellow daffodil in the middle of a lake, Maggie sitting on my dick sighing and moaning. Lowering herself up and down, up and down.

Faster then slower, up and down, up and down.

She came before I did.

I could feel the spasms inside her stomach and the rain of her pussy waters cooling the head of my dick.

It was my turn.

I turned Maggie over onto a bed of crushed pink roses and rode her pussy like a bull. I put my arms underneath her shoulders and held on for dear life. My dick became a piston drill tapping new oil; going at Maggie deeper and deeper. Each wild scream of pleasure accelerating me onward, downward, forward toward the cliff and then on until I fell, groaning into the ocean of my first coming. Shuddering, shivering, burying my face in the good-and-plenty chocolate Maggie-tits.

Spent.
We lay there. . . .
asleep.

Hours later, I was awakened by Maggie running into the room
telling me I had to get out before Cynthia got home.
I rubbed my eyes asking who was Cynthia.
Maggie threw me my clothes.
Cynthia was her daughter.
So that's what her name was.
Maggie watched me as I dressed.
Before I had finished she came to me and kissed me, sucking my
tongue as before.
I pushed her back on the bed, lifted her skirt and fucked her
some more.
She cried this time.
Cried as her rain blended with the milk of my second coming.
Again and again.
She bit my ear, then whispered that Cynthia was coming.
The thought made my dick harder.
I plunged in again.

MAY 25, 1991 — 7PM

Some real bad deals. . . .
Low.
Low items.
Waste.
Destruction.
Death fire.
Yesterday was a day of shame.
If I could rip off my skin to give life back to those innocents I
would.
Low as I am. . . . . I would.
My people. . . . .

My people. . . . . hold on. . . . .
I'm standin' at the kitchen window yesterday afternoon drinkin'
some water and I hear this shouting coming from behind my
building so I run to what used to be Lorraine's room because her
window is close to the back.
At first I couldn't see anything but I could hear a lot of shouting
and some pop-pop sounds like firecrackers. Then I see Spartacus
tearing around the corner from the direction of the Centa-Renta
and he's got a gun and he's turning around shooting at
somebody.
Spartacus keeps running.
He runs into the skelly-monkey-bar-park where there's kids
playing.
Mothers-Dads-kids-playing. . . .
People see the gun. They start screaming and running.
Then I hear more pop-pops and one little boy who was hanging
upside down on the monkey bars falls off headfirst and I can
see before he falls that his head is split open and some white-
gray stuff is showing through his skull.
There's more screaming.
This little guy runs toward Spartacus shooting at him and I
recognize the guy as the dude who beat me in the head for my
check.
People come running out the building shouting, screaming and
Spartacus and the little dude is still shooting at each other like
they're playing cowboys and Indians and they musta never took
shooting lessons because as close as they are to each other they
keep missing each other but are hitting other people who are
hiding or running. One woman in a second-floor window who
was yelling and crying was hit in the shoulder.
Finally Spartacus hits the little guy in the eye.
The little guy falls down on the ground hollering.
Spartacus runs up and stands over him and shoots him in the
head again and again and I'm shouting as the sirens are wailing
and six men grab Spartacus before he can run away.
Four kids killed.
4.7.12.13.

Including Carlino, the newspaper boy. . . .
This nice thirteen-year-old kid who delivered papers to the
whole project, every morning including Sundays and every
weekday afternoon including Saturdays.
Carlino would sometimes give me a free paper if he had any
spare after he finished his route.
Carlino was hit in the chest.
I heard he died on the way to the hospital.
I had to go outside and walk around after this happened.
I went to the playground after the police had taken Spartacus
away and the ambulance had taken the bodies away.
I looked at the chalk outlines of where the little ones had fallen.
I cried.
Hot angry tears.
Why-when-will-it-be-over-tears.
I remembered this holy-play-life-land where me and Nate used
to play skelly with our melted-crayon-filled bottle-caps. Tyrone
used to swear that his was melted glass; I never believed
him . . . we used to run until dark playing ring-a-levio among
the buildings until mama called us up; our own private never-
land where Lorraine used to fall off the monkey bars
daily . . . this was the safest place in the world . . . I used to feel
safer here than I did in my own bedroom . . .
For the first time in my life I was glad I didn't have any children
to lose to this violent stupidity that respects no age, sex, race.
I cried when-will-we-ever-learn-tears.
I could hear the sound of moaning, shouting, crying and cursing
all throughout the night.
This was these kids' home.
Home equals safety.
Innocents doing what innocents do.
Be. Play. Live. Laugh. Fight.
Cut down.
Caught.
Their lives ambushed, betrayed by an evil they didn't ask to
know or understand.
Low.

Real low.
Nasty.

MAY 28, 1991 — 12:23 PM

There are wreaths in the skelly-monkey-bar-park.
White and red carnations.
Pink roses.
Names.
Alfredo . . . Anjelica-Marie . . . Keisha . . . Carlino. . . .
It's a gray day, cool . . . the sun isn't beating down.
They had funerals for two of the kids this morning.
The funeral for Carlino is happening in Puerto Rico.
I don't know when Alfredo's funeral is.
They say his body is still in the morgue.
He was the child on the monkey bars who had his skull blown
open.
Alfredo was living here with his grandmother so they have to
wait until she can notify his parents.
Too sad to dwell on.
Too sad to look away.

I'm gonna haffta plunge back into Boston and try to tell my story
quicker.
I don't feel much like writing these days, but it takes my mind
off what's happening here.
I gotta get this all told before Lorraine goes away.
I've got to be straight by then.
'Cause after she's gone I may not have the luxury of free time.

Me and Maggie got real tight after our acid trip together. I
eventually moved out of the YMCA and in with Maggie.
It was her idea.
I went along with it.
I can see now that I was never really in charge of my life . . . ever.

I sort of did what came, not really thinking about the consequences.
I did what was presented to me.
I did whoever's will was stronger than mine.
It was a real weird setup at Maggie's.
We would hang out at Ken's until Cynthia went to school, then
we'd go home, fuck, sleep, wake up and fuck some more.
Maggie made me go out every day at 3pm and I wasn't
supposed to come back until after 9:30 pm, after Cynthia had
gone to bed. We'd get ready for work then. I don't think
Maggie wanted Cynthia to know that I was living there but the
girl wasn't stupid, she musta known what was going on.
Some days though when Maggie had sexed me to the max and I
was worn out, I would refuse to leave the apartment, especially
if it was raining outside.
At those times, Maggie would let me rest on the couch in the
living room.
She'd close the living room door, blocking me out and off from
her and Cynthia. I finally asked her about it, and she told me
that Cynthia's father was a crazy dude and if he knew that
Maggie was seeing someone there'd be trouble. He might not
pay the maintenance money for Cynthia. Maggie and him
weren't divorced yet.
I offered to move back to the YMCA, but Maggie said "Don't
worry about it," if we were cool there shouldn't be a problem.

I kinda got to know Cynthia from a distance.
We never really had a conversation.
I saw her on Sunday afternoons when she wasn't with her
daddy; then she would join me and Maggie for Sunday dinner.
Cynthia was too young and too beautiful for me to think about.
I was afraid to, and since Maggie kept her under such tight
wraps, I put Cynthia out of my mind.

I was spending a lot of time with Dalek Dali.
Down at his recording studio.
The recording process was mystifying.

Dalek sometimes got these youngish chicks he was trying to fuck into the studio to record them.

These chicks for the most part had no talent. . . .

Dalek was trying to impress them, so I'd sit in with them while he'd "produce them." These chicks would try to sing and finally, hours and hours later, Dalek would get a "performance" out of them, then for payment he'd take the girls into the back, fuck them or get them to suck his dick, then send them away. Later, somehow, Dalek would magically turn their sow-ear performances into jewels of sound.

Those recording machines can do anything.

It made me check out records more.

Dalek actually got an offer from a major recording company for one of the girls.

I was there when the contract came in.

A big forty-page motherfucker.

I sat down with Dalek and helped him understand the clauses.

I borrowed a book from the library on entertainment law and helped him construct a better contract. It took a bit, but the contract went through, he got his advance and paid me $250 for my trouble—which was like two weeks' salary at Merchants.

Dalek asked me what I was making at Merchants and I told him $125 after taxes.

He invited me to come and work for him as his PA and sort of in-house lawyer. He'd pay $150 a week to start and a percentage of his advance for every contract I dealt with.

That's how I came to quit Merchants Bank and how I got into the entertainment business.

Dalek's recording business was going great guns.

Being right next to the Berklee School of Music was a great location.

Fifty percent of his business came from the students at the school and his club, Pericles, was the hot spot of any weekend.

I was soon making $300 a week and told Maggie that I was moving out to get my own apartment.

Maggie made a scene, complaining that I had used her.

Rod Stewart's song "Maggie May" was popular at the time so I bought it and played it to her one morning as I was dicking her. She laughed, we made up, I moved out and found a nice one-bedroomed apartment on West Newton St.
After a while Maggie saw the wisdom of the move because now our affair could truly be private.
I still stayed at her place periodically until the thing happened; well not the thing but the start of the thing.

I think back to the work I was doing with Dalek in Boston, something forgotten wells up in the pit of my stomach near to my heart.
I think it's pride.
Pride mixed with sadness.
Couldda-shouldda-wouldda . . .
I was fierce.
I was the magnet that pulled business into Dalek's office.
I did it.
I remember walking one spring afternoon, browsing through the many arts and craft shops that were part of the bohemian soup that spiced the sizzling South End.
I noted that many of these shops were emptier than they should be especially as masses of affluent neon-clothed students and business types flooded the restaurants, snake-dancing in the bars that neighbored these electrically creative shops.
As I looked and thought, I hit upon an idea that would be useful to these artists and lucrative to Dalek and myself.
Commercials.
Boston needed to know what and where these shops were.

Most of mankind is blind.
The West blinded by too much.
The East starved blind by not enough.

Light is needed.
Illumination.
Commercialization.

Illumination of the idea.
Blind Boston needed light in order to see these creative craftsmen.
I would provide this light.
I . . . well, we . . . Dalek and me, could produce radio commercials for these shops, at a price they could afford.
By dealing directly with us they could bypass the hefty agency fees that stuck-up pro-ad companies would charge for their services.

I spun my idea past Dalek one evening in Kenmore Square drinking some chilled white wine, puffing some Colombian red-reefer.
"I know nothing about advertising."
Dalek exhaled the sweet aroma into the thicky-hot afternoon air.
"You don't have to!" I took the joint from him. "There's a dozen schools in the area with broadcasting departments . . . these kids pay to learn how to produce their own in-house commercials to advertise imaginary products! Shit! You've got a real-deal studio here—probably better equipped than anything they're used to. Let's get in touch with their student councils, interview some, weed out the wizards, make them a deal—and bang! You've done your bit for education and we get a whole new slice of business!" I was excited. I knew this idea was pure money.
Dalek nodded, swallowed more of the cold credit-card wine.
For the next two weeks, I pestered Dalek, bombed him with the idea, bullied him into at least letting me do some market research.
I knew this would be candy.
The rewards sticky.
Every day for the next few weeks before I went to Dalek's, I targeted two shops. Talked to the owners. Got the 411 on their turnover. Pressed them to reveal how much they'd spend if they had an advertising budget. I followed this up by sending them a flyer offering them a deal: $500 plus tape for a sixty-second commercial, that could be chopped into two thirty-second

formats—in effect they'd get three commercials for their money.
It was surefire.
When I got a list of twenty-five would-be customers, I haughtily presented my findings (but not the contact details) to Dalek who looked wide-eyed at my master-thesis, blinked up, surveying me as if I were an exotically choice and expensive piece of real estate that he'd suddenly discovered.
Dalek came over, knelt, took my right hand and kissed it.
Immediately promising me a ten percent commission on every deal secured.
We settled on fifteen percent.

My radio commercial idea boomed.
Big-time.
I found these two nineteen-year-old wizard-kids who knew their way around slick lingo, pop-beat-sounds and irresistible angles.
With Dalek at the studio controls and me to temper and customize each track, we were flawless.
The commercials supplied our keep-bills-paid money.
Dalek treated me differently after this coup.
He sought my advice and ideas.
I was mint.
An open mind of diamonds.
I was on the beam.
I was happy.

I loved my new apartment.
It was a one-bedroomed thingy with wooden floors, high ceilings and exposed brick walls. A kitchen where I'd cook up potato soup and ground-beef midnight snacks for my own special sample of the most happening of Boston's cream.
My crib was the high spot of the 'hood.
Music poured out of my front windows daily.
My amplifier would announce to the 'hood that Cornelius was in . . . ready to receive.

*My esteem was rising daily because of my services to the
business people in my area I had met while canvassing. My idea
had worked.*

*They were making money. I was making money, we were all
happy.*

*Many of these business people became my friends. They'd stop
by my crib, evenings after work, and if I was back from the
studio, we'd smoke the latest delight washed down by some
Courvoisier or Old English 800. Some nights I'd call Mercedes or
Maggie over and we'd sit with a crowd of maybe fifteen or
twenty people; all vibing to the music, sharing sensations, a joint
was always in rolling mode, we lived the high.*

Loving the feeling, loving the freedom, loving life.

There was once a day when I loved life.

I do remember that feeling.

*It's the same feeling I get now when I've had the most sublime
first hit.*

*It's the same feeling I keep chasing after; rock after rock, bowl after
bowl.*

I'm paying now for yesterday's freedom.

It was magnificent while it lasted.

I hadn't taken cocaine then.

There were too many other drugs I was busy tasting.

*My all-time favorite drug was reefer, but I liked acid, adored
quaaludes, mescaline, THC, mushrooms, freaky angel dust,
poppers. . . . I can't even remember all the drugs I've
experienced.*

*I'm sure the only reason it took me so long to get to cocaine was
that I was too busy recovering from everything else I was taking.*

*I was a perfect little Alice in a purple-poppy-laden wonderland,
eating and drinking all the "drug me"s that fought their way into
my mouth.*

If it appeared, I took it.

Sometimes I took stuff without even knowing what it was.

I remember waking up one morning after a heavy druggy

session the night before. Mercedes had stayed with me, and
while cleaning up we discovered an almost full pouch of weed
that someone had left behind.
Finders keepers!
It had no name so it was ours.
After smoking a bit of the stuff, we discovered these two little
white pills.
Mercedes and I smiled.
A find.
Neither of us had ever seen the two little white strangers before
but they were in the reefer bag so they had to be drugs! Right!
So we did the honorable thing.
We swallowed them with orange juice, smoked another joint
and waited to see what it would do to us.
That was the fun of the thing.
Waiting to see.
Would there be colors?
Visions?
Sexy feelings . . . laughs?
Terror?
I sizzled with anticipation, struggling to be alert to the second
when the goodness would kick in and the trip began.

It began without us knowing.
Me and Mercedes didn't realize how fucked we were until we
looked at a clock. Slowly, languidly focusing on the hands of the
pointing clock we saw that three hours had passed between us
silently.
Where had we been?
What had we seen?
Nowhere and nothing that we had noticed or could remember.
This shit was a time-stunner.
Everything was in slow motion.
The trip lasted several eternities.
It was a monochromatic, underwaterish caterpillar-crawl of a
trip.
Mercedes started singin' the blues in extended notated arias.

I wouldda told him to shut up if I couldda moved my lips.
I was too fucked to panic.
Half of me slept. The other half waited.

The next day I stayed thirsty and promised myself I'd never take
another mystery drug as long as I lived.
I kept my promise until later that evening when someone
commanded me to open my mouth (which I did), and they
chucked some elephantine pill down my throat.
I musta been crazy then.
Good thing I didn't have any enemies.
They couldda kilt me easily . . . but this was Aquarius
time . . . peace, love and alla that shit . . . we truly let the sunshine
in every which way we could.
By night we partied—by day we paraded ourselves like floating
peacocks down Boylston St. nodding to and hooking all the pussy
we could bag on the way.
Maggie was still my main squeeze even though I was dickin'
other girls.
Mama and Lorraine had even come up to visit me. They both
were happy that I was getting on with my life. They weren't
happy that I hadn't returned to school.
I was happy.
Life was, as Dalek put it, real swell.

Cynthia had been about eleven when I first met her.
She had been big for her age then and over the years had
blossomed into this gorgeous nymph of a creature.
Whenever I stayed at Maggie's I had to make myself keep my
eyes off her.
Cynthia was about fourteen now and thinking about men.
Not boys.
Men.
Her and Maggie would have these shouting fights when Maggie
found out that she had been hanging out at night with some
twenty-six-year-old Spanish dude down the block while Maggie
was at work.

Maggie got her work schedule switched to days so she could be home nights and things cooled out for a while.
I had no real work schedule.
I would show up at Dalek's at about noon when he got there, and would work until Dalek said I could go.
Most times I would be there until about ten at night, unless I sat in on a recording which could last forever and a day.
My time away from Maggie would give her the time she needed with Cynthia without me being there as a distraction.
I was trying to find a way to break off with Maggie because now that I was twenty-five, I wanted to settle down with this babe Shirley I had been dickin' on the side. Me and Shirley had even talked about marriage and children.
I wanted children then. And I knew Maggie, who was now forty-three, would never have them for me.
Maggie and me never talked about the future of our relationship.
I was like a son who she fed and fucked.
And big Maggie had a big appetite. . . .
She consumed me.
I needed breathing space. . . .

BUT

I also cared for Maggie deeply, and didn't want to hurt her.
I was also a little afraid of Maggie.
Maggie had a volcanic temper bigger than her universal laugh.
Volatile.
Unpredictable.
I had been there at the house once when Cynthia had done something which displeased Maggie and Maggie had beat her.
I had to pull Maggie off the girl because I thought that Maggie would kill her, then Maggie started beating me and Cynthia.
Together.
At once.
I stayed away from her house more after that which meant that Maggie had to come to me when she wanted me.
Power.

One Sunday night in '74 . . . I think . . . it must have been
January . . . right after Christmas . . . because I can still remember
the smell of dried Christmas-tree pine needles. I had just come
back from spending Christmas with Lorraine and mama.
Maggie had made this big dinner for me with wine.
Lots of it.
Cynthia had spent the weekend with her father . . . so we were
alone.
We had dinner . . . talked . . . laughed . . . drank . . . Maggie started
making plans for the next weekend . . . I tried to interject my
thoughts and feelings . . . Maggie kept talking and she was in
such a good mood I couldn't bear to bring her down . . . off to
bed we went . . . as usual it was an all-night affair . . . I didn't go
home . . . finally we slept . . . I thought at first I was dreaming
Maggie's hand on my dick . . . through the haze of sleep and
drink I allowed the dick to enlarge and grow because the hand
was tight. . . . warm. . . . sliding. . . . up. . . .
down. . . . updown. . . . updown. . . . I smiled. . . . Maggie's hand was
never so small . . . so slender . . . so much tighter . . . Maggie's hand
was larger . . . beefier . . . Maggie's hand . . . my eyes screamed
open . . . I shot up like a hit . . . of lightning in time to see Cynthia
run from the room . . . Confusion. . . . I looked at the clock. . . . It
was 11am. Maggie was at work. . . . Cynthia was supposed to be
in school . . . she was here . . . alone . . . with me . . . scared . . .
thrilled. . . . alone for the first time in two years. . . . . I knew what
she wanted. . . . . The front door slammed shut . . . I went to the
window and saw Cynthia running up the street toward her
school . . . I opened the window to call her back. . . . I got dressed
instead and left. . . . . I promised myself that I would make sure
that I wouldn't be caught in that position again. . . . literally and
figuratively . . . No more nights at Maggie's. . . . It was too
dangerous. . . . Cynthia was more luscious than any Lolita
Nabokov could fuck up. . . . I just couldn't be responsible for
what might happen if we were ever alone again . . . I stayed away
from Maggie's house for weeks. . . . I'd go home at night after
Dalek . . . I'd remember the grasp of her tiny hand on my

dick. . . . . I'd jerk myself off in memory of her sweet hand on my
dick. . . . I couldn't keep the promise . . . I began to find ways of
spending nights at Maggie's . . . Of course I never told Maggie
what had happened . . . she'd kill Cynthia. . . . Cynthia . . . Sin-thee-
A-sin-theea. . . . golden-haired . . . flower child . . . wood
nymph. . . . Woolly-long-brown-hair. . . . . hanging down her back
like a caramel Barbie Doll . . . eyes . . . browner . . . blacker . . .
deeper than the entire Grand Canyon . . . body . . . like the elastic
gymnast she was at school. . . . tight . . . taut . . . tasty. . . . .
I began spending even more nights at Maggie's . . . even Maggie
was surprised. . .
Lying to myself . . . telling myself I was in love with Maggie. . . . I
pushed away Shirley. . . . showing up at Maggie's with flowers
and wine . . . not going home . . . laying in bed alone the next day
listening with heated . . . bated . . . breath . . . heart
pounding . . . praying . . . fearing that Cynthia would come and
take my life in her hand again. . . . dick so hard it hurt.
Sometimes I'd wait in bed until 2:30 in the afternoon then my
nerve would abandon me and I'd go shamefaced back to my
apartment. . . . Once, Maggie invited me over to dinner and
Cynthia was there . . . Maggie went into the kitchen to get
something . . . I was left at the table with Cynthia . . . we looked at
each other . . . quickly looked away . . . my heart running the
Indianapolis 5000 . . . dick ripping through my jeans . . . I fucked
Maggie that night while thinking of Cynthia. . . . . I stayed that
night . . . the next day nothing happened. . . . . . caught up in this
torture hell for months . . . until precious, fragrant spring came
around. . . . . it was Cynthia's fifteenth birthday. Maggie invited
me to go out with her and Cynthia to an African restaurant for
dinner . . . her father was coming to pick her up the next day
after school to take her away on a birthday trip . . . I gave Cynthia
a bottle of perfume . . . I don't remember the brand
name . . . Maggie, as usual, did all the talking . . . Cynthia and me
speaking silly noises to each other . . . my stomach so tight . . . I
could barely eat . . . this fifteen-year-old chick had me by my nose
ring . . . I remember suggesting to Maggie that I should go home

because I had an early start the next day . . . Maggie knew I was lying . . . she kept her hand in my lap all through dinner . . . she knew my body was ready for movement . . . later that night by candle we made slow majestic love . . . I had Maggie screaming before it was over . . . I was afraid Cynthia could hear . . . and I wanted her to . . . sleep . . . dawn . . . sunlight . . . the hand was on my dick . . . I couldn't believe it! . . . . the hand was there! . . . . on my dick! . . . I knew it wasn't Maggie . . . I could smell the perfume . . . I didn't jump up, I pretended to be asleep . . . I started snoring . . . lightly . . . I opened my legs a bit . . . the hand played with my dick for what seemed like hours . . . squeezing it . . . bending it this way that way . . . rubbing it . . . up-down . . . up-down. . . . faster and slower . . . then it stopped . . . I didn't open my eyes . . . I kept snoring . . . a hot wetness . . . Cynthia's pert, apple, bow mouth was on my dick . . . her breath . . . harsh . . . heavy . . . I thought I'd die . . . I moaned in spite of myself . . . I wanted to pull her up, throw her on her back . . . fuck her brains out . . . I just lay there snoring . . . shaking . . . . she musta known I was awake . . . I don't think she cared . . . she sucked and sucked . . . sucksucksucksucksuck . . . stopped . . . playing with me . . . after a millennium I felt this fleshy, juicy softness engulfing my crying tortured dick . . . I gasped . . . this teenage child . . . this luscious-candy-Lolita-goddess was lowering her tight, hot, little pussy on my dick. . . . she was no virgin . . . she had taken big dick before . . . I could tell . . . there was no tearing . . . no blood . . . just never-ending entry . . . down she came . . . down and down . . . down . . . I filled her . . . impaled on me . . . I was her prisoner . . . laying there . . . she rocked herself . . . she forgot herself . . . putting her hands on my chest . . . rocking . . . moaning . . . laughing into my chest . . . I wanted to kiss her lips . . . stroke her hair . . . tell her I loved her . . . get her to run away with me . . . I lay still . . . snoring . . . as she rocked herself into a frenzy . . . like a dervish . . . raining all over me . . . screaming softly in her throat . . . like a pony neighing . . . she came . . . quickly got off . . . ran from the room . . . I

lay there shivering . . . shaking . . . I turned over . . . fucked the
stuffing out of the mattress. . . .

After I heard the waters of the bathroom running and then even
later after hearing the front door slam, I got up, cleaned myself
and went to work.
My mind was like a rummage sale.
Full of everything but the right thing.
I couldn't get my mind on my work.
All I could think about was Cynthia.
It got embarrassing.
I'd be standing on the bus and look down into a shocked old
woman's face, whose roving eyes couldn't help but notice my
rampant dick strainin' against my jeans, threatening to jump out
and kick her in the mouth.
I felt so guilty.
It took me nearly a week before I could get up the nerve to call
Maggie.
Luckily the bank was taking an inventory and she was too busy
to notice that I hadn't been around.
I was afraid to go over to her house but I wanted to so badly.
I needed to see Cynthia.
I tried to bury my head in work.

Dalek found these four young teenage boys from Roxbury who
were like a more aggressive version of the Jackson Five.
He was giving them free studio time because he thought they
were special, and he'd be able to get them a record deal.
They were fourteen to sixteen.
Skinny, streetwise kids with Afros as big as their dreams.
They were basically nice kids who wanted to get somewhere.
I was busy working with Dalek constructing a management
contract for them.
It was because of this that Dalek and I had our first falling out.
The contract Dalek was considering was a sell-your-soul-to-the-

devil-for-peanuts kind of document, which I thought wasn't in
the best interests of the four young brothers.
Dalek gave me a quick lesson in entertainment-business law.
Fuck them before they fuck you.
He said that he was puttin' up all the money and takin' all the
chances, writin' the songs and settin' and direction for the group,
so he argued he was only askin' for what was fair; besides, he
continued, nothing would probably happen with these guys,
who were now callin' themselves New Sensations, and if nothing
happened, the contract would be worthless anyway and he'd
release them.
These guys—the New Sensations—were hot.
They could sing in sweet, sensuous four-part harmony, create all
their own dance steps and were great at rapping, a then new
kind of talk-street-rhyme that had started in New York and was
slowly catching on across the chocolate cities of the nation.
The lead singer of the New Sensations was a precocious
fourteen-year-old named Robbie Mitchell who was especially
talented.
Dalek wanted to sign him separately, and also together with the
group. So in case he decided to ditch the group, he would still
have Robbie.
I didn't know how ethical this was but I went along with it
because Dalek's scene was moving and I wanted to be part of it.

One night as we were about to lay some music tracks down for a
demo for the Sensations, Dalek took out this aluminum foil that
had this white diamond crystal powder in it.
I had seen foil like that at home.
Heroin junkies that snorted would keep their shit in foil like that.
My heart tapped me on the head.
I never knew that Dalek was a junkie.
In my neighborhood junkies were the scum of the earth, they
were the lowest of the low.
I didn't want no part of that shit.

"Want some?"
Dalek had this steely gleam in his eye, this questioning smile on his face.
"What is it?"
I played stupid.
"Cocaine . . ."
Dalek started spooning a pile of the powder onto the glass-top table with a fingernail clip.
I was surprised and intrigued.
I had heard about cocaine.
I had never seen any.
Or knew anybody that did it.
Cocaine was a money drug.
Pimps used it.
Rock stars used it.
People I knew didn't.
"What does it do???!!!"
My eyes were fascinated by the diamond sparkle glinting off the white powder lying before me.
"It gets you high motherfucker!!!"
Dalek laughed his low home-boy-laugh.
"Gives you energy . . . keeps you up . . . try a bit. . . ."
Dalek said this so nonchalantly, so coolly, like he was offering me Coca-Cola.
I never knew that what I was about to do would change the channel of my life forever.
I never knew that I was about to chain an eight ball around my neck that would enslave me to cocaine from that day to this.
Many times I think about my seminal toots of cocaine and how my life might have been different if I had simply said no; but I didn't say no.
I said . . . . "Sure! . . . I'll try anything once . . ."
A popular and true saying of the day.
Dalek chopped up two lines for me, rolled a twenty-dollar bill into a tube, gave the tube to me.
I snorted up my first toots.

The powder hit my nostrils like a million tiny pins stinging the
inner membranes of my nose.
My eyes started watering.
I started sneezing.
Dalek screamed! "Not on the coke!"
I turned away just in time.
Tell the truth I never felt nothing.
Just an irritation in my nose and eyes.
Dalek laughed; pulled out a pouch of some primo-reefer that he
always had, sprinkled a healthy portion of cocaine into the joint,
rolled it, then lit it, inhaled a few times and passed it to me.
I smoked the whole thing.

I had never, ever, ever felt so mellow, so in charge, so sexy, so
dreamy, so wonderful in my life.
It was too good.
I bought my first twenty-five dollars' worth of cocaine from
Dalek Dali that night.
I never snorted it again because it hurt my nose. . . .

BUT

smoking it . . . well . . . earth has no sorrow that smoking cocaine
cannot heal.
So I thought.
Nobody told me it was addictive.
Nobody told me it was bad for me.
Nobody told me it can kill you.
Nobody told me it would ruin my life.
I loved getting high because I could get away from the haunts,
hurts and humdrum-ness of everyday life . . . and cocaine got
you away nice.
I didn't notice the physical changes in myself at first.
All I knew was that whenever I smoked a joint, which was often,
I wanted that joint to have cocaine in it.
I soon found out that fucking on cocaine made one a master of
the universe.

You could stay harder longer and drive a person to the brink of
insanity under the influence of cocaine.
If both of you were doing cocaine then baby as the song
says . . . "Heaven belongs to you! . . . . ."

JUNE 1, 1991 — 3:30 PM

Central Park New York City

I love the sun.
Its purity . . . warmth like pure love . . . honeyed sweet. . . . .
No matter how dark, how painful . . . how fearful those hours are
before its appearance, once the wispy slivers of light radiate
through the murk, my heart sings.
I know I'll be alright.
I know I'll make it.
I've spent the entire night here in Central Park.
Near the fountain.
I came out here yesterday evening.
Lorraine came by to see me after she finished work.
She dropped by to see me and left me some money.
I hadn't even asked her.
I certainly didn't need it . . . well I always need money but my
check had come, so I was alright.
Lorraine gave me a hundred dollars. I nearly choked. Lorraine is
so happy.
I've never seen her so happy.
It's now official. She leaves New York for San Francisco on
August 5th.
She brought a few important papers over to me because she was
starting to pack and she didn't want the papers to be lost with
her stuff.
She brought me my birth certificate, my social security card, my
welfare ID, and some letters from mama.
I put all the stuff in the box where I keep the picture of me-like-I-
usta-be, wrapped in the coat mama gave me.

Lorraine was real chatty, full of plans, full of future.
It made me feel proud to see her happy.
It's good. No matter what happens she'll be alright.
I came out here to the park after riding with Lorraine into
Brooklyn.
It was such a nice evening, warm and billowy. I didn't feel like
sitting in my place by myself so I thought I'd go uptown.
I hardly go anywhere anymore.
I hadn't been to Manhattan in light-years.
I wasn't gonna buy any rock at first but the money Lorraine gave
me was burnin' a hole in my pocket, so after I left her I went to
see the pipe-man that I know in her neighborhood and bought a
few bags. I haven't done them yet.
I'm still trying to build a will.
After I left Lorraine, I got back on the train and went to 59th St.
I got off and went in a movie. Something I hadn't done in ages.
Just like a normal person I bought a ticket and went in to see
Ghost.
I like that Whoopi Goldberg.
There's a certain honesty about her and she's funny as
shit.
I laughed so much and cried. It's a cryey movie.
When the movie finished I still didn't want to go home. I didn't
necessarily want to be with anyone but I didn't want to be
alone. It wasn't a sexual thing. I wanted to be counted and
included.
I wanted the moon to see me.
I wanted the big bright moon that was rising in the early
evening sky like a slow cake to nod and wink at me like the fairy
tales say he does.

A couple of policemen were in front of me walking towards the
park. I followed them.
I knew I'd be safe with them around.
It was starting to get dark but it wasn't pitch-black yet.
The police wound their way through the park talking intently to

each other. Trees to the side, moon above, lake straight ahead. I willed another future for myself.

A power future.

A future of hope like Lorraine's laughter.

I never noticed that the policemen were no longer in front of me.

I panicked for a moment—then laughed, realizing that I had nothing to fear. No one would bother me.

No one would come near me.

Dressed as I was in the uniform of the despised, I had become one of the feared. "A dirty-stinkin'-crack-addict!"

A leper. A Medusa.

A stay-away-keep-away person.

The only beings who will approach me are dealers and other dopers.

That Lorraine would walk down the street with me, sit with me on the train holding my hand, is a testament of her love.

I passed through the shadows of Central Park unmolested, unapproached.

The park seemed quiet.

There wasn't even as much sex-in-the-bush activity that was a staple park highlight in the '60s and '70s.

Everybody fucked in the park then.

Cruise area number one.

I guess the message of AIDS is getting through.

I saw several furtive souls sucking each other off at the end of a dark tunnel.

I never really saw them but I know the sounds of pleasure.

Finally I arrived at the fountain.

Homeless city.

Cardboard box hotels with shopping carts standing guard checkered the area around the fountain.

These were the brave souls. The regulars I guess.

Some hadn't retired for the night. They sat on the wall smoking cigarettes, drinking, chatting with sad eyes. How-did-this-happen-to-me-eyes.

BUT

it was warm and the moon shone down so it wasn't too bad.
There was just so many of them.
Old people, young people and some children. All huddled
together.
The new nomads. Urban nomads.
From the tiny sporadic lights that flickered on and off in the
darkness and from the sweetness of the smell that settled on my
nose like a friendly memory, I knew that it was pipe-time in the
park; but I didn't want to partake here. I didn't want to open
myself here.

A fifteen-year-old-boy passed me, then came back and asked me
if I had any money. I told him no, because I didn't know if he
was cool or not. He was persistent. He told me that he was
hungry. He hadn't eaten in two days.
I thought at first that he was conning me to see if I really had
any money. I started walking away.
He caught up with me and begged me to let him walk with me.
He had run away from his father in Kentucky and had stolen
away on a Greyhound bus and ended up in NYC.
His name was Mercury. He was from Florida.
His mother had sent him to stay with his father in Kentucky
because she had just gotten married again and he and her new
husband weren't getting on.
Mercury's father, in Kentucky, was a bit of a drunk, not able to
support himself, and certainly not willing to support and care for
a fifteen-year-old troubled teenager.
They had fought, and after a fierce beating Mercury had
stabbed him, taken what money he could find and bused his
way cross-country until he arrived at New York Port Authority.
He had been in the city two days.
We talked together as we toured the haven of the homeless.
Mercury looked like he was eleven. Small, Mexican-looking,
skinny body with a big head and masses of curly black hair.
A pretty boy.

Mercury could make money selling himself if he wanted to.
He would probably have to eventually if he wanted to survive.
I listened to him as he told me his history guiding ourselves
outside the park to 63rd St.
Mercury stopped talking when he realized that we were no
longer under cover but were exposed to civilization again. He
looked up at me with hungry moon eyes. I took his hand and
guided him to a delicatessen that was across the street. We
bought lots and lots of food, candy and soda. We walked back in-
to the park, back to the fountain, sat on some steps and feasted.
I gave away most of my share to some old people who asked.
I felt like Jesus with the five fishes and the loaves of bread.
And so I spent the night—talking, listening, wandering, praying
that I never come to this.
Without shelter.
Without walls of safety around me.
To be homeless would be the ultimate cruelty.
I can hardly imagine not having shelter.
God forbid.

About three or four in the morning, I found some bushes against
a rock overlooking the fountain, with some tall trees above our
heads for cover, and lay down with Mercury.
Back to back.
Mercury was crying.
I tapped him on the shoulder, he turned and flung himself into
my arms.
I cuddled him gently.
Nothing sexual.
This was a child.
Yes, I had fucked a child many years before, but that child
wanted to be fucked. This child wanted comfort. I gave him
comfort.
Mercury slept in my arms until the warm forgiving sun found us,
wakened us.
I took Mercury back to the deli, bought him breakfast.

Afterwards he ran into some kids he musta met the day before.
He smiled at me then ran off with them.
I let him go.
It was best I did.
I had nothing to offer a child.
I can barely take care of myself.
I am a child.

I walked out of the park and up toward Lincoln Center, just
looking at the people as they hurried to make money.
I watched the sellers and observed the amounts that were sold,
the amounts of money that changed hands, the numbers of
goods that stood in the windowed shops like wheat, cut, dried,
ready to be devoured.
So much.
Too much, but not enough for the dwellers in the city of the
homeless.
I walked back into the park, sat down on a bench as I am now
and wrote the memory.

And I do love the sun.
It makes everything hateful tolerable, everything painful
bearable.
I may move to Southern California just so I can keep the sun
around me all year long. I think I could beat this addiction with
the sun around me, or at least live with it more easily.
When the sun is shining, I don't really care to smoke.
It warms away the guilt.
It carries me with love and reminds me I am alive.
I have life.
I can do.
I can be.
The sun is the miracle of life.

JUNE 1, 1991 — 9:30PM

I still haven't smoked yet.
I'm gonna see if I can go till tomorrow.
It's so late.
If I smoke now I'll be up all night and want to sleep all day.
I'll miss the sun.
I'll write some more.
It takes up time.
I'm so tired after writing.
Memory is exhaustive.

After being introduced by Dalek Dali one warm May evening in
the spring of 1973, me and the big C became very close friends.
Inseparable. Just like the Natalie Cole song.
We started each day together.
My lips on his ended the day.
I lost a lot of weight.
I became very popular.
Maggie took Cynthia away for the summer of '74 which was a
big relief to me.
I was still feeling really guilty since Cynthia raped me.
She did rape me.
That's what I told myself.
I was only able to justify my actions by telling myself that she
had raped me.
Yeah, I had allowed it to happen, but what was I supposed to
do, jump up and yell at the girl? Tell Maggie, who would have
beat her to kingdom come?
That probably would have traumatized Cynthia sexually, might
have made her have sexual problems with men later. Might even
have turned her into a lesbo. We couldn't have that.
Cynthia had raped me.
Pure. Simple.
She had raped me.
And I liked it.

I wanted some more.

So Maggie taking Cynthia away solved all kinds of problems for me. I hadn't seen Maggie much since the rape.

I certainly hadn't stayed at her house.

Every time Maggie wanted me to, I told her that I was on my way to the studio, which wasn't entirely a lie.

Dalek had started the New Sensations on vocals and the first track was sounding livid. It had hit city written all over it.

I suggested to Dalek that he should press up a few records and send them 'round the college radio stations to see if it could get some airplay. If they played it, he could sell some. If he could sell some, then they'd be more attractive to a record company. We could demand a better deal.

So I wasn't lying to Maggie entirely. I was busy but I really didn't think I could face her.

I took her out for a drink the night before she was leaving. I took a break from the studio and met her at this café on West Newton St.

Maggie looked anxious. She smoked a lot of cigarettes.

She looked like she was about to cry.

"She knows!!!" I thought.

"Cynthia must have told her!!!" I almost ran out of the café.

Maggie apologized. Relief.

She was sorry she hadn't been in touch. She was real busy with Cynthia.

Cynthia was worrying her.

Maggie was sure that Cynthia was fucking.

I nearly dropped my glass.

"How do you know this?" I asked furtively.

"I can smell it on her panties . . ." Hmmmm.

Maggie looked distraught.

"I've washed that girl's diapers and panties every day since she came out of me. I know what Cynthia smells like. Lately there's been this strong, musky, mannish smell in her panties and I've found lots of come stains . . ."

"Well it couldn't be me" I thought to myself as I slowly sipped my brandy and port. Cynthia had washed herself afterward. I know she did. I remember the sound of the running water.
"Have you asked her about it?" I tried to disguise the nervousness in my voice.
"No . . ." Maggie sounded defeated.
"I know if I ask, she'll give me lots of lip and it'll be a fight. I don't take no lip from Cynthia . . . you know that."
I knew.
"I'm gonna take her away to my mama's. I don't want that girl comin' up pregnant . . . If I let her stay here this summer I know she'll end up knocked up before the summer's out and then I'd have to kill her!"
I tried to smile to lighted up things.
"Come on Maggie, don't say things like that. You know you won't do nothing like that."
Maggie stared at me sadly but evenly.
"If the bitch ever comes up pregnant before she's eighteen or married . . . whichever comes first . . . I'll kill her and the nigger responsible . . . I've warned Cynthia many times and I ain't playin'! . . . ."
I knew Maggie was serious.
I tried to change the subject because the topic was a bit too hot for me to dwell on.
The remainder of the evening was kind of pleasant.
I excused myself, went to a phone, called the studio and told Dalek that I needed the rest of the night off. Trouble at home I told him.
I took Maggie back to my place and gave her a mercy fuck because I felt so bad for her.
I promised myself that I would never touch Cynthia again.
I really wanted to keep that promise.
Maggie left in a cab early the next morning.
That would be the last time we would be together in any safe sense of the word.

■

With Maggie and Cynthia out of my beam for a while, I was able to focus on the empire that Dalek and I were furiously building. He had taken my advice and pressed up five hundred copies of the New Sensations demo.

The tune was called "Telephone Song."

At first we never heard it anywhere, and Dalek was afraid he'd be stuck with five hundred worthless pieces of plastic and loudly and often rued the day that he listened to my "hot-shit-idea," as he called it.

Then one afternoon, four weeks after we had circulated the records to the radio stations, a call came into the office from a local record shop. Several people had come into the shop requesting "Telephone Song." They had heard it on the radio. The shop had called the radio station and found out that Dalek had produced it. The shop ordered twenty copies. We celebrated that night with the Sensations.

We were all sitting in the control room smoking reefer when there was a scream from the office. "They're playin' it!!! They're playin' it!!!" We all rushed into the reception, Dalek turned up the volume and there in glorious monaural sound was the New Sensations singing "Telephone Song." I hadn't sung one note on the record and had contributed minimally to its production but I was prouder than any of them. It had been my idea to press up the tape.

The next few weeks were supersonically busy. We soon sold out of the original five hundred copies. Dalek pressed up five hundred more.

They went.

Soon we were besieged by local radio pluggers who would, for a fee, plug our record in other states.

I told Dalek that I didn't think that this was a good idea. We weren't a record label. We were producers trying to be managers. We only wanted to get the New Sensations signed to a major label. But Dalek smelled big money. He pressed up fifteen hundred copies of "Telephone Song," gave them to this *plugger guy, and that was the last we heard of him and the records. We did get calls from radio stations in other states though, saying that they were playing the record, and could they get some information on the Sensations.*

My cocaine habit wasn't too aggressive yet.
I was smoking about a hundred to a hundred and fifty dollars of the stuff a week, which wasn't too bad. I was paying my rent.
I wasn't saving any money, but I was getting by.
I did notice that the day after smoking I would usually be in a foul temper until I lit up the first big C joint of the day.
I happened to rush into Dalek's office one afternoon with a contract proposal and there was Robbie Mitchell, lead singer of the New Sensations, with his nose to a mirror snorting up an almighty long line of cocaine.
I was shocked but I said nothing.
Dalek smiled at me.
I waited until Robbie had satisfied himself and left before broaching the subject with Dalek.
"Isn't he a bit young to be doing that shit?" Robbie had just turned fifteen.
"Young!" Dalek roared with laughter. "It was his shit! . . . he turned me on!"
I didn't know what to say to that.

I made it my business to talk to Robbie later that night before a recording session. It didn't help. Robbie laughed it off. lold me that all the other guys in the group did it too. His big brother had started him on it and it made him sing better. I didn't know what to tell him.
I was smoking it.
I loved it.
It made me feel better and think better.
I thought. At the time.
I didn't know enough of the dangers of the drug to warn him off it, so I said nothing.

■

Things were hopping at Dalek's.

Three record companies had made inquiries about the Sensations, and one had made an offer. I was busy orchestrating a deal with Dalek for the Sensations when the heavy-duty shit butchered the fan.

It was the last weekend in August.

I remember it because it had been one of the hottest days that summer and this particular night was torrid.

We were doing final mixes on a new Sensations track, and it wasn't going too well. We had run out of cocaine the night before, hadn't been able to score that day, and we were all yellin' and cussin' each other. Robbie and Lentil, the bass singer, had just pulled guns out on each other and I was standin' in front of one of them and Dalek was standin' in front of the other. Teeth-eyes-tongue all hangin' out at each other and cussin' from the gut. Ready to blow each other's brains out. Pure-coke-rage. And me and Dalek had jumped simultaneously in front of each of them. Protecting the investment. They couldda shot the shit outta us and robbed us blind. That night me and Dalek realized that these young dudes, these children, these New Sensations, were truly serious about stardom.

They were ready to kill each other for it.

And the only reason they didn't kill us was because we were the only people they knew who could get stardom for them . . . That would soon change.

After persuading Robbie and Lentil that a recording contract would be much more fun than jail or death, they finally put their guns away. I was shaking like a Jew in a concentration camp.

I suggested to Dalek that we call it a night.

Dalek, nervously smoking a cigarette, agreed. We sent Robbie home in one cab and Lentil the bass singer in another, splitting the rest of the Sensations in the cabs between the two. Dalek and me smiled uneasily at each other and went to our respective homes as well.

■

I walked home from the studio checking the pro-girls and boys that were still busy trading, even though it was about 3:30 in the early morning. I got home, walked into my apartment. I was glad that I had splurged and bought myself a fan because my apartment was cooler than it was outside and for that I gave muchas gracias.

I had just rolled myself a night-cap-number when there was a manic ring on my doorbell.

I thought it might be Garcia, this Puerto Rican chick I was dickin' that lived in the 'hood. I pulled three hits off the joint, then went to open the door. There on my doorstep looking disheveled but luscious was Cynthia. Saying nothing she walked past me into the apartment. I stood on my stoop laughing. I didn't know what else to do so I laughed. Before going in I looked up and down the block praying that Maggie wasn't on the way to my door with a cavalry of policemen.

When I walked into the front room Cynthia was standing in the center with her back to me.

"Where's your mother?" I started gently.

"She's still in Florida." Cynthia answered in a quiet monotone.

"In Florida!!!" I relit my joint.

"I ran away . . . the bitch is crazy!" Cynthia didn't move. Her back was still to me.

"You shouldn't call your mother a bitch." I didn't know what to say to her.

"She is a bitch and she is crazy . . . she burnt my fingers on the stove!"

"Why'd she do that?" I tried sitting down.

"I took some money from her purse." Cynthia turned to me now. "I wanted to go to a movie with a boy I met down there and she didn't want me to go . . . so I took the money . . . she caught me before I could leave . . . she beat me, dragged me to the stove and put my fingers in the fire . . . she's a sick, evil bitch!"

At that moment something told me that I should take this woman-child to the nearest police station and leave her there to face her fate with the police and Maggie. That I should make good my mistake with this child before I made any more. Cynthia was not my responsibility.

BUT

I didn't listen to my head.
I listened to my dick.
A dick that was ballooning with blood lusting for the pussy of the not-so-innocent-child-woman standing now in my living room. Unaccompanied and totally at my mercy—or was I at hers. I made us some hot chocolate and half-listened to her tale of woe at the hands of her mother, who only wanted her to keep what little was left of her virginity intact for a later date, when she would be older and more responsible.
I said about as much to her and tried my best to do the right thing. I asked her how she had gotten to New York from Florida. She had hitched the whole way.
Wasn't she afraid of what her mother would do when she discovered her gone and then finally found her?
Cynthia didn't care.
She wasn't going back home.
Ever.
I asked her where was she gonna stay. She said that she was gonna stay with some cousins of hers that had an apartment in Mattapan, but could she stay with me for the night?
I said "Yes!" without even thinking.
The cocaine in the joint I had smoked earlier was making me hornier than a pride of rhinoceroses, but I was determined not to touch this child. I suggested that she sleep in my bed and I would sleep on the couch.
"Why?" Cynthia looked at me with those liquid almond eyes that made my skin turn inside out.
"You've already fucked me." She started taking off her clothes.
"I was asleep!" I tried to protest, I really did.
"If you were so asleep then how do you know that you've already fucked me?" Cynthia was standing too close to me.

This child beat about no bushes. She knew what she wanted and she went for it. She rubbed my dick through my jeans.
Up-down . . . up-down. . . .
She tried to grab my dick through the jeans but the jeans were too tight for her to hold on to it.
I pulled away.
"No! . . . we can't do this! . . . your mother will kill us!"
I was sweating monsoons.
Cynthia walked back toward me.
"My mother! Fuck that bitch! How is she gonna know? You gonna tell her? I didn't tell her about our first time . . . not yet . . ."
There were so many things that I wanted to say to this troubled teenager; things that I could have said that would have stopped what was about to happen.
But nothing came out.
I was twenty-six.
A hot twenty-six-year-old who had been bewitched by this teenaged temptress for the past few years. She had already fucked me and it was now time to return the favor. Perhaps if I fucked her like a woman she'd realize that she wasn't ready for a man.
Her kiss destroyed me.
Cynthia had stopped talking as I stood there silently thinking.
She had walked up to me and kissed me. Her lips torpedoed into my mouth, found my tongue and sucked on it.
Hard.
Her fingers danced on my dick.
I feebly tried to push her away but I couldn't. I caressed her hair, fingered her face. . . . . her body.
I caught her up in my arms and carried her into my bedroom like that dude did to Scarlett O'Hara in Gone With the Wind.

I don't need to tell you what I did to her because you know.
I fucked her.
I fucked her silly.

We stayed in bed for four days.
I didn't go to work.
I didn't answer the manic phone.
I was afraid to answer the door because I was sure that it would
be Maggie. We stayed naked the whole time.
We only stopped fucking long enough to eat, sleep and pee.
I would wake up and Cynthia would be straddling my dick. I
would turn her over on her back and finish her off.
There seemed to be this great need within her to be fucked. I
couldn't understand it. Her desire was savage.
She told me that a cousin of hers had popped her cherry when
she was nine and that she had been fascinated by dick ever since
then. She was on the pill so she wasn't afraid of getting
pregnant. Her cousin had been fifteen when she was nine so she
had always been attracted to older men. She had even planned
to run away with Carlos, the twenty-six-year-old Puerto Rican
guy her mother had seen her with. She loved Carlos.
Carlos was wild, and until me, he was the only man who could
fuck her for hours and hours without tiring.

JUNE 18, 1991 — 1PM

So much has happened since I last wrote.
I've spent some time in the hospital.
I nearly died.
Well it felt like I nearly died.
I've also got a roommate. I'll tell you about him in a minute.

I was doing great for a while.
I didn't smoke those rocks that I had bought with the Lorraine
money until nearly a week after I bought them.
My system was clear so the first hit off the first bag was nearly
virgin. Magical.
I saw colors.

The rushes were so intense I started sweating. It was magnificent.

I got through the first bag and got all hyper.

It looked as if an A-class binge was gonna be the order of the day, but I never got that far.

I opened the second bag, stuffed my pipe, lit up, inhaled and waited for the rush.

Soon as I lit up I knew something wasn't right. The shit didn't smell right.

The smoke hit the back of my throat like a blowtorch. It felt like my head was melting.

I had inhaled so much that I started coughing and spitting, then vomiting. The smoke was cracking my brain like sulfuric acid.

I heard like a tearing sound in my head behind my ears, then the room started swaying in front of me.

I got real para.

My heart kept accelerating and as much as I tried I couldn't calm down and I kept vomiting.

I could barely walk but I made my way down to Mr. Green's door, the neighbor friend of my mother's who looked in on me from time to time. I remember banging on his door, then blackness. I woke up in Kings County Hospital.

They put me in a ward with all these old men, old dying White men.

It was horrible.

You could smell death on them.

Some of them couldn't move without a nurse's help.

It was almost impossible to sleep at night because a few of them moaned and cried constantly.

The doctor assigned to me asked me a lot of questions. I told him very little.

I figured that he must have examined me when I was out so he had to know the deal.

The doctor asked me what drugs I was on.

I told him nothing.

The nurse told me later that I had a bad liver and there was a
bump on my scalp that they were worried about. Other than
that I was healthy. Undernourished, underweight, dirty and
generally unkempt, but healthy.
The doctor came back and told me that heavy traces of a cocaine
derivative had been found in my blood with other traces of a
toxic chemical, he told me the name of it but I forget what he
said. He said that I was very lucky.
If I had ingested much more it would have killed me.
He asked me if I was on crack.
I told him nothing.
I wouldn't even tell them my name.
In fact I didn't talk to anyone the two days and three nights I
was there. I didn't want them having any records on me.
Who knows, one day when I clean my shit up I might decide to
run for public office and I wouldn't want some rival cunt to dish
up that kind of dirt.
The doctor was cool.
He told me that if I was an addict he could refer me to an out-
patient therapist. I nearly cracked up laughing at him.
I was so tempted to tell him about Eric, but I said nothing. I just
laughed.
Perhaps another therapist could help me but I don't know. Right
now I'm trying to find my own strength. I already know the deal
with a therapist and I know what they'd say to me. They'd say to
me that it's up to me to kick. I know that already.
I was so glad to get outta that hospital.

I came home in a taxi.
They paid for it.
They said that I was still weak and that I should drink lots of
water. I told them that I didn't have the money to buy water
and that the tap water in my apartment was nasty and I couldn't
drink it.
They gave me fifty dollars' worth of food stamps, so I bought
water and some food on the way home. I saved twenty dollars
of the stamps. I could trade the stamps for rocks.

When I got home I immediately checked the bags of rock had
been smoking before I got sick, to see which rocks were the
rough ones.
I was tempted to sell the bag I had been smoking from because I
hated getting beat for my money, but I knew that if I sold it to
anyone 'round my area I'd have them on my back for all eternity
and I couldn't be bothered to go uptown.
I flushed the tainted rocks down the toilet.
I sampled a bit of rock from each of the remaining three bags;
putting a touch of rock in the pipe and lighting it and smelling
the smoke, not daring to inhale it.
I hated using so many matches but I didn't have a candle.
The rest of the batch was primo. It was a heart-warming-coming-
home-smoke.

I adore the summer.
I can deal so much better when it's warm, the pipe doesn't talk
to me so harshly, and if the pipe does talk, if I don't want to
listen I can go out on the roof of my building, one of my favorite
places, sit in the sun and blow out the pipe-talk.
I've got a roommate.
This dude I went to school with.
His name is Quentin.
He's homeless.
I hadn't seen Quentin for years.
I was on my way up to the roof three days after I got out of the
hospital, and saw all this cardboard on the landing just outside
the door leading to the roof. I paid no attention to it because in
the winter lots of homeless people take shelter in the stairwells
of the projects.
I walked outside and saw this figure in a black woolen coat
sitting with his back to me. His hair was all matted and dirty. He
looked like he was growing dreadlocks, but it just needed
cutting and was filthy. I smelled him before I saw him.
I was about to turn away and go back to my apartment when he
turned to me.
"Cornelius?!"

I knew the voice.

"Cornelius Jr.?!"

I couldn't place it though.

The dirty-bag-man stood up and grinned. "It's me! Quentin Forrest!"

My mouth fell open.

This guy Quentin Forrest was like my rival back in the day. His grades were as good as mine and in math and science almost better. We had both dicked a lot of the same girls and he was supposed to have gone on to Yale. Our parents had been friends, which was rare because his parents didn't go to church and my folks had nothing to do with ungodly people. Yet here he was standing before me, a five-star Vampire-Zombie.

My shocked expression made him laugh.

We sat down together on the roof in the sun of the hot June day afternoon.

Quentin told me his story.

What had happened to him.

Life can be real shitty, and his had been.

Quentin had just given up . . . well it really wasn't that simple. A lot of things had happened to him.

Tragic things, things that would take a week to write about.

But the gist of it was that he, like me, was feeling that life had rushed him. Life had slapped us in the face and left us bleeding in the gutter. Life had laughingly dealt us out a bunch of wild cards that we couldn't cash in and at the age of forty-four, starting over again wasn't an option. Seeing Quentin and the condition he was in made me realize that I too had given up on my life.

I wouldn't ever become the millionaire I always knew I'd be. I'd never own my own car, forget a house. This was true for both of us.

This shared confession made us both laugh. Then it made us silent.

We sat there scratching at the old days like elder roosters until nightfall.

160

The nebulous stars twinkled above our heads, while a lazy wind rushed about languidly cooling the hot angry air.

It was dark.

I wanted to go inside and have a smoke.

I got up to leave and saw an asking look in Quentin's eyes. He never said anything but I knew what he wanted.

"Look . . ." I started slowly. "They say it might rain tonight, I have a spot downstairs on the sixth floor . . . it ain't the Trump Taj Mahal but it's dry . . ." Quentin didn't say a word.

He got up, grabbed his stuff and followed me downstairs to my place. The first thing I did was make Quentin take a bath.

I put his clothes in the kitchen sink with some old bleach and soap powder that I had left and soaked them.

It wasn't so bad after he cleaned up.

I was afraid to smoke with Quentin around because I didn't know if he was into it.

So since he's come to stay with me I've been clear. Maybe it's a good thing.

Maybe we can help each other.

I was telling you about Cynthia.

How she turned up on my doorstep that sad hot August night in 1974.

It was sad because neither Cynthia or myself could have realized what terrible things would fall on our heads as a consequence of her running away to me.

To say that I was in love with Cynthia is not only too easy it is also indefinite.

I was possessed by Cynthia.

I know now that it was probably my addictive nature.

I was addicted to the girl and she was a-dick-ted to me.

Her smell . . . her taste . . . her colors . . . her eyes . . . her breath . . . every line, space and texture of her being filled me with primal cravings.

I couldn't bear to be away from Cynthia for more than fifteen minutes. I had to keep her in my view.

Othello's jealousy had nothing on me.
I could have gladly murdered in her name and for her
sake . . . Macbeth style.
I wonder what life would have been like if Cynthia and I
had been allowed to continue, to grow into man and
wife. . . . . .

BUT

like Romeo and Juliet our end was quick and tragic.

After a week of paradise . . . just the two of us together, not
seeing anyone else, not going anywhere else. I was prepared to
tell Maggie that Cynthia was mine and that I would make an
honest woman out of her.
I would wait until she was sixteen, then marry her.
I never even got a chance to talk to Maggie.
During my Eden week with Cynthia, I had gotten a couple of
harried telegrams from Dalek (I wasn't answering my phone so
Dalek sent telegrams).
A record company had come through with what he thought was
a once-in-a-lifetime deal for the New Sensations and he needed
me to check it out.
I finally called Dalek and told him that I was sick with the flu,
but if he biked the contract out I would look at it.
Which I did.
But I had to go into the office and sit down with Dalek and get
the terms of the contract right.
This contract could put Dalek, me and the New Sensations on
the map and I certainly wanted to be part of the geography. So I
went back to work.
Not wanting to keep Cynthia locked up in my apartment like
some urban Rapunzel, I went to the shoemaker, had another
set of keys made, came back, sexed her up good, gave her the
keys and went to work.
The plan being that Cynthia would go by her cousins in
Mattapan . . . let them know that she was alright, and meet me
back at the apartment later on that night.

I went to work.

Finished work and came home.

Spent a delicious night with my own-private-Venus. This became the pattern of our lives for three glorious weeks.

The evening before our last night together, I came home from work to find Cynthia upset and sitting on the stoop in front of my apartment. She had lost her keys.

Well, she didn't know if she had lost them. She thought that she might have left them at her cousins' apartment.

I told her not to worry. She could get them the next day.

"That's the problem . . . they're going away tonight for a week!" Cynthia whined like the spoiled child she was.

A child who had been given far too many caramel-chocolate-sundaes and whose every whim had been indulged by a mother who had guiltily struggled to fill every space in her daughter's life. A mother who had been father, brother, sister, friend, but was now losing the battle.

The child was now a young woman and the young woman had chosen her savior.

Me.

I savored my new role.

I cooed, calmed, clucked about her, reassuring her as I took my key, unlocked the door and led her inside. Closing the door against the world, I realized that my life was perfect and that I would never be happier.

I was right.

I rolled myself a big joint laced with cocaine and blew smoke into Cynthia's nose.

I wouldn't let her inhale it. There had to be some rules. We ran around the apartment naked playing a variation of kiss-chase. Whoever was it had to chase the other, and when caught the it person had the prize of demanding pleasure from the other.

Any pleasure.

It was the most fun I ever had to this day.

We were playing when the sun came up.

I slept for a couple of hours with Cynthia on my dick, got up and went to work.

The deal for Dalek was fantastic.
As an inducement, the record company was providing New York offices for Dalek's company. I wasn't sure about that. I pushed him to make sure that the offer was nonrecoupable and non-reversible and that the lease would be in Dalek's name.
Dalek was so pleased with my eagle-eyed acumen that he rewarded me with a two-hundred-dollar cash bonus and two grams of cocaine.
I went home to my baby exhausted, elated, excited. Cynthia was there, sunny, giggling.
"Take a bath! You smell like a pooh-bear!" She singsang her wishes as she set about cooking dinner for us.
I wanted to take her out, but she insisted on cooking, so we feasted on pig-in-a-blanket with baked beans and corn-on-the-cob. We happily ate our Coney Island dinner, never knowing that it would be our last supper together.
I was so tired after eating that I didn't even fuck Cynthia . . .
Well not the way we usually coupled. She climbed into my arms, lowered herself onto me, locking herself on my key.
We slept thus.

Two screams.
One. Outraged. Livid.
The other. Pained.
Deathly.
I opened my eyes.
Standing above us, face contorted into a gargantua of anger, disbelief, betrayal was mama Maggie. Something flashed in her hand.
A thing that she crashed down, then quickly raised again and again. Each time she crashed down, Cynthia screamed as if boiling hot water was being thrown over her.
Still embedded inside Cynthia, I rolled over to protect her from Maggie's frenzied blows.

It was my turn.
The steely thing, cold, blood-moistened—Cynthia's blood—
caught me in the shoulder, then the back.
I tried to move, but Cynthia, stilled, was underneath me, and
Maggie lay on top. Crucifying me. Nailing me to the tree of
lifeless Cynthia.
Cyn-thee-a. . . . Sin-thee-a.
Darkness.

Centuries later.
Awakened by pain.
Tumultuous pain.
Blinding pain.
Hot light. Bright light.
Lorraine and mama's voices above me.
Furtive . . . trepidated voices.
"His eyes are flickering!"
"Thank you Jesus! Thank you Father!"
Bells, tubes and wires.
Machines.
Life-factory machines.
I had become Nate.
A Nate nightmare.
Then I remembered.
Cynthia.
Maggie.
Mama and Lorraine terrified above me.
Like Maggie had been.
I tried to move, passed out again.
Sadness.

Since it happened I have tried to erase the story of Maggie and
Cynthia from my mental history.
I have never been able to fully accept responsibility for what
happened.
They were events that ran over me like an angry army of
steamrollers.

I stayed in the hospital for two months.
They told me I was in a coma for nearly three weeks.
It musta been a video nightmare replayed for mama and
Lorraine. They thought I was gonna die.
All the Washington men would be gone then. An entire dynasty
gone in one fell swoop.
With no heirs.

Cynthia was dead.
Maggie in jail.
In custody awaiting trial.
I slept most of my stay in the hospital.
Every time I woke up and thought about Cynthia and Maggie I
got tired and fell asleep again.
A harried but worried Dalek came to see me several times with
masses of paper. The nurse told him that I was totally unable to
deal with any kind of business. Dalek would stare at her, curse,
then leave.
He came back a week later with more papers and a smoking
canister. An ingenious creation that enabled you to smoke a
joint, and all the residual smoke that you didn't or couldn't
inhale would be caught up in the canister.
I looked at the papers.
Dalek told me that he had signed the deal and was moving the
next week. He left me the address and telephone number of his
new headquarters, and said that my job would be waiting for
me in New York whenever I got there.
Mama and Lorraine stayed until they were sure I was out of
danger.
The police had spoken to mama.
I didn't know what they had told her.
I knew that mama had a million questions but she never
troubled me with them.
Mama never scolded. Never judged.
I loved her for that.
The police also spent a lot of time with me after I came round.

They told me that I could be prosecuted for underaged sex with a minor.

I lied.

I told them that I thought that Cynthia was eighteen.

They also told me that Maggie had said nothing to them since her arrest. They told me it was Maggie who had called the police. They had found my key among her personal effects. Whether or not Cynthia's cousins had called Maggie and given her my key I never found out. They asked the nature of our relationship and wanted to know why she would kill her own daughter. I told them that Maggie and I had been lovers, and that I had wanted to break it off because I thought she was too old for me. I said Maggie had gotten angry and didn't want to discuss it. I said she had told me that she was going away to Florida to think things out. I told them that Cynthia had run away from Florida after a vicious fight with Maggie and had come to me for help, and our relationship had started then.

I explained that me and Cynthia had just happened, had only been going for a month. We went to bed one night and the next morning Maggie was there. I said that I believed that Maggie killed Cynthia out of jealousy. The police told me that I couldn't leave the state until after the trial because my testimony was necessary.

The trial was scheduled for early November, right before Thanksgiving.

I left the hospital.

I walked along the banks of the Charles River behind Back Bay, behind Emerson College.

Brown, red, orange autumn leaves lay like a thick moldy scab on the skin of the water.

It was almost winter now.

Boston was cold.

Electric cold.

The kind that shoots through your bones like a bowling ball knocking down tenpins.

I mourned.
I cried for Cynthia.
I cried for Maggie.
I remember feeling confused.
Not wanting to feel guilty but knowing that I should.
The trial was the next week.
I would be home for Thanksgiving.
I didn't feel too thankful.
I was too confused.
I never almost died before.
It was a confusingly strange feeling.

I signed on for unemployment because I had no job and no money and I wasn't gonna stay in Boston long enough to get a job. They gave me an emergency stipend.
I bought cocaine and reefer.
I smoked away the next few days.
I didn't do anything . . . I didn't want to do anything . . . I was in mourning.
I really had loved Cynthia.
I have never loved another woman since, as much as I loved Cynthia.
I guess that makes me a pervert.
I don't care.
It was unbearable living in that apartment after what had happened. I couldn't wait for the trial to be over so I could move away from Boston and the memory of Cynthia.
I had requested to visit Maggie in jail but I was told that she wouldn't see me.
I was told that Maggie would behave violently whenever my name was mentioned.
Maggie had never said it but perhaps she had loved me.

The trial was uneventful.
They couldn't press charges against me, because they couldn't prove that I knew that Cynthia was underage. I certainly hadn't

raped her, and since Maggie wouldn't talk to them, she didn't
refute my testimony.
Maggie didn't even take the stand.
A statement was read out by her lawyer.
As I remember, it only said that she had indeed killed Cynthia for
her own reasons, that she was sorry Cynthia was dead but she
wasn't sorry she had killed her, and if she had to live it all again
she would do the same thing.
The lawyer in me became puzzled.
Maggie could have gotten off if her lawyer had been smart.
She could have got off on diminished responsibility, or even
some manslaughter technicality. Instead the all-White jury found
her guilty of first-degree murder and sent her away for thirty
years.
I learned later that she didn't even want to appeal the verdict.
Maggie sat in the courtroom with her back to me. Those once
proud shoulders slouched forward. Burdened. Her head tilted
down, her hand shading her eyes. She would cough every now
and then. Before I took the stand she was led away. I told the
court exactly what I had told the police.
Just as my lawyer had instructed me.
Even though I wasn't on trial I felt that I was.
My lawyer was good.
He presented me to the court as a normal pussy-hungry young
man, who had been caught up in a triangular sexual situation
that I had desperately tried to get out of. The daughter had
thrown herself onto me, and in a moment of weakness I had
entered into a relationship with her which led to her spurned,
jealous mother killing her and trying to kill me. He said I was an
innocent who only wanted to forget this situation and get on
with my life.
He was right.
The jury believed him.
The judge believed him.
Maggie went to jail. I went free.

■

Lying in my bed during my last days in Boston, I realized that death had touched my life quite a few times in my twenty-six soon to be twenty-seven years.

I left Boston quietly.

Mournfully.

In a shadow.

I didn't even have a going-away party.

I arrived at Lorraine's in New York City on November 21, 1974.

Three days before my twenty-seventh birthday.

Lorraine wanted to give me a combined birthday and welcome-home party but I wasn't in party mode.

I walked around New York somber . . . chastened.

The cloud that now hung over me would hover there for the next seventeen years. It was just a little cumulonimbus then, but the forecast was not good and the cloud was growing larger daily.

It would rain.

Soon.

JUNE 23, 1991 — 4AM

Having Quentin here is becoming a fuckin' hassle.

I am at this moment locked up in the bathroom.

I've been sittin' here ever since he passed out in my living room chair. Quentin does not sleep. He passes out.

The boy's a fuckin' alcoholic.

He drinks like Moby Dick.

If I smoked as much as he drank I'd be in an asylum tearing my hair out and punching in walls.

From the moment he wakes up to the moment he passes out he is constantly in a bottle.

Wait a minute, I think I hear him stirring. He has bad nightmares.

He fights an unseen assailant; cursing, thrashing through the night.
The first time I heard him I thought somebody had broken in.
The boy is getting on my last nerve.
He definitely doesn't smoke, and for the first few days I didn't either.
Both of us was hiding our dirty laundry from each other. Dirty denial.
I didn't even see him take a drink those first few days.
But early one morning I heard these moans and crashes as if somebody was banging my chair against the wall. I went into the living room to find Quentin shaking like autumn leaves caught in a hurricane. His arms and legs and head were knocking feverishly. They were literally rattling. Like a whizzer who had taken too much speed. I had to throw water over him to calm him down. When the liquor store opened I had to spend a little of the welfare money I had left to buy him a bottle of Seagram's. I told him when he had calmed down that I couldn't afford to take care of his habit.
"I've got habits of my own!" I said.
Quentin went out and came back with a whole crate of Seagram's.
I don't know how he got it.
I didn't ask.
Anyway, he started on this drunken binge which has been going on for the last three days.
I'm gonna haffta ask him to leave.
He depresses me.
I've started back in smoking and I was doing so well without it.
Quentin gets so juiced you can't even carry on a coherent conversation with him. He gets mad with the mystery person he fights in his sleep, then he's off into the twilight zone. When he gets into that state there's no rhyme or reason to him.
I mean shit! I've just smoked and I can keep it together enough to write my shit down, but Quentin licks the bottle and gets totally narcotized.

It's scary.

Wait. . . . . . . I hear him breathing out there.

Fuck!!!!!

I need my space.

Alone.

I don't like him being here.

Shit!!! He could murder me right in my own bed!!!!

He could get confused and think I'm that person he fights in his sleep every night and attack me—and me trying to help him too.

Some people are so fuckin' ungrateful!!!!

Fuckin'-drunken-Black-mothafuckin'-bitch!!!!

That's why his ass is out on the street! 'Cause he's a fuckin' alkie!!!

Alkies are the Grandfathers of Vampire-Zombies!!! . . . . In fact they are the original Vampire-Zombies.

In the beginning was the bottle. . . . . . .

I'm throwin' his ass out!!!

I can't even smoke in the privacy of my own home!!!

Gotta come here in my stink-bathroom and sneak a smoke like a fuckin'-twisted teenager gotta open the window and blow my shit out the window.

What a waste!!!!

I can't even let the goodness collect in the air and get an open high!!!

And for why?!!!!

Because Quentin the drunken-shit-wonder is here!!!

This is my place!!!!

He don't even seem to care if I see him piss-ass-stinkin'-drunk!!!

He ain't got no kinda fuckin' dignity!!!!

Tomorrow. he goes. He might not even be Quentin Forrest!

He might be an agent!!! Someone sent from the ghost-people to check me out!!!!

How do I even know he's Quentin?!!!

He never showed me no ID or nothing!

I must be fuckin' crazy lettin' that cunt in here!!!!

JUNE 23, 1991 — 6AM

I had to stop writing for an hour.
I was sittin' there in the dark (my candle had gone out) and I saw
this big fuckin' spider flying in front of me.
This spider was at least two feet around.
A-big-monster-fucker!
I screamed and ran into the living room and fell over Quentin,
who had graduated from the couch to the floor.
I turned around to see where the spider was and realized that I
had been hallucinating again.
I wouldda laughed but I'm too tired.
I'm gonna catch some sleep then throw Quentin's ass out of here.
The boy's got me seeing spiders.
And that ain't on!

JUNE 25, 1991 — 3PM

A good thing happened today.
I woke up hungry for a change and searched the fridge for a
munch.
Like ol' Mother Hubbard my cupboards were truly bare, and it
being the end of the month my cash was nearly zero.
I will definitely have to run rocks at the Centa-Renta today to
get high.
Anyway, I was hungry and I wasn't in the mood for terrorizing—
the sun is shining, it's warm, basically too nice a day, so I went
for a walk to see what I could see, and get away from Quentin
for a while.
I went down to the Safeway and checked its garbage bins.
They throw away a lot of good stuff, but the bins were empty.
The garbage dump trucks had beat me to it.
I went into the Safeway.
It had been my intention to only walk around and eat what I
could, then split.

I had just picked up a Hostess Twinkie, was about to open it,
when this young White checkout girl turned into the aisle
nearly runnin' into me.
I didn't know rightly what to do so I just started eating.
I figured that she was gonna bust me, call one of the guards and
have him throw me out, so I thought I'd at least leave with
something in my stomach but the White chick just smiled at me,
winked, then continued down the aisle.
I wandered around the store eating till I was full, then left.
I was really grateful to that White chick.
White women have more humanity than White men.
Pia used to tell me that.
I used to think that White women were generally silly until I
met Pia.
Pia might have been a lot of things but silly she wasn't.
She was the only White woman in the world I would have
fucked in the pussy. She was the only woman, White or Black,
that I truly think I could have married.
If only.
She wouldda done great things for me.
She fed my mind in a way that no one ever had or has done
since.
Maybe it's because we weren't fuckin' that we found other
things to share.
Once you start fuckin' a woman the relationship changes.
A weird kind of tension creeps in.
That never happened with me and Pia.
Pia was the only woman I knew (outside the women in my
family) that didn't give me sexual grief.
I don't even think Pia ever saw me as a sexual object.
I don't think I was her type.
I miss Pia.

JUNE 27, 1991 — 2PM

Quentin is still here.
I tried to throw him out.
He started crying.
I wasn't having it.
I grabbed him by the neck and dragged him to the door.
He was squealing like a pig about to be slaughtered.
I didn't give a shit.
Out he was going.
"Wait! . . . . . wait!!" he was screaming and then before I could get
the door open he jerked away from me and ran into my
bedroom down the hall. He turned around and screamed
"Wait!!!" He reached into a pocket of his once-gray-blackened-
trench-raincoat and fished out all this money!!!! I couldn't
fuckin' believe it!!!
This drunken-stinkin'-slimy-sad-once-was-a-schoolmate-shit
standin' in my bedroom was holdin' $576!!
I counted it!!!
Well, Quentin didn't want to go and I wasn't gonna let him go,
not with all that money.
I persuaded him to give it to me.
He begged me to take it.
Man, my mind was hijacked!
Quentin had enough money to get his own place, yet he lived in
the street.
He could be dressed in Gucci and Pucci, yet he is a living-
walking-toilet-shit-rag.
I asked him what he was doing with all that cash.
He told me it belonged to a leprechaun and that there was
more!
"Oh yeah!?" I said . . . "Where?"
Quentin smiled mysteriously.
He couldn't tell me.
But Saturday at midnight he'd take me to it. Today is Thursday.
Hmmmmm . . .

He said that it had to be at midnight because the Devil left the tree where the money was at midnight, and we couldn't get the money if the Devil was at the tree.

Sheeeiiiittttt!!!! . . . .

I didn't want to hear no more shit about leprechauns and devils. The boy was clearly loony-tunes.

I asked Quentin why, if he had so much money, he lived in the street. He turned away from me.

His shoulders started shaking.

"I'm cursed . . . I'm a walking Dutchman. . . ."

I hollered! I hadn't laughed so hard in eons!

"I can't have my own place because the walls wouldn't have me . . . the walls haven't forgiven me . . . they would swallow me up . . . you haven't made them angry, they won't swallow you up, so I can stay with you . . . you are my salvation . . ."

Hmmmmmm . . .

I didn't know what to say to that.

Change the subject.

Why . . . I asked didn't he buy some new threads?

"New clothes would burn my skin . . . after these fall away from my bones then I will be worthy for the new . . ."

I said "Shiiiiit!!!! What did you do??!!!!"

And as soon as I asked Quentin that question, I knew I shouldn't have, and that the answer was unimportant because Quentin is truly loony-tunes!

Out of his fuckin' skull!

The alcohol has pickled his brain—the story he came out with was truly surreal.

Quentin told me that fourteen years ago when he was really low, he had decided to commit suicide and had worked out how to do it. He had decided that he was going to go to the Brooklyn Bridge at midnight and jump off. He figured he'd make the papers.

Y'see Quentin had been this real high-flyer when we were kids in school. We used to call him Quentin the Famous—he always

176

had his picture in the local paper for being a basketball-playing-golden-hero. He had been given a scholarship to play basketball for some university somewhere . . . I thought I heard he had gone to Yale.
We all just knew that he'd wind up professional, in the major league. . . .

BUT

Quentin spent one semester in school and got promptly thrown out. He got the President of the University's daughter (this White Jew chick) pregnant and her father went all hysterical. Anyway Quentin returned to the 'hood in disgrace. He settled into major obscurity as a nobody and stayed that way until fourteen years ago. Then, suddenly he was real cool, cool for about six or seven years. I heard he was on his way up again. He had a good job in the city, a condominium—that kind of shit. But just as suddenly his degeneration began anew and I hadn't heard or seen much of him until I discovered him on my roof.
Anyway, Quentin thought that on his way to his death he'd jump off the Brooklyn Bridge and make the papers. At least he'd end it all in a blaze of media glory. . . .
Well, as he came up on the Brooklyn Bridge, he passed this graveyard and saw this light in the distance.
The light was coming toward him.
If it hadda been me I wouldda got the fuck outta there, but Quentin was always a bit of a brave idiot so he stayed there until the light was right in front of him, and out of the light walked his father, who wasn't dead but lived somewhere in Connecticut. Quentin said he was freaked so he started talking to his father-of-the-light. His father put his finger to his lips as if silencing him and beckoned him into the graveyard. Before Quentin could get right next to him, his father started walking farther into the graveyard.
Quentin, still freaked, followed him.
When they got deep into the graveyard, away from the sidewalk and the road, his father turned around and asked Quentin for

*his heart. Quentin said that he was scared and didn't know what
to say. He asked his father why he wasn't in Connecticut.*
*His father said that he came to get Quentin's heart, and if
Quentin gave him his heart then he and his father would have
everything they ever wanted. They would live like kings and
princes, but he needed Quentin's heart to make the deal
stick.*
"I have already given my heart and now I need yours."
*And with that, Quentin said, his father stuck his hand in his chest
and snatched out his heart.*
*Quentin said it was steaming, hot, black, bloody and still
beating. Well I didn't want to hear any more.*
*This shit was getting too deep for my liking. I mean this was
Ninja shit!*
*Quentin said that as soon as his father snatched out his heart, his
father turned into the Devil; big, bogus and laughing at him. He
said that the Devil was White too.*
Gray-white, like the color of chitlins.
*He said that the Devil laughed and told him he would give him
his heart back in seven years. Then the Devil disappeared.*
Weird thing was, everything that the Devil said happened.
*His father and his self became like property barons overnight
and their shit was great for seven years.*
Then in 1984 they hit the skids.
His father got done for fraud, had a heart attack and died.
Quentin lost his nerve after that.
He hit the bottle and has been in it ever since.
*He says every night he fights the Devil who tries to give him
back his heart. He doesn't want it because he's afraid that if he
gets it back he will die and go to hell.*
*Well, I made Quentin hush after all that . . . I couldn't take any
more. I had to go outside and think about that shit. I was ready
to put his ass out again.*
*Still every night when he's fightin' the mystery man, he's always
shoutin' out "You keep it! I don't fuckin' want it!!!" and there is
this nasty scar where his heart ought to be.*
Crazy shit.

The boy is bugged.
I don't want to know about no Devil shit.
But I do want to see if there is any more money.
I know that I've just been on a fuckin' huge tangent and that I
shouldda been telling you my-story but this Quentin shit was so
unbelievable that I just had to write it down.
Money ina tree ina graveyard. . . .
Saturday.
We'll see.

It took me ages to resettle in New York.
Lorraine was a true angel.
She was—is everything the word sister means and stands for.
Lorraine was—is more brother to me than any man could boast
to be.
I love Lorraine.
She cajoled and teased life back into my wounded, stricken soul.
I didn't want to see anyone or go anywhere the first few weeks
after I got back from Boston.
Lorraine left me alone to sleep.
Healing sleep.
Mama called; wanted to know our plans for Christmas.
I had forgotten about Christmas.
Had no money.
Couldn't face a job.
Had nothing to give. Getting wasn't an issue.
I couldn't care about Christmas.
My baby was dead.
Cynthia was still in my skin.
Her smell still in my clothes, her face burned into my mind.
Sometimes while standing at the window in the then
comfortable living room, I'd think that I'd seen Cynthia and
would bolt to the door then realize that I couldn't have possibly
glimpsed my angel. . . .
My angel was in Lolita heaven.
I hate the finality of death.

■

It was decided by mama that she'd come to New York and spend Christmas with Lorraine and me.

One Saturday evening a week before mama was due to arrive, Lorraine kicked me out of bed, dragged me out of the apartment, took me by the hand, like she still does, pulled me to the subway, pushed me through the token-thing and onto the A train which delivered us to 72nd St. We got out and hurried through the cold, moody, frayed-at-the-edges Manhattan night.

The swishing streets were littered with has-been-hippies, hustler clowns.

It was the end of the day called Aquarius.

The rising disco moon's silver lining sparkled like the rhinestones on the dance-suits of the cocained glitterati that shook multi-plumed colored tail feathers in jump-joints across the Manhattan continent.

It was to one of these jump-joints that Lorraine dragged me.

"Insouciance" was the name of the place, tucked down a flight of stairs of a brownstone apartment building.

Insouciance's clientele were admitted to the club only if their attire and attitude echoed the name of the club.

Lorraine was dating one of the owners of the club at the time so it didn't matter how we were attired or what our attitude was; we were on the guest list. In we went.

The interior of Insouciance—a direct lift from the sets of the movie 2001, all white, gleaming without a practical chair in the place.

The inhabitants of Insouciance—these I'm-cooler-than-you-could-ever-hope-to-be types. People who broke their necks trying to ignore you. People who walked into doors trying not to see you turn-it-out on the dance floor, in gold-braided-sequined-Versace hot-pants.

People who walked around in Yoko Ono sunglasses, sniffing, being darling-lovely to those they knew, or thought worth knowing.

180

Who you were mattered.
Who you knew mattered more.

Lorraine asked me what I wanted to drink, I remember that,
because the lights in the dance floor in front of us started
blinking red.
Boa-feathered dancers flew off to clear the dance floor as it
revolved and became a stage, complete with three-piece band
and singer.
I knew she was a diva the moment the light snapped onto her
Blacker than Africa face. Blessed with Cleopatra's body,
Nefertiti's elegance. She didn't move. Not even a blink.
Every last Kool-Aid head in the joint committed attitudinal hara-
kiri after beholding this Black Angel, they had to.
On stage, in front of them, in a floor-length-purple-velvet-
trimmed-in-gold gown was someone cooler than both polar caps
put together.
She was announced as Ms. René Anastasia.
Don't remember the band.
Barely remember her singing . . . her singing didn't matter.
Here was a Black regal Goddess.
I felt like genuflecting.
She was super natural.
Hair cornrowed into a crown 'round her Somali-boned features.
I stared.
Mouth open.
I remember Lorraine punching at me to take the drink she had
bought me. She pulled me down to a table in front.
The original-land beauty above us tilted her head forward ever
so slightly and nodded at Lorraine!
The Empress had noted our presence.
I couldn't believe that Lorraine knew her.
I sat there listening to her set, thinking of what I would say to
her later.

■

*As the last of the applause evaporated, I pulled Lorraine out of
her seat so we could go backstage and meet this golden diva.
I almost cried when Lorraine said that Ms. René Anastasia never
received visitors in her dressing room. . . .*

BUT

*we were invited back to her apartment on West 87th St.
I couldn't leave that dreary and insipid style-prison fast enough.
I did have to wait while Lorraine played some networking nice-
nice-games with acquaintances from a company she wanted to
work for.
After the last hug-peck-handshake we fled the Insouciance,
captured a cab and headed uptown to where her majesty lived.*

*We were buzzed in.
Immediately.
A little tan boy with black horn-rimmed glasses politely
answered the door. Her majesty hadn't arrived but we were
expected, and were ushered into a spacious Afrocentrically
furnished apartment in this old brownstone that badly needed
exterior modernization.
The little tan boy's name was Ramoses.
He was the most together little ten-year-old since me.
The me-I-usta-be.
He played perfect host.
Prepared and delivered our drinks with a coolness that several
patrons of Insouciance would envy.
He was definitely his mama's son.
Graceful, nimble but resolutely masculine, even at such a young
age.
It was very clear that he was "the man" of the house.
Finally her regalness arrived.
Ms. René Anastasia rolled into the room—kissing Lorraine,
shaking my hand, hugging, kissing Ramoses and checking her
messages off the neat little yellow slips that Ramoses gave her.
Accepting a chilled margarita from her prince, she folded herself
into a leather-and-wood throne of an armchair.*

Ramoses made his final pleasantries and retired to his
bedchamber.

Searching eyes are all I remember of the ensuing conversation
between the golden one, Lorraine and myself.
Eyes that found, read, analyzed every visible portion of my
being, as I sat there witnessing her mouth saying one thing, her
eyes doing something else.
Ms. René Anastasia was weighing me up like some government
foreign policy proposal.
Was I worth her time.
Did I measure up.
Sex and lust had nothing to do with this.
Ms. René Anastasia was a Queen.
Her consort had to be at least a Prince or a Prince-in-training.

"Did you enjoy my performance?"
More a command than a question.
That voice.
Darkened at the ends.
Lilting tones.
Sung almost.
She was a singer.
She held court with Lorraine.
I found out that Ms. René wasn't a full-time performer.
Her day job was as supervisor at the bank where Lorraine
worked.
"Yes . . . I'd love to record . . . not for the sake of being a star, even
though the experience would be cute . . . I want to record the
fullness of my feeling . . . I want to record the state of my life
today as expressed through my voice . . ."
She licked a bit of the salt from the rim of her lucky glass.
I shivered as her pink tongue played against the hardness of the
delicate fluting.
I thought about Dalek and how useful it was that he was in New
York.
I resolved to call him very soon.

Ms. René didn't talk much to me, but at the end of the evening as we pecked cheeks and shook hands she pressed a bit of paper into my sweating hand.

I remember feeling like Rip Van Winkle brought back from his deep sleep as Lorraine dozed with her head on my shoulder during the interminable subway ride back to East Brooklyn.
I was awake again.
The Maggie-Cynthia-horror-movie became just that; a flickering nightmare consigned to the vault on a reel of memories marked **FORGOTTEN**.
I didn't need or want nightmared memories, not when there was a living, breathing Black Venus pressing telephone numbers into my waiting palms.

I called Dalek the next week to let him know I was back in town.
He was ecstatic.
He sent a limousine to pick me up and deliver me to his West 15th St. New York offices. There I found an old-steel-concrete warehouse with "Dalek's" in five-foot-high iced-blue neon letters displayed gaudily above the door.
It was a sprawling place.
A bigger studio with all the latest gizmos—a rehearsal room for the New Sensations, who were now Dalek's number one priority —a games room—a kitchen and a restful reception room.
The deal with the recording company seemed to be sticking.

All work stopped as soon as I stepped through the metal doors into the office reception area.
The new secretary, I think her name was Crystal, buzzed me into Dalek's inner office.
Inside were Dalek, the New Sensations, and an A&R man from the record company who I'd never met before.
Dalek and the New Sensations seemed really wired.

On the middle of the table, on a cake plate, was an almighty mountain of sparkling cocaine.

There was so much there that I became para.

There had to be at least ten thousand dollars' worth of cocaine on that plate.

My nose started itching.

Dalek, the New Sensations and the A&R guy were feeding their noses with plastic milk straws like hungry infants.

They were laughing, snorting, planning, and at times would look up grinning and leering at me in that I-own-the-world cocained glaze.

We talked no business that week because it was Christmastime and there were plenty of parties to go to.

The record company had two limousines sent to us every day. We used them to the max.

Dalek advanced me a month's salary, sold me two ounces of Colombian gold reefer and two grams of cocaine.

I was ready.

In that week of manic partying, I realized that I hated the recording industry. Well not what it does, because as a source of communicating and sharing ideas and feelings, no business does it better, but because there is so much money to be made and stolen the industry attracts the most diseased souls, the most malevolent creations any universe could spawn.

The recording business is not about talent.

A dog could be a recording star.

With enough money to buy allegiance from the gods—radio, DJs, promoters and shopkeepers—a dog could be made into the new Elvis Presley.

Talent is at the bottom of the list of criteria needed to become a pop star.

At the record company Christmas parties that I attended with Dalek, I encountered some of the slimiest, drug-driven ego-maniacs that I ever had the misfortune to spend an evening with, and these weren't the artists.

A&R men who couldn't hear a hit record if Stevie Wonder played it to them **after** their ears had been cleaned out with Drāno. A&R men who gushed and flung multimillion-dollar contracts at anything White that moved. It didn't matter if it couldn't talk, sing, play or read—if it was weird and White it got a deal. The only Blacks that got deals during those mindless '70s were disco-ducks and most of them were one-hit-wonder-accidentals. That the New Sensations were even getting a look-in was a rarity in itself. The New Sensations only had a deal because I had insisted Dalek press up those records in Boston, the track was played on the radio, and was selling. If Dalek and I had sent a tape to some A&R person, there wouldn't have been a deal. Even the divine and talented Ms. Donna Summer wouldn't have happened if she hadn't been an American in exile in Germany. To be fair there were a few major companies with some integrity who held their artists' interests, Black and White, in some regard, but these were the exceptions.

New York City was cowboy-independent-record-company-land. There were small independent labels everywhere.

Basically these labels were owned by RWBs (Rich White Boys) who were attracted to the glamour and excitement of the music business but were clueless as to what made the industry work. But that didn't stop them from finding and recording dance acts for little or no money, then selling on the product to some major, without caring if the artists got anything out of the deal or not.

To my dismay I found out that the "major company" that Dalek had signed himself and the New Sensations to was one of those cowboy outfits who had their own deal with a bona-fide major company.

This meant that the New Sensations would be getting a reduced royalty after paying this cowboy outfit, who did nothing for them except pass their product on to the real company.

I had originally wanted the New Sensations to be signed direct, and had advised Dalek to hold off closing this deal, when the Maggie massacre happened.

*Against my advice, Dalek went ahead and got himself involved
with those pirates.
I tried to bring these fears of mine to Dalek's attention during
that Christmas week but he only wanted to party, and pose with
the New Sensations for photographs that he hoped would be
displayed in the disco sections of Record World and Billboard
magazines.*

JUNE 28, 1991 — 5PM

*I had to stop writing yesterday, 'cause I was tired.
Quentin being around didn't help either.*

*The next week was Christmas.
Me. Mama. Lorraine.
Hands held around a table laden.
Mama cooked goodness.
Prayers and hopes for a healthy coming year.
Sadness for those gone on before.
Names we could only bear to whisper.
Nate. Daddy.
Mama was coping.
She was well and was as happy as could be expected in North
Carolina.
Me and Lorraine kept trying to convince her to think about
remarrying.
Mama needed someone to look after her, but mama assured us
that her personal freedom was more important to her than
future security.
I knew how she felt.
We all went to church together.
The church where Nate and Daddy had been funeralized.
I was surprised at Lorraine's composure.
The sisters and brothers were happy to see us.*

Mama and I hadn't been there in years.
Lorraine still went occasionally.
I felt uncomfortable being around those church people. It
reminded me too much of Daddy and Nate.

Since I had some money, I took mama and Lorraine to a movie
and dinner afterwards.
I don't remember what we saw.
At dinner I remember there being huge slabs of awkward silence.
Mama's eyes locked into mine.
Lips struggling to ask questions she had hid in her heart all those
weeks.
We still hadn't discussed the Maggie situation.
I wasn't ready to.
It was too close.
I didn't have any answers for myself.
Lorraine broached the subject first.
"How did you meet Maggie?"
I remember looking at both of them.
Trying to read their eyes.
I'm sure Lorraine was asking for mama's benefit.
She hadn't asked about it during the previous weeks after my
return from Boston.
I looked at my mama.
Small.
Hunched.
Worried.
Holding her pink crocheted sweater around herself as if to
protect her heart from the revelations that were not
forthcoming from me.
Mama looked at Lorraine then back to me.
About to say something, but instead raised her glass, looked
inside as if the answer to Lorraine's question lay like an ice cube
on the bottom.
"How's your back?" mama finally asked.
The "k" of the word cracking in her throat.

*"It's still sore . . . I'll be sleeping on my stomach till next Christmas
I think . . ."*
I tried to lighten things up.
*"Lorraine make sure you keep rubbing that cocoa butter on
them stitches till he gets his color back . . ."*
Lorraine nodded. Embarrassed that she had forgotten all about
the cocoa butter treatment.
I had too.
Mama hooked radar eyes on me.
"The Lord is a good God . . ."
My eyes scurried away from the hot searchlights of mama's
stare.
"Yes he is ma . . ." was all I could manage to croak out.
Full moments of silence elapsed.
All eyes on me.
Demanding-an-explanation eyes.
I saw daddy rise from behind mama's chair, pointing mama's
finger.
His voice was mama's voice.
Mama-daddy-words.
*"Cornelius . . . you gotta be careful baby . . . you can't be getting
yourself mixed up with alla these kinda people . . . these people
ain't got no God honey . . . ain't even thinkin' 'bout him . . . these
people out here will kill you Cornelius if you let 'em . . . you a
young man . . . my eldest baby . . . be smart Cornelius . . . be
careful . . . watch yourself . . . it's you me and Lorraine gots to look
to, to take care of us . . . you the head of the house now . . . the
priest of the family, like Moses was . . ."*
There were tears in mama's daddy-eyes.
That was the most words I had ever heard my mama say to me at
one time.
Mama never talked much.
She was silent.
Like me.
I am her son.
I stayed silent.

My taciturnity angering me.
My only true blood sat before me.
Mother.
Sister.
They, my blood, had stood above me every hour of the day for
nearly three weeks while I was away, caught between death and
life.
My blood had prayed to the Ancients of Power, had begged,
bargained back my life.
I had to tell my blood something.
I sat there breathing—instead of the silence that might have
been my memory.
Nate.
Daddy.
Cornelius.
Easily could have been.
I owed them some explanation.
I started hesitantly, haltingly, trying to search out words that
wouldn't tell too much or betray me too quickly.
I wanted mama and Lorraine to like Maggie, even if I had never
loved her as maybe I should have.
I wanted them to understand Cynthia and not condemn her
and me.
"How old was she?" was followed by "And how old are you?"
Then mama was silent.
Lorraine became uncomfortable.
She got up to call a cab.
Alone with mama.
At the table.
Her head bowed as if in a guillotine waiting for the inevitable.
Looking guilty as if it were her fault.
All of myself flew to my mama, pulled her to her feet and cried
into her arms. It was hard to remember the last time I had cried
to my mama.
My mama forgave me that evening. She put her arms around
me, hugged and comforted me as I cried the bottom of my
Maggie-Cynthia-grief onto her shoulders.

Lorraine found us sitting together.
Smiling.
In silence.

Christmas went and so did mama.
The year changed.
So did I.
I was determined to make my mark in New York with or without
Dalek, who I felt was wasting himself and not furthering his
credibility as manager of the New Sensations.
Their single, "Telephone Song," had been remixed dramatically
by some Manhattan DJ with little, if any, of Dalek's original
ideas featured.
The boys sounded serious.
"Telephone Song" hit the air in New York on Black radio. Clubs
started playing it. It was a smoochy song—chicks craved it and
dudes that were sniffing made sure it was playing as the
background music to a seduction.
Things were happening too quickly.
Suddenly everybody wanted to know, and we weren't ready.
I booked a rehearsal hall for the New Sensations, away from the
office and the drugs that lived there, and set them up with a
piece of heaven.
Another coup.
Another stroke of genius.
I knew the New Sensations would have to be the coolest group
in New York in order to impress the tish-ass-snobby-media-
writers, who could make these raggedy-roughnecks into over-
night stars.
A big negative mark against them already was that they were
from Boston. To geophobic New Yorkers, Boston was a disease
that turned people into friendly, country optimists—a disease as
fatal to up-nosed New Yorkers as water was to Dorothy's wicked
witch.
The New Sensations had to be iced.
They had to be too cool for the sun.

There was only one person I knew who dripped cool, had cool to
spare.
I called her.

She teased me.
Kissed me.
Then stopped.
Held me in her arms.
"Incest must feel like this . . ." I remember thinking.
A-mothered-caress. . . .
I didn't want to play baby.
She already had a finely tuned Ramoses.

Her touch had fingers.
Fully clothed, she undressed me. . . .
. . . . slowly.
Taunting the fabric into tantalizing ribbons of foreplay.
She wouldn't let me touch her.
I wanted her tits!
No!
Breasts.
Even the word breasts doesn't bless and dignify enough the
firmness that she denied me.
Not even a glimpse.
Her caress worked me.
Her touch expelled me.
Ms. René Anastasia laughed.
Later, over coffee and Billie Holiday I desperately wanted a joint,
but Ms. René looked at me as if she'd slap my face when I
produced one, so I hastily put it away. That hiccup aside, the rest of
the evening was pleasant and she accepted my offer to direct
the staging and choreography for all of the New Sensations'
shows.
Her majesty was a pro.
There and then she drew up a contract that paid her $250 a

week. She would come to the studio every day after finishing her job at the bank.

"When I'm finished with them they'll be ready for Carnegie Hall!" I knew Dalek would never agree to a piece of paper promising $250 to anyone, even if the name on that paper was Ms. René Anastasia.

I didn't want her royal highness to think me a no-power-flunky, so I asked her to delay signing her contract until she had "auditioned" the New Sensations. This would give me time to clear it with Dalek.

"You might be too much for them . . ." I crooned. "They may not be able to pick up your steps quickly—if they need more time, and I've only contracted you for two weeks . . ."

She smiled a benediction.

"Touché . . . Call me in the morning . . . we'll set a time for the audition . . ."

I should not be sitting here in a moribund apartment digging up bones of past treasures.

I should be commander-in-chief of some global firm.

For nearly two years I ran Dalek's operation.

I was Manhattan at night.

The New Sensations, with Ms. René Anastasia directing, became the hottest newcomers on the scene.

I found other acts for Dalek but he never did anything with them—my main concern was the New Sensations.

Dalek was beginning to get more and more lethargic.

He was becoming just a front, it was his operation in name only. I was the power.

Dalek busied himself running a club on the top floor of the warehouse. He called it Cinderella's.

I was against the club idea. It gave us too much profile. It made us too vulnerable, too accessible. It attracted the wrong kind of people to our operation.

Ms. René became my corporate inspiration.

The office began to shine with her positivity and élan.

For nearly two years we waved the purple-cool flag above all the small management companies that were saying something in New York's club-land.

It was hard trying to keep hold of the New Sensations. I heard rumors that two of them were sensationally fucking two of the vice-pressies at the parent record company. I didn't say anything because I thought it wasn't any of my business—and if the rumor was true, I thought having a couple of big dicks in the right places might be useful.

Every week it seemed some larger, more connected management company was trying to snatch the New Sensations from us. Lucky for me, Ms. René was now my leading lady, and the New Sensations adored her, and hungrily picked up on every nuance that flicked from her manicured fingers.

Robbie Mitchell, the lead singer, was her most dedicated student. He was also the one I had to keep outta trouble most often. Robbie's cocaine habit was becoming expensive. I warned Dalek, but he shrugged it off saying "That's show business . . ." Dalek was involved with some shadowy figures that I shouldda been watching as well, but I couldn't do everything.

Dalek was spending money too confidently.

I assumed it was profits from Cinderella's—the club was always packed, and as Dalek was my boss, I didn't see it as my job to pry into his business. I was kept on my toes building colored smoke-screens around the more nefarious antics surrounding Dalek's operation.

Ms. René would have left in a flash if she had had any idea of the level of drugs and drug-related activities that were part of the ordinary life there.

I kept Ms. René and the New Sensations busy rehearsing new routines and material in a dance studio away from the main office.

I kept Ms. René away from the recording sessions and made sure the office was "clean" whenever she came down to see me or Dalek.

■

The first New Sensations' album came out late spring in '77. It took that long to materialize because we had to wait until our "major" company came up with the money from its "major" company.

The album was a hit on the East Coast and we were about to take the Sensations to their first dates on the West Coast, when the shadows that had been floating around Dalek decided to manifest themselves on a permanent basis.

I will never forget walking into the meeting that Dalek had called, and seeing those two shadows I had noticed hanging around Cinderella's. Dalek introduced them as his two new partners, and said that they would be handling the day-to-day running of the business, and would be responsible for finances as well.

I could see trouble bright as a halo around Dalek's head.

His eyes couldn't meet mine.

He acted like a man at his own funeral.

I tried talking to him later, but one of the shadows was always at his side. When Dalek left the office to go home, one went with him.

When I tried calling Dalek at home one of the shadows would answer the phone. Finally I grabbed Dalek one morning as he got in the elevator—his shadow was busy paying the cab. I pushed the button to go before the shadow could get in, and stopped the elevator between floors.

Dalek still wouldn't say anything.

He looked like he was gonna cry.

All he told me was to get out before it got too hot.

"These are big men . . . we're babies . . ."

I didn't know what to make of Dalek's cryptic message but I soon found out that the shadows had substance.

Suddenly everything had to be okayed by these guys.

The New Sensations' West Coast tour didn't happen.

Suddenly our records weren't getting played, and stock wasn't

reaching the shops. Every time we called the "major" company no one would talk to me or Dalek.
The shadows were in control.

All was revealed one warm autumn day in '77.
Ira, the A&R man I had seen snorting cocaine with Dalek and the New Sensations, paid us a visit. I was at my wits' end because Dalek had not turned up for work and Ira quickly told me why.
We were being closed.
Shut down.
The parent record company had decided that they wanted the New Sensations for themselves as a direct signing.
According to Ira, Dalek had proven to be, over the last couple of years, unfit to manage an act with their million-dollar-potential.
Ira cited Dalek's drug problems as the reason.
Dalek had apparently spent royalties due to the New Sensations on drugs, and Cinderella's was about to be investigated as a probable "laundering" room for drug-gained cash.
The shadows I had seen Dalek with were underworld civvies who, strangely enough, worked for the same record company that Ira worked for.
Ira was there to wind up Dalek's business and to offer me a job at the parent company.
I was so freaked that I just walked out of the building.
I had built Dalek's.
I was Dalek's, and it was being stolen away from me.
I went to Central Park, sat on a bench and smoked a reefer laced with lots of cocaine, there, in broad daylight.
I didn't care.
I called Ms. René.
She wouldn't talk to me.
I went by her apartment.
She wouldn't open the door.
She would only talk to me over the intercom.
She called me a liar.

■

Several days later, a letter arrived from her.
Included was a copy of a letter she had received from RCR
records, the parent company of the "major" company.
The letter was from Ira, who turned out to be the head of A&R
for RCR's Black Music division.
I couldn't believe it!
A White-Jew-boy head of Black music . . . it made no sense.
The letter thanked her for her "help" with the New Sensations,
but said that the boys needed more professional direction and
management, and that I had suggested they hire some White
choreographer because I felt that this new director could "take
the New Sensations to heights René Anastasia knew nothing of."
These, according to the letter, were quoted as my words.
I exploded.
I called Ms. René but her phone had been disconnected.
I went by her apartment. No one answered.
A neighbor passed by as I pushed the button again and again,
and told me that she thought that Ms. Anastasia had moved.
I ran over to Insouciance.
Everybody had heard about what I had done to their star.
No one would talk to me.
One of the waitresses did tell me that René had left New York
for a while.
She had been humiliated and hurt.
Everyone knew she was the driving force behind the New
Sensations, and now all of club-land New York knew she had
been fired.
It was even reported in the trade periodicals.
My name was mentioned as going to a new job at RCR!!!
I felt like suing someone.
I twirled around looking for direction during the following
weeks.
Dalek wouldn't or couldn't see me.
The New Sensations had been spirited away and set up on the
West Coast near to the main offices of RCR records.
The "job" I had been promised at the record company was in the
mail room.

A joke job.
This was the end of my career.
I was finished, right before my twenty-ninth birthday.

Yeah, I did try to cut my losses and fight my way back in. I
thought about suing but I didn't have the capital. Maybe I
should have taken the job in the mail room, but I couldn't.
I was being punished. And for why?
All I had done was take a nothing company and build it into an
exciting, money-making outfit.
I trusted too much.
I had run the office as if it had been mine, but it wasn't.
I became para.
The New Sensations went on to fulfill their promise and became
one of the biggest acts in the business. I get ill when I hear their
records.
They're still around.

I began to think that I was cursed.
I began to think more about Nate and Cynthia.
Mama always said what goes around comes around.
Maybe mine was coming around.

I had made lots of friends during my years in business in New
York, and some of those connections kept me in work for a
while, but the scene was changing again, and by the turn of the
decade we all were looking for jobs.
By the early '80s, disco was dead.
Black people couldn't get nothing in record companies.
They were looking for the American equivalent of White English
punk bands, like the Sex Pistols.

I took whatever jobs I could get.
Flitting like a barfly from one job to another. Aimlessly.
I lived with Lorraine, who even then was becoming what she is
now. A success.

A rip-roaring success.
I never worried about money or rent or food or even clothes, because Lorraine took care of everything. She was gonna have a roof, so her brother had a roof as well.

I, like everyone else, partied, pussied and drugged in the early '80s.
What money I got I spent on drugs and lived in Studio 54.
I wouldda got a job there if I couldda.
But that was the spot.
Everybody wanted to work there.
Instead, I spent time working as a coat-check boy at the Under Line—this Jewishy-live-musicy-place down in the Village near to where I used to live. I saw a bunch of great acts down there.
Acts like The Voices of East Harlem, Ashford & Simpson, some White-boy groups whose names I can't remember, and Prince.
I saw a Prince gig at the Under Line.
I was workin' the coat-check room, fucked out of my mind on cocaine and this high-yella-pretty-ass-skinny-short-shit struts on stage wearin' nothin' but a skimpy tiger-print bikini and some boots; he strapped on a guitar and proceeded to take the world apart. The bitches were screamin'! The pimps were screamin'! The intelligentsia were screamin'!
Even the White folks were screamin'!
I knew that boy would be a star!
Fuck Purple Rain!
Prince was the best when he was on a little stage in a little shitty club called the Under line.

I met lots of people druggin'.
Cocaine loves company.
I ran into some kids who were in Dreamgirls.
A Black hit musical that was a hot ticket on Broadway. One guy in particular took a liking to me.
I hung around this guy, who I'll call Sid, because he always had cocaine and he was kinda interesting.

All I had to do was let him suck my dick and I could get all the cocaine I wanted.

I guess this started my "trade" days.

"Trade" is a gay term for somebody who is willing to engage in sexual encounters with gay people.

Now I'm no homo.

Outside of Eric, I have never had any lasting sexual relationships with men . . .

BUT

from time to time whenever I needed something, usually money for food or drugs (mostly drugs) I've "traded" my dick to get what I wanted.

Sid was cool.

All he wanted to do was suck me off.

So I let him.

I'd meet him at the theater after his show and we'd either go to a club or his place and "trade."

He used to go to this place called the Continental Baths, this real scary place where gays (mostly White) would hang out, watch a show around a swimming pool in the basement, or cruise the hallways and cubicles upstairs.

The Continental Baths was a try-out spot for hot new, almost alternative musical and comedy acts. If an act got the "queens" screaming, chances are it'd be picked up and booked into classier uptown clubs like Reno Sweeney or Backstage.

I once saw Bette Midler down at the swimming pool.

BUT

the action upstairs was where the party was at. While the men downstairs were screaming and clapping, pleasured by the antics on stage, upstairs the men screamed—moaning to a pleasure of another kind. . . .

Sid would get a room and we'd sit there and smoke and he'd suck me off, then we'd smoke some more. Then Sid would go walking about, "cruising" the place as he called it.

I never liked the Baths.
I always felt like a slab of hamburger meat there.
It was usually so dark that you couldn't see who you were
dealing with. I don't think people wanted to see.
Some dude would come up to you and put his hand on your dick
to see how big you were and if you passed the size test and
were willing, then off you'd go to cubicle-land to sex the time
away until you or he was bored, then off you'd go in search of
another "piece of trade."
I saw some wild shit at the Baths.
Group orgies where one dude would be fucked by five or six
guys.
People snortin' poppers.
Poppers were these bottles of amyl nitrite that some guys would
snort to heighten their senses during sex.
I couldn't stand the place.
It was too impersonal.
No one cared about you as a person.
All they cared about was the size of your dick.
I saw one sad, lonely dude who kept getting rejected by
everybody. He turned to me, dropping his towel, and I saw why.
Between his legs was an inch and a wrinkle.
Nobody wanted smallies.
Size was everything.
I only went to the Baths with Sid a couple of times.
And after a while I stopped seeing him.
He was too rampant.
I didn't want him to give me any kind of weird disease he might
have picked up in a place like that.
I learned later that he was killed in a fire at another popular
bathhouse whose name I can't recall.
The last real job I had was in 1982.
I lasted three months.
I got fired because I was getting advances on my salary (to buy
drugs) and then not showing up the next week for work. I didn't
want to work.

I only wanted to smoke cocaine.

I didn't care about anything else.

Lorraine probably had an idea of what I was up to but she didn't say much because she really didn't know for sure.

I would sleep all day while she was out at work and would be out looking for a party before she got home.

I didn't get involved in any serious female relationships during this time. These chicks were looking for yuppies and buppies.

Guys with millions on the way and though I could look the part when I wanted to I didn't have the ducats to back it up.

THE BIG WHY??????

I look back and wonder why I let this happen to me and I can't really say. I think it had something to do with freedom. I was trying to find out what I wanted to do.

Not what Cornelius Sr. or mama or Maggie or Cynthia or Dalek or Lorraine or school or a job wanted me to do.

I wanted to do what Cornelius Jr. wanted to do.

But what I didn't understand then was that all I really wanted to do was to smoke cocaine. I couldn't admit that to myself.

I was an addict in denial.

I thought that the cocaine was something I just did to help me pass the time, like drinking water or orange juice. I didn't see that it was an occupation.

But it was.

A big job.

Finding it.

Finding the source.

Finding the money.

Dreaming up the schemes to get the money.

Finding the people who had it if I didn't, and what they wanted in return for it. It was a full-time occupation.

Once high, it wasn't like I would just get up and go to work. After staying up all night, cocained up, all I wanted to do the next day was sleep. Lorraine hollered at times when my money

202

was funny, and to appease her I took any odd-job I could find to help pay the bills.

What Lorraine still didn't see was that I had no ambition.

I wasn't aiming anymore.

The fire and enthusiasm I had as a teenager and young man was pissed on and eventually drowned out by this thing called freedom.

Freedom is only elevated when chained to discipline.

Freedom without discipline is laziness.

I had never learned that.

When I had been disciplined, it was inflicted. A Cornelius Sr. or mama or school discipline.

It had never been coupled with freedom.

Or choice.

I had never learned to develop a will.

Just because a man can do what he wants does not mean that man is ambitious.

Without a will, that man will do doody-squat! Neeesch!

Nada. Nunca.

Nothing!

I did want to succeed.

I did want to become a millionaire.

I dreamed about the big car and the big house, but whenever I confronted the job of what I had to do to make these dreams possible, my mind would ache, I would roll me a big fat joint, smoke it and say "Tomorrow . . . I'll do it tomorrow . . . I'll start looking tomorrow."

Tomorrow became my anthem.

My bible.

Maybe I didn't want it bad enough.

Ambition is hard, dirty work.

Yeah, I wanted money but not at the exclusion of a good time.

I had spent my childhood working and running to be excellent, to be number one, and all for the praise of my daddy. I had no daddy now to crack the whip.

I had never been excellent for myself.

For my own self-satisfaction.
Mama was well taken care of, so I didn't have to work and be
excellent for her; besides she wasn't around to appreciate any
achievements I might have accomplished!
I was still a hero in Lorraine's eyes.

I hadn't started crackin' the pipe yet and somewhere deep inside
me, I did feel the need to excel but I knew I needed a huge push.
A bit of direction.
Some discipline.
So I joined the Army.
Well, actually, I tried to join the Army.
I was really too old for the armed services as I soon found out.
Ideally a young man, and the operative word is young, should
go into the armed services at around seventeen years of age
when his mind is fresh and malleable and his body is pliable
and strong.
I signed up for military service in July 1983. I was thirty-five
years old.
America was not at war.
The induction officer nearly laughed at me when I told him how
old I was.
He wasn't sure that I could even join, but my educational
qualifications were impeccable, so they let me fill in the papers
and take the physical that day.

Smells.
Funky locker room smells.
Funky male bodies . . .
Funky sweating underwear.
Funky athletes-feet-smelling socks.
Sitting in the funky basement medical room waiting for an Army
doctor to hold my balls while I coughed conjured up memories
of funky High School Physical Education. I laughed mournfully to
myself as I looked at the other three candidates for armed
service.
We were the stragglers.

There was no war.

There was no real reason why any one of us should have been waiting to see an Army doctor at 8:30 in the morning on a funky, muggy, hot summer's day.

We were funky stragglers.

We had no direction and needed daddy Army to show us the way.

There I was with one white boy, about twenty-two, and this other brother.

The brother had to be at least thirty.

He was fatter than two cages of elephants. I knew that he'd never pass the physical.

We both knew that we were there to get a job that we couldn't find outside in the real world. This was our last chance before family critics implored us to do something with our lives.

The White boy went in.

Me and the brother looked at each other.

Shook our heads and laughed.

He went in next. I never saw him again.

I went in, took the physical, took an eye exam and took a written exam which was easy. I told them that I wanted a job that dealt with communications. They laughed.

I went home and waited.

Two weeks later I got a letter that said I had been accepted which depressed me no end.

I had been praying that something would be wrong with me so that I wouldn't have to put myself through the coming torture, and I knew that it would be true torture.

Dealing with White folks is almost always truly torturous.

Mama and Lorraine were surprised that I had made such a decision.

Mama was glad that I was "doing something with my life" but wasn't sure if the Army was good enough for me.

"Why not the Marines?" she asked.

Lorraine, who asked nothing of me and gave everything, was supportive as usual, and declared that she was happy if I was happy. I smiled and made happy noises but I was miserable.

I was sleepwalking.
I was stalling.

I smoked away my last few days of freedom, went to this Army
depot on Crescent St. early one morning and took the bus to Fort
Dix in New Jersey. My military career lasted twenty-one days.
Eleven of those I spent in the brig or in observation. I hated
every microsecond of it.
I was not ready for the yelling, the pushing, the pestering and
the shock of routine. I was in a foul mood from having to cold
turkey my cocaine addiction. I went from smoking all day almost
every day to nothing in less than twenty-four hours.
I was an essay in contrariness.
Whenever the squad leader barked out at us, I made a point of
doing exactly the opposite, and I did it in my own time.
I was para but was determined not to let them know that they
were intimidating me.
I was stupid.
I couldda made a go of the Army but I didn't want to be there.
My drill sergeant was this White Hollywood Hills boy who had
watched The Dirty Dozen one time too many.
He had been briefed about me and came down on my case
cement-style.
Immediately.
After being shown my barracks, and seeing where I was gonna
be living for the months ahead while I completed basic training,
I realized that I had made a huge and terrifying mistake.
I had to do whatever was necessary to get myself out of this awful place.
I had sign-locked myself in for four years! Four! Years!!!
I knew I'd never make it past the fourth day.
In twenty-four hours they tried to take away my identity, my
pride and my own reasoning yardstick—that was what they
were supposed to do.
For fuck's sake this was the Army not some sleep-away-welfare-
camp—even though sometimes it reminded me of just that.

The third day in the barracks after sleeping with twenty-one strangers (who I never talked to the entire time I was there) and eating the nastiest food ever imagined, I knew I had to run away. When the platoon leader came to switch on the lights at the end of reveille, I refused to get up, which made me the object of his morning ire.

"Get your ass up Washington! This ain't no whorehouse!" He grabbed me by the neck of my undershirt. I turned over and kicked him off me. He came in at me again and we fought. He had to call for reinforcements.

They beat my ass.

Big-time.

I was thrown into solitary confinement.

I was stupid.

I was so angry and deranged.

It never occurred to me to just go and try to talk to somebody about the mistake I had made, and what my options were. But on the other hand, nobody in this place talked.

They all shouted and barked at you like you were a mongrel dog.

I was no child.

I was a grown man.

A shiftless drug-driven aimless thirty-five-year-old, but a man still.

The Army was like having 26,000 Cornelius Srs. shouting and yelling at you from every angle all day. My first sergeant came in to see me while I was in confinement. He sat down with me like a human being. For the first time since I was there. I told him that I had made a huge mistake joining the Army. I couldn't make it.

I wanted to leave.

He laughed.

He told me that I had signed for four years.

He said that I was only homesick and that I should at least take time to think it over.

He left me to think it over for eleven days.

And think I did. I made so many promises to myself sitting in that dark, airless,
small, wooden room. I hope the Lord didn't write them all
down.
I promised myself that as soon as I got out I'd get a job and
never touch cocaine again.
I promised myself that I'd find a wife and start a family before it
got too late.

I had my first nervous breakdown alone in that brig.
It was after my fourth day.
After breakfast.
I started laughing hysterically.
tI didn't know why I was laughing but laughter erupted from me
in heaves like a hacking cough.
Then I started crying and beating the walls. No one came.
I quieted down and started playing mind games with myself.
I told myself that I was the Christ and that I was awaiting trial
and that I had to die on the cross to save mankind from their
sins. Man I was real loony-tunes.
The platoon leader came to see me on the sixth day and had me
sent up to the hospital for observation after I greeted him with a
full kiss on the lips, called him Judas, told him that I and my
Father forgave him and that I was ready for the cross.
They gave me a battery of tests.
Gave me drugs.
I don't know why they thought that drugs were necessary but I
guess they wanted to calm me down. I talked to several
psychiatrists who asked the same questions over and over again.
Namely why had I enlisted and was I sure I wanted out. I
told them over and over again . . . . . "I made a mistake . . . I can't
take this . . . I want to go home . . ."
They sent me back to the brig.
Finally on the eleventh day I was let out of the brig.
I was handed a letter saying that I would be medically
discharged within ten days.

Reason. I had flat feet!
No shit!!!
Of all the reasons they could have concocted and created, flat
feet was what they came up with.
I spent the last days of my military career in the library reading.
I had refused to take part in any kind of duty until I was let out.
In all fairness the Army had been real lenient with me.
I had heard all kinds of horror stories about brothers being
harassed and even medically experimented on, but the Army
was fairly cool with me considering I was the one creating all the
havoc.
Hey the Army is the Army.
It's supposed to be a mind-fuck.

I returned to civilian life and surprised the hell out of Lorraine
who had met Kenneth, her husband-to-be, earlier that summer
and had moved him into the apartment while I was away in the
Army.
I was home.
I was weird.
I was in the way.
My baby sister Lorraine was beginning to realize that things
weren't quite right with her heroic big brother.

JUNE 30, 1991 — 2AM

I have just come back from the graveyard.
I left Quentin there.
I hope he's alright.
The scene was just too weird for me.
I didn't even wait to see if there was any more money.
I just hope Quentin is alright.
I shouldn't have left him there but he started shaking, spitting
and ranting so loud that I had to get out.
I was afraid someone would hear us and call the police.

I don't know why I went down there in the first place.
The train ride down was real embarrassing.
There was this mother on the train with a five-year-old.
This precocious little brat kept pointing to me and Quentin and
asking his mother "Why? . . . Mommy why . . . they look like
that . . . why? . . . they look so dirty Mommy why? . . ." Well the
poor mother was mortified and a bit scared. Even with clean
clothes Quentin looks like an urban refugee and I don't look
much better. Thankfully the mother took the child off the train
and moved to another car.
Quentin is cracked.
He probably found the hiding place of some drug baron.
Dealers are known to hide their drug money in weird places
where no person in his right mind would think of going; and we
all know that Quentin isn't in his right mind.
If the money he's got is drug money I don't want to be around
when the dealer finds out that someone has been tampering
with it. So I left Quentin in the graveyard. I won't be letting him
back in.

I'm glad it's the end of the month.
After tomorrow I get my check money.
Quentin musta took the money, the $576 he said I could have,
out of the box underneath my bed where I keep the picture of
me-like-I-usta-be because when I looked there after I got back
from the graveyard, the money was gone.
Crazy come.
Crazy go.

After fleeing the Army, realizing the grounding hope of my life
had turned to quicksand, I quaked.
I was almost thirty-six.
With no job.
No prospects.
No ideas.
Emotionally frayed.

Idealistically tired.
Quiet and somber.
I retreated into myself.
I don't remember much about that time.
I just remember feeling depressed and tired for most of it.
I only did what I had to do to keep myself high.
I would spend days sitting in my room staring at the walls.
Living some vapid alter-life in my head. Hours would pass as I traversed the globe in my mind.
I didn't have to speak using my lips.
I had mental telepathy.
I could communicate with all human and animal life through my mind. I didn't know it at the time but I was having another mental breakdown. After fighting with Lorraine about how many peas she had put on my plate one evening during dinner, she and Kenneth knew something was wrong. They called 911. I woke up the next day to find that the mythical men-in-white were indeed in the front room waiting for me. They took me to Queens General Hospital where I was put on lithium.
I stayed there for three weeks.
Lorraine came to see me.
Told me I couldn't come home.
She wanted a life with Kenneth.
I would be in the way.
This didn't sound like Lorraine.
It sounded like someone had put her up to this. Someone like Kenneth.
I hated my sister then.
I felt betrayed.
When the doctors and social workers came to ask me what my plans were after I was to be released from the hospital, I convulsed in tears. I blubbered that I had nowhere to go.
My sister didn't want me at home.
They told me not to worry.
I would be given welfare and Medicaid.
The breakdown was a cursed blessing.

As long as I stayed crazy I can still get the checks.
I'd be given a room in a welfare hotel in Manhattan and
welfare food stamps. I hadn't realized that Lorraine had met
with my doctors and social worker beforehand to work out this
little "package" to start me back on the road to self-
determination.

I left the hospital after three weeks.
All my belongings in the world were in a black garbage bag that
I carried down my back like an Afroed Santa Claus carrying his
Christmas gifts.
It was raining that day.
I was gloomed, irked and strangely embarrassed.
I had no socks.
My sneakers were falling apart.
I felt and looked like a bum.
I hated Lorraine.
I was to live at a place called the Hotel Operatic on 77th St. and
Broadway.

The lobby of the Hotel Operatic was this mishmash of Oriental
horror-movie bric-a-brac, on top of wearied-worn-gray-lounge
carpets, underneath the torn leather couches which sat silently
empty . . . "No sitting" signs beautified the walls . . . the reception
desk was a bullet-proof-cubicle through which I paid my first
two weeks' rent in advance . . . a middle-aged, toothless, haggish-
looking hippy-woman ran the elevator and took me up to my
room 1021.
There were no buttons on the floors for anyone to ring the
elevator so everyone had to scream and yell out their floor-
destination and pray that the elevator mistress heard their
fevered cries. As I was hauled up to my new abode, a chorus of
"21! Down!," "8! . . . Up! . . . mothafucker I said 8! Up! Bitch I'll
shoot you" etc. greeted me and sonically introduced me to my
new neighbors—a coterie of pimps, prostitutes, addicts, single-
lost-people, criminals, multi-everything students and transients

that helped to make up the nameless-faceless-forgettable-
masses that you see ghosting through the streets of Manhattan
24–7.
Going nowhere in particular, floating through another day.
One seriation from the gutter we were.
The common link chaining through all our lives was our welfare
dependency.
Our drug dependency.
Dependent ones.

The Hotel Operatic became my home.
Room 1021 was approximately four feet wide and ten feet long.
It had a sink. A bed. a closet. A drawer.
The bathroom was halfway down the hall. I shared it with
this Puerto Rican junkie who ritually beat-the-shit out of
his wife/girlfriend then would fuck her in a frenzy of
contrition.
I lived in this box for four years until Lorraine and Kenneth got
married in December 1989 and moved into the apartment in
Brooklyn where they live now.
Kenny never really liked me.
He didn't understand why Lorraine was devoted to me. Kenny
met me when my shit was starting to dissolve.
I detested my little-cake-box-of-a-room at first. I hated Lorraine
and Kenneth for finding each other. I hated mama for not
rescuing me. . . . . .

BUT
I found some old Broadway show posters in the basement of the
hotel and stuck them on the wall; I found a flea-eaten cactus
plant in a garbage dump behind this Chinese restaurant and
gave it pride-of-place on my windowsill at the foot of my bed.
I named it Trigger.
The protector. My symbolic gun.
I spent $10 of my check money (a-bit-of-an-extravagance) on a
two-burner hot plate and soon learned to make extraterrestrial

meals out of baked beans, tuna, rice, onions, garlic, peppers and
mushrooms.
Strangely and slowly . . . I began to fall in love with my
esoterically-bohemian sublife . . . I discovered candles, and would
sit in my flickered-lit-room . . . listening . . . to the publicly-private
lives of the miseries who also called the Hotel Operatic home.
The place was well named.
The tragedies and comedies that played out in the grand lobby
of the Hotel Operatic are legendary. Its inhabitants were as
hugely-colorfully-eccentric as any Wagnerian hero or Puccini
diva.

I learned in Grand Guignol style how to be a nobody.
Welfare is a wonderful thing.
It teaches you how to lie, cheat and steal to keep getting your
bimonthly-hand-to-mouth-out. It gives you no incentive to do
better. If (and a big "if") you should find a flake of a job while
waiting for your next hand-to-mouth-out and you tell them
about it (like you're supposed to do) they bleed you. So you lie
and steal whatever extra money you can, any way you can, and
still collect your welfare.
I began to understand purse snatchers.
I began to always walk with my head down, looking to find
money. I learned how to shoplift.
I mostly shoplifted food.
I would walk around the store and eat the cakes, pies, cookies,
fruit, yogurt, ice cream, potato chips—anything that I wanted
but could not afford to buy after my food stamps had run out.
Even if I wanted to see Lorraine I usually couldn't afford the
train fare.
I became a prisoner of Manhattan.
I got high though.
The citizens of the Hotel Operatic stayed high.

BIG TIME!!!

If we never had food we always had drugs.
All kinds.
If you didn't have any someone on any floor had some. We did share.
I found out the true meaning of "getting high" while living at the Hotel Operatic.

Summers weren't too bad in the Hotel because if it got too claustrophobic, you could escape to Central Park right down the street.
You had to pass this huge, ancient, Rocky-Horror-Show-looking-building to get to the park. I once saw Roberta Flack get out of a limo and go inside this funeral-parlor-looking-building. She lived there. So did John Lennon.
Once in the park, you could maybe find some loving in the bushes if you were lucky. But there is nothing drearier than a cold, rainy February morning in a Manhattan welfare hotel when the heat has been off for two days, you have no food stamps and the elevator is not working.
I used to get high before I got out of bed just to ghost me through the day. Those days I was smoking reefer mixed with tobacco.
I could hardly ever afford cocaine.
Only when I took the chance to cheat welfare with a temporary job.

I began to make friends.
There was Wanda-Fay, a transvestite/drag queen (I couldn't figure out which) who lived on the sixteenth floor, who had just broken up with her/his pimp, who lived on the twelfth floor.
The pimp was named Marcel. He was from Birmingham Alabama.
He looked like a 450lb. Little Richard.
The middle-aged-haggish-looking elevator operator was Myles.
She once danced in Annie Get Your Gun *with Ethel Merman.*
She had an Equity card. Myles would regale you with stories of

her Broadway triumphs as she chauffeured you between the floors of infamy and destitution.

The specifics of my life at the Hotel Operatic are not important. What is critical about the time I spent there is that it was the breeding ground of my addiction.
I began to cultivate a negatively regressive personality.
I pushed myself to work only when drugs pushed me.
Most times me and my friends reveled in our inertia.
We used to have contests to see who could sleep the farthest into a day. The winner was whoever could sleep the whole day away and miss the tedium and boredom that were the playmates of the unlucky many who had actually gotten up to engage.

I had two main spars at the Hotel Operatic. The weird thing was that these two dudes didn't even live at the Hotel. Since I couldn't afford to splurge money on buses and subways (fuck cabs) I used to walk everywhere. I met Kicker, a drummer, and Skeets, this singer, in a punk club in the East Village. I think the club was called the Tin Angel or something like that, though it might have been CBGB's.
I used to go to CBGB's to smoke angel dust and watch the White boys make fools of themselves as they tried to pull some of the most luscious White girls you have ever seen this side of New Orleans. Not just White girls, Oriental exotic girls. The only reason I met up with Kicker and Skeets in the first place was that they were sitting at the same table as this Oriental vision of air-brushed gorgeousness.
This Seuno as I found her name to be.
Seuno nearly made me well just by looking at her. I wasn't piping then but I couldda given up the pipe if Seuno had told me I could be her baby and have her pussy for all eternity.
Seuno was fine.
Seuno also liked . . . no . . . loved pussy more than I did. Seuno's lover Chika was also fine.
They loved only each other. Seuno and Chika broke my heart.

Many times.

Anyway I met Kicker and Skeets because of Seuno and we all became good friends.

Kicker and Skeets were in this jazz funk group called Black Magic and they both lived in the basement storage hovel where they rehearsed. The hovel was on Bleecker St. Kicker with Skeets, after a night of haunting the clubs and not scoring a pussy-with-a-roof, would arrive at the rehearsal hovel with milk and bread stolen from the doorsteps of the neighboring Bleecker St. merchants. They'd sleep the day away to await the 6pm arrival of the other band members who had homes, and jobs to finance the band.

One of those types was Mornay, this White-boy guitar player who was a sound engineer at Electric Ladyland Studios. Jimi Hendrix's studio. Mornay had a loft on Bond St.—Black Magic was his band.

Mornay was also a drug dealer.

He, together with his girlfriend Tish, an Off Broadway actress who dreamed of working with Divine in Tom Eyen shows, were The Drug Dealers Emeritus of the East Village from NYU to 2nd Avenue.

Their Bond St. loft was across the street from the top-floor loft of Seuno and Chika.

Mornay is important to this story in as much as he was the one who introduced me, Kicker, Skeets, Seuno, Chika and a few others to the pipe one wintry afternoon in 1986.

Kicker and Skeets were indebted to me after I saved their asses from the cold early one morning after we all had been to the clubs. We hadn't scored with the chickies and they were going to show me their lair. The idea being I would crash with them at their place then make the walk uptown later in the day when the sun was shining. We arrived at their place to find the metal gate leading downstairs to their hovel had been double-locked by the landlord who had found out that Kicker and Skeets had been squatting there.

So I invited them up to my place. It took us about one hour to
walk from Bleecker St. to West 77th, I remember us smoking
reefer all the way uptown. The mad Kicker cussing the landlord.
His long red dreadlocks flicking in time with every hurled epithet
that missiled from his thickened, tan lips. Kicker was from Belize
and could have been a model or a movie star if he had had the
desire and the drive.
Chicks loved Kicker until they realized that he expected them to
take care of him. Kicker shouldda been dickin' with me sixteen
years earlier. Them hippy girls wouldda kissed his ass and
loved it.
These new power-pussy-chicks expected champagne and caviar
with breakfast lunch AND dinner, a Testarossa and a treble of
Platinum-Gold credit cards before they even considered the
possibility of a lasting relationship.
Kicker loved them uptown chicks for whom his looks and dick
might be cool for a brief flingy between corporate romances,
but rough trade like Kicker and Skeets were not to be taken
seriously.
I liked them though.
Skeets was a good-looking Black boy who stayed so high all the
time he could never finish his sentences, so you would never
really know what he was talking about. I thought Skeets was
just stupid when I first met him. Most people thought he was
always drunk.
I learnt a lot about them that night they stayed with me at the
Hotel Operatic.

After that we spent many a time sitting on my bed smoking up
found treasures of get-high.
Kicker and Skeets had porcelain dreams of greater rock-n-roll-
glory.
Kicker would boast . . . "We just fuckin' wit' dis jazz funk shit just
to toughen out our chops . . . after we nervy-up, we drop an
anchor on them slits and kick the real rough-rock!"
Kicker had a vision of a hot-ass four-piece rock-n-roll band. Him

on drums, Skeets the frontman, a Japanese guitarist and a six-foot Swedish blond babe on bass. Kicker wanted to call the band Testi-Vagj.
He liked the obscure sound of it.
They both hated disco even though Skeets had done vocals on a twelve-inch disco record the week before for $250.
"I'll never promote . . . even if . . . selling out . . . that's what . . . I . . . never . . . I" were Skeets's comments on the subject.
We all shook our heads and sucked on the umpteenth joint.

I was a ghost-in-training during this period.
I hovered near the cutting edge of sub-urban-city life.
I knew the movers. I got high with the shakers but I hovered.
Touching neither the ground nor any tangible aspect of anyone's life.
I initiated nothing.
I contributed nothing except maybe space and form.
I half-listened. My antennae honed on to talk of drugs and sex and money if the getting was good and easy.
It was a nomadic yet static, spontaneous yet premeditated, engrossing yet mind-numbing existence with no end in sight.
No prize to be won.
That is why the pipe seemed so tantalizing. It asked for nothing and gave everything.
It seemed.

I had heard about crack but had associated it with the underprivileged-gangsta-youth that ran rampantly through the South Bronx . . . I didn't know that I knew anyone who used it.
Reefer was starting to get reeeeaalll expensive and crack came into my life as an economically-miraculous-life-saver.
A good high for cheap. "A great high for cheap . . ." is how Mornay introduced the subject of crack to the group assembled at he and Tish's groovy loft that wintry afternoon in 1986.

"Today we're gonna try something new!" Mornay wouldn't even tell us what it was.
He just said that it was a "get high" and to trust him.
Mornay put some Dire Straits on and fashion-showed us the rock-star paraphernalia.
Seuno the gorgeous was the first candidate.
When her languid eyes popped like flashbulbs and she passed out in front of us after just one hit!!! our collective pulses quickened, our tongues hung out, salivating for our turn in line.
I remember my very first hit just like a saved and sanctified Pentecostal remembers the day, the hour and the year that they first met Jesus.
I remember taking the pipe in my mouth and mounting its cold hardness between my lips and teeth.
I remember the hot-holy-ghost-smoke-like-a-mighty-rushing-wind engulfing my lungs.
I remember it tasting like peppermints. My favorite candy.
I remember the electric shock of the dooooooeeeeeeee bells blistering my ears and the world turning upside down.
I remember feeling small and shrinking till there was nothing left of me and thinking that the crack between the floor and the bottom of the door was bigger, wider, darker and stranger than five black-holed-galaxies.
I remember the cruel crash.
The cold in the pit of my stomach.
Feeling naked and exposed in the harshest of the brightest light.
Dying to return to the heat of the rush.
The protection of the high.
An aquarium of safety.
An incubator of protection.
"Naked without the high is!!" became my favorite proverb.
The pipe became the perfect accessory to my ghostly-alter-sub-life, the perfect condiment to a dinner of destruction.
If you must crack up . . . crack does it best.
It's hard to even write the word.
Crack.

Pipin' is easier to think.
Denial is easy to feel.

JULY 2, 1991 — 12 NOON

My fuckin' check hasn't arrived.
It was supposed to get here yesterday.
I waited downstairs from 8:30 this morning till a half hour ago
for the mail to come.
To make sure none of the ghost-people stole my shit.
I kinda wish Quentin was around with his money.

Lorraine came by yesterday with my rent book.
I didn't ask her for any money since she gave me so much last
month.
Her moving date is only three days away.
I can't even think about it.
Lorraine paid my rent for July. Starting August it's up to me.
She's directed my rent check straight to me so now I have yet
another fuckin' piece of paper to look out for, to protect and
keep grubby fuckin' ghost hands off.
Maybe I'll take a walk to a phone booth and call the welfare
and see what happened to my money; but calling them folks is
like trying to call the fuckin' Pentagon.
Maybe I'll call them.
I feel the monsoon of responsibility hitting me full in the face
like a gale wind and I don't like it.
I don't like it one bit.
But paying the rent is the price I must pay to keep a roof over
my head. Just a walk down the street.
Easy-peasy.
That's not what I'm worried about.
I worry about the will.
The doing of the right thing . . . That's what scares me.
In the heat of a pipe-lust, will I be strong enough to do the right

thing even with the thought of becoming a Vampire-Zombie
staring me in the face?
Is homelessness threatening enough to force my will to
save some monies for the roof over my head as opposed to
the roof in my head where the pipe-monster lives who
dictates my actions according to its needs and desires?
And the fact that I have to think about choosing between home
and the pipe scares me even more.
Back to the past.
It's safer and further away.

Lorraine and Kenneth didn't have a church wedding.
They got married at a Justice of the Peace then went down to
North Carolina for a honeymoon celebration at our mama's and
his mama's houses. I didn't go.
I wasn't interested, and I didn't have no money.
I was happy for Lorraine but I thought that Kenneth was a bit of
a jerk. I had no reason to think that, he was actually a lot like
the me-I-usta-be.
Ambitious. Hard-working. Dependable.
Commendable qualities.
A husband any girl would want.
I knew my sister would be taken care of. Excellently.
That's probably why I hated him.

It was mama's suggestion that I move back into the apartment
when Lorraine and Kenneth announced that they would be
leaving the Washington homestead to live in their own
mortgaged condominium downtown in beautiful Brooklyn.
I guess mama wanted to make sure that she still had a link and
access to what was once our family's stomping ground.
At first I didn't want to leave the Hotel Operatic.
I was enjoying my carefree existence in the company of those
like myself who didn't give a shit for the manic-rat-racers that
fanned the flames for the Vanitic Bonfires of the yuppied
'80s.

222

BUT

I had lost the company of one of my main spars, Skeets. Against
all the odds, Skeets had lucked-up. Big Time.
He was sitting on my bed one afternoon sucking on a joint,
glancing through Back Stage (an entertainment business want-
ads magazine) when he announced . . . "I should . . . this
audition . . . London . . . big . . . . later . . . !" and with that he glanced
at his watch and left.
Me and Kicker looked at each other, shook our heads, laughed,
finished the joint and started another one.
We heard later that Skeets had gotten a job in a show that took
him to London, England!!!
Skeets who couldn't string two sentences together but could
sing his ass off musta had a good mind. A will.

Those not in your view become dead to you.
One day you're in a place surrounded by a community of faces
that have been a part of your window-life for the past four
years . . . then you go away.
You never see those faces again.
Your life has a different window that you see through now.
Somewhere that parted community of faces lives in someone
else's window.
The faces are dead to you.
I just wish I knew what happened to them. . . . .

Two things decided for me that moving back to mama's house
was probably my best option:
1. The Hotel Operatic had been sold to a property developer
and was being converted into condominiums (everybody wanted
one) and I'd haffta move anyway.
2. Lorraine and Kenneth came to visit me after coming back
from North Carolina after their honeymoon. Kenneth sniffed at
my room like a White-boy stuffed in an elevator packed with
niggers the entire time he visited me in my tiny cell.

Lorraine kept saying "This is no place for you to live . . . they're animals here . . . you need space . . . I'd go crazy in this tiny box."

She was right.
I had gone crazy.
Stark. Raving.
I had lost my mind. My will.
Two of the most important treasures any man or woman needs to make it through this mangled journey of life.
I sat there and listened.
If I couldda cared I would have been mildly angry.
Lorraine and Kenneth were acting as if they'd never seen where I lived.
Both had come to see me at the Hotel Operatic several times but I guess me being here at the now animalistic and tiny box was preferable to me living at mama's with them, but now that they were moving . . . well it's a different leopard entirely?
Isn't it?
I sat there.
And listened.
I said nothing.

It was decided for me that I would move out that very night.
I put my clothes into another black plastic bag, took my hot plate, Trigger, my plant, and left.
I left my Broadway posters on the wall as a memento.
I had spent four years of my life at the Hotel Operatic but I turned my back on it as if I had only stayed there for an hour.
There were no tears of nostalgia. No good-byes.
Myles, the elevator mistress, wished me well and told me she wouldn't say nothing to the dragon lady at the reception desk.
She thought I was trying to sneak out without paying; which was the norm at the Hotel Operatic once a person decided they were going. The most monumental thing I took away from the Hotel Operatic was my newly engaged lover . . . the drug . . . crack.

I loved . . . looooovvvveeeeed crack.
It was miles cheaper than reefer and cocaine, the high was more
intense—just briefer.
I wasn't an addict at this point.
I only smoked crack if I didn't have enough money for reefer, or
just wanted something different, and crack, partly because of its
cost, was starting to rule the 'hood, as I soon found out in a few
weeks after returning to the John H. Blue Houses, the name of
the project in Brooklyn where I'd grown up and where I was
now returning to as a man of forty-one.

I wasn't returning a King, in glory, to show the neighbors, who
were still there and who remembered me as a youth, that I had
accomplished something with my life.
No.
I was returning as a bloodied casualty.
A walking wounded.
No.
A walking ghost.
I had lost the war.
I had become one of the contemptible ones.
A ghost-person.
I had a master's degree in dependency.
That I wasn't a fully fledged Vampire-Zombie was the only thing
I could congratulate myself on.

I assumed the responsibility of the apartment and was doing
quite well until I discovered, a few months after arriving, the
crack spots. Places I've already told you about.
The Centa-Renta and Sexpo's.
My crack intake increased sharply and regularly once I started
hanging out in my 'hood, at those places.
Lorraine had left most of the furniture that mama had bought
us in the apartment so I was very comfortable at first.
After I sold the television and the stereo for pipe-money, I
freaked and knew that I needed help.

I found Eric.
You already know what happened with me and him.

I now think that at the time I sold my things because
unconsciously I was trying to shrink my possessions; and in
shrinking my possessions I would shrink my responsibility.
I hadn't had creature comforts during those four years at the
Operatic.
I guess I was trying to make my new house like the ghost house
I'd just left.
Empty and spare.

I never told Lorraine that I was doing crack.
She found that out herself, on one of her regular visits to make
sure I was OK.
I remember the night Lorraine discovered me in the bathroom
standing on the toilet seat.
Petrified.
Cracked out of my skull.
Hallucinating wildly.
I had been smoking in the bathroom and had been staring at
the ceramic tiles that covered the bathroom floor.
I got lost in the cracks.
I thought that I was gonna fall eternally through the cracks
and be lost in white-crack-land and no one would ever find
me, so I stood on the toilet seat until Lorraine rescued
me.
Lorraine didn't know at first what was wrong with me. She put
me to bed but I wasn't sleepy. She called Kenneth (I still had a
phone then) and told him she'd be staying with me until the
morning. Since I didn't admit to her what was wrong with me,
Lorraine took me to the clinic the next day. The doctor took a
urine sample and a blood sample and after a few days the
doctor told Lorraine what the deal was.
I had never seen Lorraine so angry.
Not since Nate died.

She punched me.
She battered me in the face then convulsed, in an aria of tears,
into my aimless arms.

To say that I couldn't help what was happening to me would be
the truth but not the whole truth. . . . .
Life was running around me.
Action was my enemy.
I existed in a world of thought.
If the thought of doing some task tired me then I knew the
action would finish me.
I was beyond lazy.

Lorraine took over the paying of my rent after I spent my rent
money, two months running, on crack. She had found the final
demand letters from the Housing Authority.
I ripped the phone out the wall one night after hearing the
conversations of the whole of the building, in the living room of
my mind, while pipin'.
They were all talkin' about me.
I refused to have a phone after that which made contact with
mama difficult.
I didn't know if Lorraine had told mama.
She probably had.
But I didn't know what my mama made of me until the night
Lorraine and Kenneth drove me down to North Carolina at
mama's request.

By then I hadn't seen Lorraine for months as I've already told
you. She was angry at me after the incident with me and
Spartacus and the bloodied check that I signed over to him.
I told you about that already.

JULY 4, 1991 — 11:30PM

My check came yesterday.
Hallelujah!!
I bought some pipe stuff of course.
Can't celebrate the Nation's Birthday without some get-high!!!
I had been invited to Lorraine's for the Fourth of July celebration
bar-b-q and going-away party for her and Kenneth but I
couldn't handle it.
So I just stayed home and smoked.
What else is new.
I didn't smoke that much.
Just enough to get away from remembering that Lorraine is
leaving me. To get away from the feeling that when she leaves
my life is over. I don't know what I'm so scared about but I'm
terrified. That's probably why I didn't go to the party because I
knew I'd make an awkward scene . . . I'd blubber and cry and beg
Lorraine not to leave me.
I feel pathetic.
It's time to tell you about Pia.
And after I've told you about Pia, I will have opened all my sores.
I will have let out all the yellowed pus.
And I will be free.
But free to do what?
Get-a-fuckin' job?!!!
As usual, time concerts my efforts.
The US is in a recession.
Even high-flyers are crashing.
If they can't keep the jobs they have, what makes me think I'll
find one?
Pipe logic.
Makes sense.

It took a long time to get to North Carolina.
Kenneth was a safe driver.
It took nearly twelve hours.

Neither Lorraine or Kenneth spoke to me the entire time.
They only asked me if I was hungry then passed fried chicken,
potato salad and boiled eggs back to me.
We stopped only to piss, then continued making our way down
the dark Southern roads arriving at mama's place about 1pm the
following afternoon.
Lorraine and Kenneth slept and immediately went back to New
York City.
They had to be at work on Monday.
Lorraine kissed me before she left me and Kenneth shook my
hand.

When mama first walked out the house on our arrival and saw
me, she looked shocked. She hadn't seen me since Christmas
1985 when she had come up to see us and stayed at the
apartment with Lorraine and Kenneth. I had taken the train
from Manhattan to Brooklyn and had spent the night with the
family.
One of my rare times away from the Hotel Operatic.
I arrived in North Carolina to stay at mama's house in September
1990.

There's something about the smell of mama. I think it's the
womb smell.
A comforting mixture of sweated pleasure, perpetual pain,
panicked, worrisome futures coalesced with chicken fat, baked
ham and fish-on-friday.
Mama smells.
A look of love curled at the lip, lightning-flashed eyes, knowing
she could kill you with the next whack.
Porcelain knickknacks, Wedgwood bells and plastic on the
sofa. . . .
"Don't sit there . . . that's for company. . . ."
A gate across the most beautiful room in the house.
Daddy kept fish in there—a mother's day gift for Grandma.
Big tanks full.

Nate and me used to clean them.
Lorraine watched.
Women.
Stink-smells.
Dead-shitty-fish smells.
"You look tired Cornelius. . . ."
Mama as vulture . . . circling . . . a kind benevolent vulture . . . but a
vulture still. With claws.
Never questions.
Only open snake-pit-statements. . . .
I take my time fielding through mama's imploring eyes. Fearful
eyes. Dreading my answers . . . praying I'll say . . . "Yes, ma I'm
tired . . . I've been working very hard . . ." I say nothing.
I drink another glass of milk.
I eat another piece of mama-sweet-potato-pie. I can't lie with
my mouth full.
Drawing up a chair, mama closer to me than I can remember my
heart jumps and I need a smoke.
Badly.
My brow wets up.
Face to face.
Family lines tracing the sad waiting eyes.
Mama eyes.
"You were such a loud baby . . . jumping everywhere . . . shouting
the world down . . . jumping out your crib before you could walk . . ."
I can't run away from this; there is no Clark Kent corner even
though mama does believe in Superman.
How do I tell my mama that I've forgotten how to fly?
"Your daddy used to dog-leash you to your crib to keep you from
jumping out and cracking your head . . ." I nod. I smile.
My stomach hurts. And I can see flotillas of guilt crazies misting
in mama's eyes.
I wish she'd fuckin' shout!!!!
I wish she'd pick up a big fuckin' stick and beat the living shit
outta me.
Like daddy used to.
"Tell me I'm a shit!" I want to yell at her!

"Tell me I'm a fuck-up . . . on my way to death! . . . Tell me I need
Jesus! . . . tell me I need something! . . . tell me anything
mama . . . just don't look at me like that . . ."
I wanted to say all that to my mama and so much more . . . I
wanted to kneel at her feet and cry and tell her everything.
"Mama . . . I need to confess . . . my sins . . . I need absolution . . . I
can see my angels parading the rooms, fingers raised in
accusation . . . I see Satan's triumphant smile flicking wickedly
from the eye of a cracked crystal pipe bowl and I can feel the
power of the Holy Throne but I can't see His Holiness's
face . . . and I'll never see his face as I am. . . ."
The trickling tear spidering down my mama's face damns me.
Sentences and silences me.
Mama picks herself up, rag in hand, and cleans the cleanest table
in the world. Puts things away. Cuts off the light.
Mama comes to me in darkness . . . will she let it be . . . kisses me
on the side of my head near to my mouth . . . grabs my head like
a protective lioness. . . .
Breathes a sigh as huge as my secrets . . . mama plows my head
with her fingers like she did when I was a boy to comfort me
when daddy was mad at me because I didn't know my Sunday
School lesson.
Mama turns, goes to her bed, leaving me with anxieties I had
forgotten I had.
How do I tell my mama that I've forgotten how to fly . . . ?

Me and mama spent the next days like shadows playing at life.
When we went visiting I played, as best I could, reverential,
supportive son to her should-be proud mother. The questions
from her friends made me squirm like an eel awaiting the
boiling water.
"Cornelius what kind of job you got? . . . you married
Cornelius? . . . you a lawyer yet Cornelius? . . . I bet you got you a
big old condominium up there in New York Cornelius!" I had
forgotten that achievements are the miracles of a son that deify
the mother. Wreathes her head in glory.
Holy son. Goddess mother.

At a critical point in the scrutiny I got mad.

I stormed out of the preacher's house and walked out to the dirt road in front. I turned, ran down the red mud road to the gas station at the end.

I rushed into the store banging the door, loudly.

"Don't break my fuckin' door! I ain't done nothing to you!"

I turned to meet the voice.

The reddest hair. Long. To the waist. The bluest eyes. The creamiest face. Slight and balletic body. Short. Almost a dwarf. Maybe thirty-two.

The voice finished waiting on the antique red-necked gentleman who had come in for a chili-dog.

"You tell 'em Pia! Doors cost money!" The elderly croaker turned, as he left me alone with the voice.

"You want something?" The voice was irritated, bored, wanted to go home and needed me to know it.

I had stormed out of the preacher's house with no coins. "I forgot my money . . ." I found my voice. It was jumpy.

"Well you can't buy nothin' with no money . . . any fool knows that . . ."

I let that nugget of wisdom from the voice be my exit line.

I was to hear a lot of that voice in the three months I spent in North Carolina with mama.

I almost married that voice.

That voice was the magnificent Pia.

I hated Pia at first.

I thought she was an uppity-old-White-trashed-girl.

I hated going to her store.

I wouldda cursed her out a few times at first but I didn't want to make trouble for my ma.

I had to go to Pia's one wet Sunday afternoon after church to get mama some cranberry sauce for the stuffed-roast-chicken.

"You stupid dog-faced-shit!" Pia was castigating some poor,

unwitting White youth who had just tracked mud onto her freshly cleaned floor.

"I just mopped that fuckin' floor! You got the brain of a limp dick!" The boy blushed purple.

"You got the nastiest mouth I've ever heard on a woman!" I had to say something, "Words like that shouldn't even grace a woman's lips!"

The White youth took advantage of the cover, slipped his dollar onto the counter and slinked out leaving me to bear the brunt of Pia's acerbic onslaught.

Which didn't come.

Pia looked at me like I was some turd left by a Martian, then exploded into howls of laughter. Pia laughed so hard and long that she choked.

Then came the tears.

Raging tears of contempt and frustration.

"I hate this fuckin' place! . . . this backward hinterland of stupidity! . . ."

I put the tin of cranberry sauce onto the counter, grabbed a packet of tissues, ripped it open and handed one to Pia.

She looked at me strangely as she dabbed her eyes and honked her nose.

Me and Pia became strange friends after that day.

We had everything and nothing in common.

Many are the times I've thought back to Pia and wished on every known and unknown star in the galaxy that I'd never said anything to Pia.

You never know when you meet someone what part of their destiny you will be held accountable for . . . I had learned enough about myself to worry about people who came into my orbit . . . There was something about me that aroused the dormant calamity factor chancing the lives of those I got close to . . . I made another promise to myself, not to, for any reason, allow myself to get emotionally or physically involved with Pia. I thought it would be an easy promise to keep . . . we had everything and nothing in common . . . I had never had a White

female lover. I usually found White women to be sensationally silly.
Stupid even.
Uptight and frigidly condescending. To tell the truth I felt sorry for most White people and wondered how they ever had acquired their misplaced superiority complex.

Pia was a sad soul.
She cried a lot that first day of understanding.
I had never seen a flesh-and-blood White girl cry in such despair before.
Not even Doris Day or Patty Duke in their movies.
Pia's tears touched the tears in my own soul.
We became soul mates.
We were never lovers.
We became someone that the other could talk to and confide in.
We both hated where we were.
It wasn't even an intellectual thing.
It was a North Carolina thing.

Pia had grown up in New Jersey, had married a career Air Force officer who had gotten himself killed in a car accident in Germany, leaving Pia pregnant with twin boys six years before.
The Air Force had dumped Pia in North Carolina where her husband's family lived.
Pia's own family was one subject she chose not to talk about with the exception of her younger brother Dukey who also lived in North Carolina.
With her husband's Government settlement, Pia bought herself a house and the gasoline-grocery store and slowly fell into the rut of small-town Southern life. It was good for her to be in North Carolina only because she was able to get some help and support with her twin boys from her husband's family.
Pia had spent some time in New York City so there was a lot we could talk about.

Our relationship was talk.
We talked about everything, everyone.
And the arguments!
Tempers flying like shards of glass!
Nostrils flaring!
Pia was Super-Glued to her convictions. Even if she was wrong,
she reserved her right to be wrong.

Pia's store became my second home.
I spent so much time there that Pia hired me to help out on busy
days.
After 5pm when the twins, Jacoub and Esau, came home from
the nursery, I ran the store for her so she could do some catch-up
mothering.
It bothered me at first that I could be so open with a White
woman.
I could tell Pia things that I'd never told any of my family.
I didn't tell her about the pipe because I didn't want to scare her
away but I told her about Nate and Eric (sort of) and Maggie
and Cynthia.
She listened without emotion or judgment until I finished and
then she stomped me. Pia quartered and hung me.
She told me "Your life is one whole but broken excuse! . . . grow
up or shoot yourself!"
There was no sentimentality in her.
Those first tears I had witnessed were a fluke, not a real part of
her emotional makeup.
She hadn't even cried while mourning her husband.
Pity was not a word that she included in her vocabulary.
Pia was hard.
"The trouble with the world is men! You guys have been fuckin'
it up for so long that chaos is the only thing you know how to
create!"
I argued that the White men were responsible. Pia snarled.
"Famous last words of an oppressed people . . . If I were Black I
wouldn't give two shits about the White man 'cause he sure as

shit don't give two fucks about you . . . you Black people . . ." She
started, and I called her to the floor about her "You Black people" tone.
Pia told me to fuck off and stop being so White.
"Why should you care what I call you . . . I ain't nobody! . . . You
give the White man too much credit. He ain't that smart . . . he's
a killer-fighter though . . . your people need to learn how to fight
and I don't mean that shooting each other shit! . . . I mean
fighting for your life . . . for your right even if it ain't your fuckin'
right . . . The White man is a master-thief, everything he's got
he's stolen. Maybe it's where you came from . . . Africa . . . the
sun . . . easy life . . . the White man had to crawl his way down the
mountains of Caucasia. Naked. No shoes. Killing other White
men for food, which is why he loses no sleep killing you . . . he
has no conscience . . . Your people need to get rid of your
conscience . . . it's all bullshit! . . . relative moral bullshit! . . ."
Pia'd go on like that until I couldn't stand to hear any more and
I'd rage against her with every righteous-Afrocentric-bone I had
left in my body.
I'd call her "naïve! . . . stupid! and racist! and backward-thinking!"
and the store would rock! We'd fight as we served people.

Fighting with Pia with such ferocity and intensity made it easier
for me to open up to mama and as the days slid like molasses
into weeks I'd slowly, slowly tell mama what she wanted to
know about me in measures. Nothing too strong but enough to
bring my mama to the door of my heart. But not enough to
scare her.

The townspeople started whispering about me and Pia and Pia
would laugh. "Fuckin'-stupid-know-nothings!" she'd call them.
Most nights I'd walk Pia home after closing up the store. One
twin asleep on my neck the other in Pia's arms. She would never
ask me in and I'd never ask. I'd go home, eat some mama-food
and go to bed.
I didn't smoke anything for the first two months I was in North
Carolina.
Pia-talk replaced pipe-talk.

236

"Get rid of your conscience . . ." Pia's words haunted me.
"A conscience is for cowards!" I stringently disagreed with her
but perhaps not strongly enough to persuade her that she could
be wrong.

It was a wonder rediscovering my mama, remembering how
much I loved her and after a while it didn't matter that I was
languishing in the land-that-time-forgot—North Carolina. The
priceless gift was that I was with my mama and I was getting
well.
I was.
The smoke was clearing out of my system.
The ice-cycles were melting in my mind.
After a while, since there was no pipe-stuff to be found (well
none that I wanted to find) I even stopped thinking about it. If
things got too clear and the desire to float raged me out of my
reverie, I'd have a couple of beer and get tipsy.
I didn't dare search out any pipe-stuff because I didn't want
anyone chatting to my mama about her son's secret life.
Especially as I'd edited out all details of drug-taking in my heart-
to-hearts with mama. I knew mama wasn't stupid and she
probably knew what was up but she hadn't brought it up and I
wasn't going to and I certainly didn't want any of her friends
pulling her slip and informing her of what they saw me do.
I knew there was pipe-stuff in the area.
I had heard tell of northern GITS (Gangsters-In-Training) who
had relocated to the South, setting up their own drug baronies
because there was less fierce competition. Some of these youths
had been sent down South by their worried families to save their
lives from violence—get a new start or a respite from the inner-
city-madness-blues.
If I had seriously wanted to search out the rock I could have
found it. But searching would have meant asking questions and
asking questions usually posed questions in the minds of the
people you were askin'; and I didn't want anyone askin' me any
questions whose answers might get back to my mama.
If I couldn't give my mother a past of mine she could be proud

of I certainly wasn't gonna dirty-up the fragile present I was
trying to share with her.

To say I could have kicked my addiction had I stayed in North
Carolina is too big a statement and may not have worked out to
be true.
Familiarity breeds confidence as well as contempt.
The longer I stayed in North Carolina the more people I would
have met and sooner or later I would have run into a circle of
people outside my mother's orbit and I would have joined their
game, because still at that time I didn't want to give up the pipe.
I didn't have anything rock-solid to replace it with. . . .

BUT

Pia helped decorate my life and kept my interest engaged. Pia
and mama helped stem the boredom that in the city made the
pipe the most exciting event of my day.
Being with them gave me a reason to get up in the morning,
and I had become devoted to Jacoub and Esau, Pia's twin angel
sons.
Jacoub was eight minutes older than Esau. Both boys adored the
beautiful reflection of themselves that they saw in each other's
eyes. The memory of them scorches me to such an indescribable
degree.
I gotta stop here.
I gotta chill.

JULY 10, 1991 — 9AM

Rent Office

I am sitting here waiting for the Rent Officer to see me.
They need a specimen of my signature for my new rent card.

This is the place I'll have to come the first of each month to pay
my rent.
The receptionist blanked me.
I guess I wasn't dressed for the occasion.
I have on a T-shirt and a pair of old green army khakis. I made
sure I kept my army outfits. Clothes are clothes.
I washed.
My clothes aren't that dirty.
I certainly don't smell like a Vampire-Zombie but the
receptionist still looked at me like I didn't deserve the breath
within me.
"What are you doing here?!"
No "Good morning! . . . Can I help you?!!!"
Judged.
I couldn't possibly have no business here so . . . "What are you
doing here?!!!"
In my best two-years-of-Columbia-University-accented-lawyer-
voice, I said, "The Housing Authority needs a specimen of my
signature for my rent records . . ."
Not impressed, her eyes Amanda Donahoed me.
"You live here . . . in John H. Blue!!!!??????"
She said that like "here" was the Taj Mahal or Calvary . . .
somewhere magnificent and holy . . .
Not the shitty two-steps-away-from-a-bomb-site degeneracy that
it is.
I had to flash the letter from the Housing Authority plus my
welfare ID check-cashing card before she believed me. I'm glad I
have them with me.
She's putting me through all this palaver shit, and they asked me
to come in.
I came in to identify myself.
To say like "Hey! I'm the one this piece of paper says I am!!!!"
Like somebody else is gonna come in and give them money for
my rent. White people are so fucked.
Anyway Nurse Ratched-secretary-type finally allowed me to sit
down and wait for the Rent Officer which is what I'm doing
now.

The door is opening and a grown-up Leave-It-to-Beaver-type is emerging. Perhaps he's the Rent Officer.
We'll see.

JULY 19, 1991—4 PM

Two weeks to D day when Lorraine has her moving day. Monday August 5.
The vans arrive at 9am.
They fly out to San Francisco at 7pm that evening. I've never seen Lorraine so manic.
She told me today that mama is coming up on August 1 to help her pack up and that she will be flying to San Francisco to help Lorraine get ready to have the baby.
Mama will be out there indefinitely.
I will well and truly be alone then.
All of my family will be on the West Coast. Well . . . .
Fuck it!
If that's where they want to be . . . so-fuckin'-be-it! I'll be fine.
I'm always fine.
I may be fucked out of my head. . . . . .
Or dead. . . . .
But I'll be fine.

I went to see Eric last night.
This time I smoked up all his rock and I wouldn't let him fuck me.
I punched his fuckin' face in.
Eric was more stunned than hurt.
He lay there on the floor lookin' at me as if I had cut off his twelve-foot dick. Next time I will.

I've been ragin' all week.
Cussin' at people in the street.
Cussin' people I don't know.

I even went into the Safeway and knocked over a whole shelf of food. I screamed and cussed the place down.
I knew the security guard.
Arty.
Fisher Styler, a kid I went to High School with, his little brother Arty. Arty didn't rough me up. Took me by my hand like I was a five-year-old and led me out the store. He flashed those "I-feel-so-sorry-for-you" eyes at me and pressed $10 in my hand.
I went straight to the Centa-Renta and bought me some fuckin' rock. I smoked it there too.
I was loud and rowdy and the regulars looked at me as if I'd smoked some zippy shit.
I don't know what to do with myself.
In the sky of my mind, a black thought is rising like an early moon. Lorraine and mama are going to the West Coast to be rid of me. They are tired of me.
They are tired of taking care of me and I am taking too long to die.
I didn't die conveniently prematurely like Nate and daddy.
Maybe mama and Lorraine killed Nate and daddy.
Poisoned them.
Who'd know.
Slow poisoning is almost untraceable.
STOP THINKING STUPID!!!!!!!!!!!!!!
I'm so para.
Para to the core.
But they are all going to the West Coast.
All.
Except me.
They got a new life that's coming into the clan. Gotta make his/her way straight.
Can't taint his/her chances by being related to a fuckin'-stinkin'-dirty-crack-head.
WE CAN'T HAVE THAT! CAN WE!!!!!
Lowers the tone. Doesn't it!!!
No we can't have no stinkin'-fuckin'-base-freaks.
On our doorsteps.

No we have a clean-pure-soul coming.
He doesn't need an uncle.
He's got a daddy.
Fuckin' Kenneth.
Mr. Self-righteous.
He shouldda met Pia.
Pia wouldda put him in his place.
Pia hated all those wanna-be-White Black-folks.

And I don't know if it's fair to say that Kenneth really wants to
be White. I guess it's White America's demand that those Black
people admitted to its inner sanctums of power must adhere to
a checklist of White correctness before they are given a green badge of
acceptance and a job.
It's strange.
You can turn on the TV or even listen to the radio and the Blacks
that appear there have become so homogenized, so white-ti-fied;
and then you plug into the street culture, i.e. music,
entertainment, and the White-boys are killing themselves trying
to be Black.
There's no rhyme or reason to it and it leaves me raving and
ranting as I am now, Pia would have given me a tongue-lashing
and thrown me out of her house.

I did finally get into Pia's house.
Not that I really cared to, or that she really wanted me to—it
just happened. It happened after we had finished for the day in
her store and I was walking her back to her house with the two
sleeping twins.
Pia put her key in the door, the door opened to her without her
turning her key. We looked at each other. It was one of the few
times I can remember Pia's metallic composure slipping.
I had never seen her afraid.
I gave the twin I was holding to Pia and went in before her. Pia
was directly behind me, her hand on my shoulder.
I went into the foyer. A low light burning in another room led
me on into the house.

There was a blond, short, stocky young man, about twenty-seven, seated on the couch weighing up reefer on a scale. "Dukey!" Pia's voice shot out like a cannon. "If you can't fuckin' lock my front door when you come in here, I'm takin' back my key! . . . you scared the shit outta me and I told you to be finished up with your mess before I got back here with my babies!!! . . . Corny this is my stupid-ass brother Dukey . . ." Pia called me Corny because she said Cornelius sounded like the name of a Broadway musical show.

The blonded White boy shot an easy grin at me. "Wanna roll one up?" He pointed to the grass.

"Not in here you don't!" Pia answered for me. "You wanna smoke that shit, you go out back to the woods!"

Dukey grinned again. A toothy-goofy-I-been-high-all-day-grin, grabbed a couple of big buds, rolled them quickly into a giant joint and walked toward me . . .

"You comin'?" My stomach started hurting.

The same kind of pain I'd get just after I gave the pipe-man my money and he was putting the bag of rocks in my hand. Could it be possible that Dukey, Pia's jocund little brother, had access to the rocks that I had managed to stay away from for months? I half-prayed that he didn't.

"You comin'?" Dukey was almost out the door.

"No . . . I . . . should be getting home . . . it's late . . ." I sweated out an answer.

Dukey shrugged, grinned and went out into the night. Pia had already gone upstairs to put the twins to bed.

"You want some coffee!?" She yelled from upstairs.

"Put a light under the kettle . . . the kitchen is to your left . . . straight back . . ." I found it, found some matches and lit up the old gaseous stove. I had always hated gas stoves.

I thought they were dangerous.

I didn't trust them.

I didn't understand how anyone could sleep comfortably with one of them in their house.

Pia came downstairs just as the kettle was boiling.

She was smiling.

Over coffee she told me that Dukey was the only member of her family that she halfway had anything to do with.

"He's a good kid," she said. He just needed to find himself and decide what he was gonna do with his life.

"Why didn't you go and have a smoke with him? I don't give a shit whether you smoke or not."

I told Pia that part of the reason I was in North Carolina was that I was trying to give up drugs. Well.

That launched Pia into another one of her sermons on the evils of drug-taking. Dukey came in five minutes later, caught wind of the conversation, put his drugs and paraphernalia away in this black leather bag, made his apologies and left. I actually felt better after he left. I stopped sweating and my stomach stopped hurting.

Pia kept me up half the night talking about this and that, her hopes for the future, her fears for her sons. She wanted to find a suitable dependable man who'd be a good role model for her boys. As if on cue we heard a slap-slap-slap on the stairs and into the wooden-walled kitchen waddled Esau, the younger twin. He climbed Pia's monkey-bar-body and nestled in her arms.

Yawning, trying to brush the sleep outta his eyes.

A beautiful, blue-eyed-honeyed-blond-pure-soul.

This is too hard to continue.

The memory of Pia, rivers of hair, streaming down her face, cuddling the blonded-blue-eyed-Esau or cautioning the brave-warrior-child-Jacoub (just as blonded and blue-eyed as his photo-copied twin), hangs around my neck like a skyscraper of guilt.

I can't blame Dukey.

Dukey was only the source.

This thing, this addiction is the Devil.

It finds you.

No matter how far you run away.

It finds you.

Pia was the best and possibly only friend I had in North Carolina. I spent more time with her than I did with my mama. Pia helped me to be strong.

I thought that some of her abrasive assertiveness was rubbing off on me. I kinda thought I loved Pia but I never got around to finding that out. I tell myself now that I could have married Pia, and I could have.

I don't know if I could have made love to her the way I made love to Black girls, because I still had this "thing" about White women, but the more I got to know Pia, the less "White" she became and the more human she seemed. I learned that the colors Black and White as well as being descriptions of race were also descriptions of states of mind . . . i.e., Black meaning all things safe and positive, White meaning all things dangerous and negative. I found out that there were White people with Black minds, and vice versa. Pia was a safe White girl. She certainly wasn't silly.

Mama knew Pia because mama bought from her store. Mama would have liked Pia.

There was something about Pia that reminded me of Lorraine. I think it was her drive.

Both were extremely ambitious, you got the sense that both Pia and Lorraine would complete whatever goal they had in life with or without anyone's help. So yes I could have married Pia and perhaps if I hadda asked her she wouldda laughed and said "Corny you crazy!" as she said to me countless times a day. I never got the chance to propose.

Pia's brother Dukey was the local drug dealer.

Of all the things he couldda been, he turned out to be the local drug dealer. Dealers know their customers as well as they know their drugs. Some good dealers can just look at you and tell what kind of drug you do. Anyway, after spending that first evening at Pia's, I became a welcome guest there. My mama began to see very little of me.

I would work all day at Pia's store then spend most of the night at Pia's house drinking coffee maybe watching a video and talking. Pia loved videos. Her favorite one was The Accused. Yeah, that Jodie Foster—she was her kind of woman.

I still hadn't gotten high with Dukey and I was proud of myself for that. One Sunday afternoon after I got back from church with mama, and before I could get over to Pia's store, mama's doorbell rang. I ran to answer it. Standin' on the porch was Dukey.
I was surprised to see him.
I didn't ask him in.
He grinned his goofy-grin, pulled off his baseball cap and asked me if I was busy.
I said no.
He asked me if I would take a walk with him. I shouldn't have, but a denied part of me wanted to. My stomach started hurting.
My dick even started to get hard which made no sense to me at all. I didn't need a jacket, it was warm, but I did need my key. I ran into mama's eyes.
She had been standing right behind me.
She had seen Dukey.
She looked at me and just said "Be careful . . ." turned and walked away.

So into the woods we went.
Dukey and me.
Trees.
Ancient as Methuselah blocking out the hot afternoon sun.
Miles of moss, green like paradise carpets.
Snakes.
Crawling in the distance before us.
We took a turn to the right.
I hoped that Dukey knew the way back because I didn't have a clue where we were or where we were going.

We found a small clearing surrounded by a cluster of maple oaks. Dukey sat down in a circle of sunlight; he took off his jacket and made a pallet on the steaming ground, stretched and lay down.

"Open the bag . . . take out what you want . . ." Dukey shielded his eyes from the sun.

I opened the bag slowly as if a cobra was inside.

My stomach knotted, sweat beading my forehead like virgin pearls. Dukey had pouches and pouches of grass.

I kept searching, hoping against hope that what my mind craved would be there. I felt a glass tube, then plastic.

Hardness.

White hardness.

Rocks.

It was there.

I flinched, my fingers burned with excitement.

"Found something you like?" Dukey's voice sounded like a winded echo as if coming from a cave.

I didn't answer Dukey.

I was busy loading the pipe.

Found the matches.

Pipe to mouth.

Stomach turning somersaults.

Light to pipe.

Inhale.

Inhale.

Blinding bells of light.

DOOOOOOOOOOOEEEEEEEEEEEEEEEEE. . . . . . .

Hark!

The Herald Angels Sang

DOOOOOOOOOOOEEEEEEEEEEEEEEEEE. . . . . . .

And I'm on the ground on top of Dukey.

Dukey laughing like a rodeo full of cowboys.

"I know what you did!!! . . . . . I know what you did. . . ." Dukey laughing and pushing me off him onto the moist grassy bed.

The earth swallowing me in one gulp and I'm fighting as if in quicksand. Dukey sitting in front of me gulping the goodness like beer.

We stayed in the woods until the sun started to go down, until we could see the forest fairies peeping out from the trees.
We could hear the pixies laughing at us while they waved their wands of darkness and the shades of night lowered.
We knew it was time to find our way out.
We musta walked around in the woods for two hours laughing and freaking. Dukey rolled up a joint.
This gave us a better sense of direction.
Sudden car lights from the highway found us, pointing out the way home. Dukey went to Pia's.
I crept into mama's house and slid into my bed. I couldn't sleep. I listened to the silence of the house whispering accusations. Shadows replayed the day's actions on the wallpaper of my bedroom. I fell into a black hole of guilt.
I hated Pia for being Dukey's sister.
I hated mama for living next to Pia's store.
I hated myself for hating the innocence of these supporting players in my tragedy of guilt.
I hated Dukey because he knew my need.
The sunlight returned and I slept.

I caught mama staring at me intently at the table.
I ate my chicken quickly, saying nothing.
It was Monday and I had slept away the best part of the day. Pia would be turbulent.
I kissed mama good-bye, never knowing that it would be the last time I would be with my mama.
I still haven't seen her since then. I've talked to her on the telephone but I've not seen her since that day.
I walked out mama's door and ran to Pia's store.
Pia flung machete glares at me as she finished serving a customer. She didn't talk to me.

The blonded-angel twins were busy playing building blocks with
the cereal boxes in the aisles.
They ran up to me jabbering happily.
"Where you been Corny? . . . we had icecream, and chicken . . ."
Happy, careless, free, safe.
"You seen Dukey today?" Pia finally smiled a question at me. I
told her that I'd seen him the day before.
"He came in here looking for you . . . he told me to give you
this . . ." Pia handed me a bulky but small envelope. She looked at
me as if she expected me not to accept it.
I took it, put it in my pocket without looking in it.

We finished the day in silence, prepared the store for the next
morning.
Brave Jacoub and Mighty Esau lay asleep under the counter in
each other's arms like Romulus and Remus.

Me and Pia didn't talk much during the slow walk in the
moonlight to her place. For some dark reason I remember
feeling sad.
The entire trip had a kind of swan-song musicality about it. Just
like my last time with Nate on the train.
"What's wrong with you . . . cat got your tongue?" Pia noticed my
mood right away. "You've been smokin' drugs . . . I thought you
were trying to stay away from them . . . I know Dukey is a
charmer but you can't spend a lot of time with him . . . Dukey is a
businessman . . . he could sell crack to the Pope and hook him
too . . . Dukey has no conscience . . . he'll go far . . . he doesn't
understand the word no . . ." I was beginning to wonder if Dukey
had been talking to Pia but I didn't ask. I didn't want to talk
about it.

We got to Pia's house.
I tried to beg off and go straight home because I was feeling a
bit uncomfortable with all this talk of Dukey and I was dying to
get somewhere private so I could open the envelope.

249

Pia wouldn't hear of my going.

"I'll just put the boys to bed and we'll have coffee . . . Hell, I haven't even hollered at you all day, you owe me one good yell at least." With that Pia sailed upstairs to put the twins down to sleep.

With Pia gone, I took the opportunity to peek inside the envelope from Dukey. I knew what it was before I opened it. Well I knew what most of it was; what I wasn't expecting from Dukey was a bill. There, along with a pipe and a bag of rocks, was a bill for seventy-five dollars.

Me and Dukey musta smoked up about fifty to sixty dollars' worth of rocks the day before. Not a huge amount, but Dukey was charging me for the portion that I had smoked.

"Open the bag, take out what you want," Dukey had said. I didn't know he was inviting me to pay him.

The bag of rocks in the envelope was worth at the most twenty-five dollars, which meant that Dukey was charging me twenty or thirty dollars for a pipe I never even asked for.

Shit.

Fuck a pipe.

If I really wanted a smoke I could use a broken bottle neck or a soda can. I certainly didn't need no expensive pipe. Dukey had some fuckin' nerve.

I would pay him for the rocks but that's all, I thought to myself as I sniffed the aroma of the coffee.

Pia returned to the kitchen with candles and a quiet smile. She lit the candles, poured out the coffee. We talked.

We musta talked for hours.

Well, Pia talked.

I listened.

She had such plans.

She was gonna sell the store and move to Connecticut. She wanted to go to Yale.

Two bottles of wine replaced the coffee and soon Pia was tipsy; touching me lightly on the arm as she revealed her thousand points of hope.

Yawns replaced the laughter.
"I'm going upstairs to pee . . . I'll be back."
I waited for her and waited for her but she never came down.
I tiptoed upstairs to see if she was alright. Pia lay on her bed
fetal-like, snoring loudly.
I decided I would have one last cup of strong black coffee so I
wouldn't be too drunk on my walk home. I tipped downstairs
and lit the gas stove, sat and waited for the coffee to heat up.
I fingered the glass hardness through the envelope in my
pocket.
My stomach thudded in anticipation of a midnight smoke in the
darkness out back while I waited for the coffee to brew. I
grabbed one of Pia's candles. It seemed like an easy idea at the
time. I'd have a hit then drink some coffee.
The thought of the hit-in-the-dark propelled me out the door
which clicked-shut behind me, locking me out.
Pia had one of those automatic-lock doors, but it didn't matter
because I forgot myself.
As soon as the goodness ignited my mind and the smoke ran
around my lungs like an Olympic sprinter chasing gold, all
thoughts of Pia, the twins, coffee, candles and the lit gas stove
vanished. There was only me.
The pipe.
The moon.
And darkness.
I forgot myself.
Again and again I lit the pipe and inhaled, walking toward
home. Not even remembering how I got there.
I found myself ut my mama's house, sat on the porch and
boldly lit up again and again until the plastic bag was empty
and my smoke-drenched mind was reeling and I actually
felt good.
I felt like a seven-year-old being naughty while mama slept
blissfully unaware in the next room.
There musta not been too much speed in Dukey's rocks because I
actually fell asleep on the porch.

Dawn woke me.
I opened mama's front door went up to my room and slept some more.

It was past noon when I woke again.
I jumped into my clothes and ran all the way to Pia's store.
Mama had gone to church for noon-day prayer, so I thankfully
didn't have to deal with her.
I knew something was wrong before I got to the store. There
were three or four people standing out front. One of them was
crying.
The store was still padlocked.
There was a policeman there talking to two firemen.
I detoured and made my way over to Pia's house.

Above the green trees that stood sentry before Pia's house, I
could see gray smoke rising to meet the blue afternoon sky. I
walked quickly to where Pia's house once was. Blackened wood.
White-gray smoke.
Red-brown-crumpled brick. More smoke.
There was no house.
I stopped a distance from the small crowd of people that stood
outside the burned pyre.
Cruel memory replayed last night's events to my mind. Candles,
the hissing gas under the waiting coffeepot.
I had left the stove fired up when I went out to fire up my pipe.
I had forgotten.
I couldn't bring myself to imagine what had happened after I
left. I ran forward to find Pia and the twins.
"All of 'em dead . . . they took the bodies out in bags an hour
ago . . ." I tried not to hear the words of one neighbor to another
as I stood before the once-upon-a-time porch.
Before I could ask anyone about Pia, I had been told. The answer
gutted me.
Knocked the air from my lungs.
Threw me on my knees.
Pia.

Jacoub.
Esau.
Gone.
My fault.

A few of the people there knew me from the store.
One of them, a Mr. Andrews, came over to me and helped me to
my feet. I remember children's laughter.
It's amazing how innocently children can laugh in the face of
calamity. Children's laughter.
I turned to see, hoping that it was Jacoub and Esau.
"All of 'em dead . . . they took the bodies out in bags an hour ago . . ."
Suddenly it was too hot.
Sweat swam down my face.
I had to get away.
I started running.
Refusing to focus on the horror.
Hoping I would wake up and find it was all a drug-induced
nightmare. Responsibility and action ran with me, holding
my arms, pushing my feet forward. I had to get away.
There would be questions.
Had anyone seen me at Pia's last night?
It didn't have to be me. Maybe Dukey came back last night.
Maybe the candles had burned down to the old lace tablecloth.
It probably had nothing to do with the fired-old-coffeepot on
the ancient gas stove.

I entered the coolness of the still house.
Mama was still at church.
Thank God.
I had to get out of my mama's house before my nerves ruptured.
Panicked crying.
Cry-baby.
Again . . . as usual . . . I cried . . . Pia would have slapped
me. . . . Pia!!!!!!!!!
"All of them dead. . . . . . ."
Pia. . . . .

Jacoub . . . . . Esau. . . . .
What would mama say. . . . .
I had to escape.
I ran upstairs, threw the few things I had brought with me into
the wooden suitcase Lorraine had lent me when we came down
to North Carolina.
I sadly left the clothes that my mama made me during my stay in
the oaken walk-in closet in my bedroom.
I left them as an offering.
An atonement.
I ran out the front door, imploring all the gods that I didn't run
into my mama, and found my way to the train station.
I had about fifty dollars in my pocket.
Not enough for the train fare but I was getting out of North
Carolina. I stopped at a telephone booth and called Amtrak. The
next train to New York was in an hour.
Thank you Jesus.

•

I walked around and around the Amtrak station singing "Jesus
keep me near the cross" over and over again.
I had to.
I wouldn't . . . couldn't allow myself to think about
Pia . . . Jacoub . . . Esau . . . mama . . . I didn't go into the station.
I didn't want anyone to see me.
Especially my mother.
I didn't want anyone to ask me any questions. The train arrived
after an eternity.
I stole away inside like an invisible man, found a ladies' toilet in
the last car of the train.
Women are more patient than men.
I locked myself in.
I cried then.
I cried for the entire ten hours that the train took to get to New
York. Countless women knocked on the door of the toilet and I
was sure one of them would bring the conductor who would
find me and discover me guilty. . . . . .

BUT

since I was in the last car I guess it was easier for the women to
find another toilet than to bother with me.
I got away with it.
Just like I had gotten away with all the other scarlet-lettered
horror stories that were stitched into the cloth of my life.
I got away with it.
And guilt was the only punishment that heaped itself like coals
of fire on my heart and mind. My soul too.
Guilt married me.
Guilt became my groom.
My husband.
Guilt fucked me.
I became impregnated.
I bore guilty children.
I named them Guilt Crazies.
I gave birth to them Caesarean-style.
I delivered them myself.
The umbilical cords never severed.
My children are nurtured and fed by the revolving memories—
showcased and screened endlessly for their pleasure in the
cinema of my mind.
Their playground.
Only the pipe can stop the Guilt Crazies from crying out to me.
The pipe is their milk bottle as well as mine.
A pacifier that stops their crying and gives me peace. A respite.
Whether or not I accept responsibility for my actions is
unimportant. What is very clear is that I do have a conscience. I
know what I did, what I caused . . . . . and I suffer.

JUNE 23, 1992

Psychiatric Ward, Kings County Hospital, NYC

*There's a school of thought that says, and it might be some kind
of philosophical bullshit, but it says that before birth we make a
contract with fate.
That we choose the pieces of our future that will lead to our
destiny. We choose the lessons we need to learn in this life. We
choose our parents.
We choose our poverty or wealth.
We choose our successes and misfortunes.
We choose our husbands, wives, children.
We choose the number of years we are to live. We choose our
death.
Well. . . .
If that is so then I musta been a real motherfucker of a genius in
my last life.
Life musta been real golden; because this life, the life I'm in
now, is a real zero.
In fact this life now for most of us earthlings in 1992 is real
shitty. We as a world full of souls musta been all those Emperors
and Kings and Czars and Queens and billionaires, traders and
builders, respected artists, fulfilled dreamers. Generals of war,
great thinkers and teachers that created the beauty, riches and
knowledge recorded, unrecorded and lost in history from day
one. We all musta binged on the fatness of the earth in bygone
centuries because we as a world are truly paying for it in blood
now. But the wheel keeps turning.
There are only a lucky few who have gone to heaven and they
seem to have everything . . . people like the Queen of England,
Michael Jackson, Madonna, Forbes, The Pope . . . people like that.
Them people musta been some dangerous Hitlers in some
bygone eras because they have never had it as good as they
have it now.
The rest of us are serfs in the hinder parts of hell.*

■

I laughed when the orderly threw this notebook at me.
"Washington," he barked at me. "Think fast!" and threw this
notebook at me.
This my-story.
I thought I had finished this shit.
I had left it back at my apartment . . . well I didn't actually leave
it. After the Housing Authority people poured Super Glue in my
lock and chained my door shut, soon after New Year's,
everything that was in the apartment stayed there including this
notebook. I didn't think I'd ever see it again.
I've been trying to read it.
My handwriting is kind of weird.
Some funny shit is in this notebook.
A lot of sad scary shit too.
I was told that several of the psychiatrists assigned to my case
read it too. They think it would be a good project for me to
continue it. I don't know.
I always get suspicious when one of these brain-scratchers
suggests anything to me.
I don't trust them.
They could be setting me up.
A trap.
I've not talked to any of them since I been here.
I guess they thought that if I started writing they could get a
hold of my diary and read what they want to know.
But I got news for them.
They will never get their hands on this again.
I'm gonna keep writing but only because I want to, and then I'm
gonna burn it up. My reasons for my life are my reasons and I
don't want no White bearded-lentil-eating-can't-dance-mother-
fucker trying to analyze me. I don't care how long they keep me
here. I have nothing waiting for me outside.
I do know that once they tell the courts that I'm in a sound
frame of mind, they'll probably want to try me, but I don't ever
plan to be in a sound frame of mind again.

Ever.
I've just got back the use of my legs a few weeks ago.
I've been fucked up.
Real fucked up.
My back and legs got broke when them people threw me off the roof.
I did a real number that time.
I thought it was the end.
But that got fucked up too.
I'm still alive.

I've been through some real deep shit since the last time I wrote.
It was predictable shit but real deep.
Even stilts couldn't have helped me.
I've dubbed myself Cornelius the Harbinger of Doom.
Hopefully my doom days are over.
I think I'll stay here for the rest of my days and be taken care of.
I'll write little ditties like this and maybe get one of those White-liberal-hearted-do-gooder-social-workers to find me a publisher who'll publish my shit.
In fact I've changed my mind.
I ain't gonna burn this notebook up.
I've been writing this thing for over a year. It's the only piece of "work" that I've done in years.
I mean real consistent work.
Who knows, maybe some crazy addict might read this and check what I've been through and stay away from you-know-what. I can't bring myself to say the word these days.
I haven't had a smoke since the end of December. That is the best thing about this place. I don't know anybody on the outside who could sneak any in to me. I don't want any anyway. My family. My mother, sister, brother-in-law, niece, nephew, are on the West Coast busy with their lives. As far as I know, I am dead to them. I'm sure they're worried about me but it's best this way. I need time to flush my whole life out and I'm gonna take that

time and even if I die before I'm successful I'm gonna stay right here and flush.
It's warm.
I have my own bed.
They feed me.
I have a shelter over my head.
I know what it's like to be homeless and I never want to be in that position again.
I'd kill myself.
I'd do it right this time.
I hated myself for a long time, especially after all that Pia shit.
Pia haunted me for a long time.
She still does.
She comes to me silently with a sad questioning look in her eyes, shaking her head from side to side.

The last dated entry in this diary is July 19, 1991. Almost a year ago. What a difference a year makes.
Strange, but if things had gone the way I did them (not even the way I wanted them to go because a year ago I didn't know how I wanted anything to go; I just went with the flow as the 'hood boys used to say), then I wouldn't be sitting here now at this game table in this nut ward at this hospital.
I wouldda been dead.

After Lorraine, mama and Kenneth left New York for San Francisco, my whole existence literally evaporated in a puff of smoke.
I thought I used to get high but after Lorraine left I truly got HIGH!!
I stayed high.
I didn't want rationality. I didn't want logic. Strangely enough I did want understanding. I know that now but I didn't then.
In any case I didn't know how to get understanding. All I knew about was alienation and oblivion.

I was hurt and angry.
I was being abandoned and I didn't like it. It was my fault.
I had used up all my chances with my family.
I was a grown man . . . in fact I was a middle-aged grown man. I
had been dependent on them off and on since 1983.
Lorraine had borne the brunt of the responsibility for me ever
since I moved back to the apartment after living at the Hotel
Operatic.
This time last year she was getting ready to have a baby and she
needed all of herself to give to this new life. Lorraine had given
most of herself to me for too long.
I knew this but I didn't want to accept it; and mama . . . well
mama had thrown up her hands in disgust with me after I had
run away from her without so much as a good-bye, let alone
some explanation.
Lorraine told me that the police had been 'round to mama's
house asking questions about me after the Pia incident. Mama
had told them that I had worked for Pia but that's all she knew.
She didn't know where I was or why I had left. I was surprised
that the police hadn't followed me to New York but why should
they? I hadn't murdered Pia. What happened was an accident.
Yes it might have been my fault, yes I might have been able to
prevent it, but it was as much Pia's fault as mine.
She had left the candles burning and she should have gotten rid
of that leaky gas stove. I have told myself these things endlessly
ever since the Pia thing happened.
Only now can I accept the responsibility of my mistake. A tragic
mistake but a mistake nevertheless.

When mama came up to help Lorraine move she didn't come to
see me. I called Lorraine and spoke to mama on the phone. She
was polite, concerned but distant. I didn't even go over to
Lorraine's house while she was moving out. Her and Kenneth
came over to see me the night before they flew out but I was
over at the Centa-Renta getting high so I missed them. They left
me a note and twenty-five dollars.

I read the note then went back to the Centa-Renta with the money and bought some you-know-what.
I guess I stayed high as a protest of sorts.

I allowed my life to unravel.
I paid no bills.
I dared the worst to happen to me and the worst did.
My electricity was the first thing to go. They cut me off in October.
Candles kept me company when I could afford them, when I couldn't it was me and the dark.
I heard from Lorraine a few times but I didn't write back. She gave birth to twins.
A boy and a girl.
She named the boy Nathaniel Cornelius and the girl Cora Lorraine.
I didn't even write her to congratulate her.
Mr. Green came by to see me more often than he used to.
I guess Lorraine and mama musta called him and told him to look after me.
My welfare checks stopped right before Thanksgiving.
I had ignored all the letters for my follow-up sessions. The sessions were to ascertain my economic and mental situation, to see if I still needed welfare. It was real crazy of me not to go.
Soon I had no money.
So Mr. Green saw a lot of me then.
I was at his door almost every three days hoping to borrow some money. Mama sent me two hundred dollars once with a letter begging me to get some help. I ripped up the letter and went and binged the money. I didn't care.
No one cared about me, I reasoned, or else they wouldn't have left me. I was a pathetic-walking-well of self-pity. Bent on destroying myself.

I did things during this period that I had never done before.
One cold November night, after my electricity and welfare had

been cut off, I picked up a steel bar that I had found in one of the abandoned lots across the street next to the subway train yard, and waited next to the liquor store in a doorway for a suitable victim to come past. This old White man with a herring-bone coat who didn't live in our project came out the store. He looked like he had some money. He had a big bag of drink. I followed him until he got to the corner and was about to turn into Crescent Street. I quickened my pace and got in front of him. Brandishing my weapon, I demanded his bag and his money. He immediately handed them over which surprised me. He gave me those things and I should have left him.

I should have just gone home and got drunk or spent the seventy-five dollars he had left in his wallet on rocks (which I did anyway), but I didn't.

I hit the man.

Again and again.

I hit him on the head, the back, across the body, his face. . . . I actually enjoyed feeling the leaden pressure against his flesh and skull. All the pent-up rage and frustration I had been smoking out of my system (so I thought) I took out on this poor-old-helpless-little-White-man. I don't know if the man died. He should have the way I had beaten him but at the time I couldn't care.

I was not myself.

I was beyond being a ghost-person.

I was slowly becoming the thing I hated most.

I was becoming a Vampire-Zombie.

A heartless-mindless-dirty-stinkin'-fiend.

With no money comin' I vamped everyone I knew.

I stood on the corner outside the check-cashing place with my white Styrofoam coffee cup vamping total strangers.

I didn't care who I got money from just as long as I got. Food was not a priority.

Rocks and alcohol became my food.

I still had a roof over my head but I was about to lose that too.

*Something within me tried to push me toward the Rent Office
on more than one occasion, especially after I received a spate of
final warnings and the eviction notices that followed shortly
after. I ripped them all up and threw them down the incinerator.
Out of sight. Out of my mind.
I dared the worst.
I cursed the worst.
The worst cursed me back with a vengeance.*

*I tried to shut the holiday season out of my life.
I smoked all night Thanksgiving eve so I was able to sleep away
that turkey day; awakening when most people were settling
and relaxing, nursing their overfilled stomachs.
The home-cooked smells lingered in the hallway triggering
memories of the Washington family around the hearth on Thanksgiving day. Pictures which I tried to pipe-smoke away every time a
vision of turkey gobbled into my mind. Christmas and New Year's
weren't that easy to sidestep. The Christmas tree lights did me in.
The colorful patterns boxing eighty-five percent of all the
windows in our project reduced me many-a-night during that
holiday month to a blubbering two-year-old.
I loved Christmas tree lights as a child.
Visions of Santa Claus, toys, reindeer.
I remember once as a ten-year-old convincing Nate that I had
seen Santa Claus land on the roof of our project. We didn't have
a chimney so I figured Santa must have dropped down into the
incinerator vault. I just couldn't figure out how he could pull his
bag of toys through the small incinerator flap door. I remember
earnestly asking daddy how Santa Claus accomplished this.
Cornelius Sr. smiled me a loving-daddy-smile, and assured me
that in the project Santa Claus would take the stairs from the
roof which made much more sense to me.
I remembered all this during last year's dreary and dismal
holiday season.
I received a care package of gifts and money from my San*

Franciscoed family so I had Christmas pipe-money which I used to maximum effect.

I smoked away all the twelve days of Christmas, New Year's eve, New Year's day and the week after ensconced in the Centa-Renta smokin' wreaths of good cheer with my fellow addicts as we familied ourselves together. We dared not come down.

We dared not address our bleak situations.

It was a new year and it was far from happy but we still parroted the traditional pleasantries to one another each time we lit up.

We got so baked that we soon forgot why we were even wishing each other "Happy New Year!"

It became something to say like "bottoms up!" or "cheers!"

I remember stumbling out of the Centa-Renta one night in the third week of January.

I was dirty.

Stinkin'.

I hadn't changed my underwear since before Christmas, on the day my family sent me the care package.

My thoughts swam around turdlike.

Bobbing up and down in my head.

I was full of curses and bile.

A human cesspool.

Even when I saw the chain that was wrapped around my door-knob and snaked through my peephole, I didn't believe it.

I stood outside my door trying to force my key into the glued lock. I shouted and ranted.

I raved and screamed like a vampire who had arrived back at his coffin to find it filled with garlic, holy water and crucifixes. I finally sat outside my door and cried. All night.

All through that cold and eerie night one bit of scripture that daddy used to read to us kept circling through my mind like a never-ending loop. It was a verse from the book of Job.

"For the thing which I greatly feared is come upon me and that which I was afraid of is come unto me . . ."

It was so apropos.

264

I was now a fully-fledged-card-carrying-mindless-heartless-homeless Vampire-Zombie.

The sun came up and found me still outside my locked apartment. I never slept.

I sat there dazed, then started my rant anew.

I refused to leave the hallway outside my locked door.

I kept banging and shouting to what my neighbors thought was an intruder who had locked me out of my apartment.

They called the police.

The men in blue arrived and found me raving. They tried to explain to me that I had been locked out and should contact the Housing Authority but I wasn't having it. I raved incoherently on.

Finally they forcibly removed me from the floor and carried me outside the building, warning me that if I disturbed anyone else and they had to come out again I'd be locked up in jail.

This information sunk into my rock-encrusted brain and silenced me for a spell.

Until you've been made homeless, you can never know what a terrifying feeling it is.

It stops being a condition and becomes a feeling. A hopeless panicky feeling.

And especially on a freezing cold January morning and I'm thankin' what few lucky stars I have left that I did happen to have my treasured warm woolen coat, that mama sent me one Christmas, on my back when I got locked out.

Hours and days stretch ahead into each other and you're embarrassed to tell anyone what has happened.

Another denial to add to the growing list.

And I bless Mr. Green's name.

He did let me come in and take a bath a couple of times. And he did loan me underwear but I wouldn't sleep in his house.

I told him my water had been cut off but I couldn't tell him I had been locked out because I was afraid he would tell my family.

And I couldn't bear the thought that I had lost the family homestead. And in my derangement I couldn't see that perhaps if I had told him and he had contacted them, they could have helped me and spared me the horrors that were to come.

Most of the time I lived at the Centa-Renta running rocks so I could get high.

Word got 'round that I was on the skids. People started looking at me weirdly.

Maybe I just thought they were.

I was para all the time.

When my body odor got too rank and customers complained to the dealers that I was stinkin', I was fired from my rock-running job and banished to the bathroom of the Centa-Renta which was the domain of the other Vampire-Zombies.

Fighting for floor space on the cold, hard cement slabs that became my nightly bed until I took to sleeping hunched in a corner because of the sores that had opened up on my body from the hard edges and bumps of the cement floor that poked and pinched into my skin like a cement-rock bed-of-nails.

Not being able to run rocks for money, my dirtied and foul-smelling body making even begging impossible, I was forced at last to sell my coat of many memories for twenty-five dollars' worth of rocks.

I smoked each rock slowly.

Not wanting to think ahead.

It was still January.

I was not some rodent or reptile that could hibernate until the sky welcomed back the sun.

I had to face the cold.

Cold that clamped itself to your skin and bit until you were blue. Until you couldn't feel anything anymore. Until you wished that you were dead.

Afraid to go to sleep at night because you knew you wouldn't wake up. I saw a couple of Vampire-Zombies leave this earth that way during that hellish winter.

The dealers who cleaned up the bathroom would haul their bodies out like sacks of sand and fling them onto the garbage dump behind the building. These had probably been school-friends of theirs, but it didn't matter; that was then and this was now, and now they were dead-useless-stinkin' and in the way. So out the back on the garbage dump they went.

I remember my last day as a Vampire-Zombie. I woke up with a pain in my stomach.

It took me a few minutes to fathom that it was pangs of hunger I felt. I wrapped my shoulders in a huge sheet of brown wrapping paper that I had found in the Safeway garbage dump the night before while I was searching for thrown-away food that I could trade for rocks. The brown paper didn't really keep out the cold but it was something. I remember stinkin' so bad that I couldn't stand the stench and wanted to go to Mr. Green's and beg him for a bath.

This was a Sunday and I remember the Jesus people in their finery making their way to church. I approached one family and instinctively held out my hand—they all pinched their noses, fled to their car and sped off. So much for Christian charity.

I approached a few more people on the way to my building but no one gave me anything.

They treated me like the derelict tramp I was.

I found Mr. Green's door and knocked and knocked but no one answered.

This angered me no end.

I went outside to the cold and the smiling bright sunshine which didn't make the cold any easier to take.

I pulled the brown paper over my head and walked back to the Centa-Renta. I saw a bottle of what I thought was wine sitting against a building, left no doubt by some surprised wino who musta gone in a hurry. It turned out to be a three-quarter bottle of vodka. I downed the whole thing in two gulps.

It seemed to burn away the hunger for food but woke up the mighty pipe demon who started shouting boldly to my crucified mind. The pipe demon reminded me of my destitute and worthless state as I ambled aimlessly in no apparent direction. I couldn't go back into the Centa-Renta without money.
It wasn't night and they only let us Vampire-Zombies sleep there when the night came, so it meant that I'd have to walk around yet another day in the cold. I couldn't face it.
Not again.
I had to get some money . . . . any way I could.

I noticed the baby carriage in front of the corner store as I walked in to beg. The owner cursed me before I could say anything.
I didn't even think. I walked out the store, looked into the carriage, picked up the blue bundle and ran off in the direction of my building.
The scream behind me alerted me to the knowledge that the mother of the blue bundle I was carrying was in hot pursuit of me. Everything happened too fast.
I didn't wait for the elevator.
I ran up the twelve flights of stairs to the roof level.
A chorus of panicked disapproval shouted its way up the stairs.
I ran across the roof until there was nowhere else to go except back to the entrance to the roof—which was now crowded with thirty or forty angry but terror-stricken former neighbors of mine—or over the edge of the roof to the ground twelve stories below.
The mother of the blue bundle ran forward.
Fear in her eyes.
Anger on her lips.
"Gimme my baby!" she pleaded.
I never realized that I was holding the blue bundle above my head like some animated football.
"Gimme money!" I heard the voice coming thickly from my lips and then all sound ceased. All I could hear was the

DOOOOOOOOOEEEEEEEEEE bells that I always heard when I was getting an excellent rush from some excellent rocks.
I even saw what musta been the blue bundle's father rip open his wallet and throw wads of money at me.
Hitting me in the face.
He was crying and foaming at the mouth and for some strange reason this was hysterically funny to me.
I started laughing.
I forgot myself.
I forgot about the blue bundle that was still in my hand above me—a hand that was now stretched out into the air, away from the roof, above the two-hundred-foot drop.
I even forgot why I was on the roof with these screaming, crying Black people dancing fear in front of me; imploring me like so many centipedes and spiders, stretching their hands to me, reaching out to me.
And I never liked centipedes and I hated spiders so I moved away from them, even closer to the edge of the roof and the mother fainted and the father lunged at me and I brought my hands together to defend myself and I didn't see or hear the blue bundle as it fell into space, to meet the hard concrete, so far below.
And the crowd screamed a bloodthirsty scream and fell upon me like ravenous wolves, kicking and beating me.
I learned later that they threw my unconscious body over the side of the building to join the tiny, broken, bloodied corpse that had landed there on the ground before me.

The next thing I remember is waking up in too much pain in this hospital. There were weeks of tubes and wires. Months of hardened plaster and nurses attending me and doctors and police questioning me.

BUT

I recovered.
I didn't escape.
When I came to myself and the fullness of what I had done hit
me square between the eyes, I found a bunch of pills. Swallowed
them.
But the nurses caught me, pumped my stomach and revived me.
I didn't escape.
I lived.

And the pipe still talked and raged but there was nothing I
could do about it. I was on too many other drugs to even think
about catering to one that had utterly and completely destroyed
my life. And when I could get around a bit, the sessions with the
brain-scratchers started.
I told them that I didn't remember anything. That seemed to
appease them.
Now they're waiting for me to get better so I can reveal myself
to them. . . . .

So here I sit behind lock and key in this world for mentally
deranged killers and rapists.
And I belong here . . . . . I am a murderer and a rapist.
If nothing else, I murdered my life and raped my soul.
I did that to myself willingly . . . consciously . . . but I never meant
to hurt anyone else . . . it just turned out that way.
But the brain-scratchers wouldn't understand that. I wouldn't
expect anyone else to either.
I don't even understand how all this got so fucked. So I tell the
brain-scratchers nothing.
But then one day they'll read this and realize that I do
remember. I remember it all.
And I am guilty, and it is my fault, but it isn't all my fault.

I don't know what the coming days will bring.
I know I'll eventually have to go to court but I don't care, I'll get

*through that just like I've gotten through every other event in
this blistered cracked up life of mine.
Justice will prevail . . . I owe too much to too many souls . . . I will
pay the price of my deeds.*

*I always thought that I'd grow up to be a rich lawyer or
chairman of some megacorporation or at least a millionaire.
I always knew that I'd be somebody that kids could look up to
and respect.
As a teenager, my friends would embarrass me by telling me
that their mamas, when they were upset with them for being
unruly and not getting good grades, would ask them why they
couldn't be more like Cora and Cornelius's oldest boy, smart and
ambitious.
Why couldn't they be like Cornelius Edward Washington Jr.?
"That boy is going places!" they'd say. . . . . .
Well, like the song says:
"If my friends could see me now. . . . ."*

Acknowledgments

All praises to the Holy One in whom all names are blessed!
The highest thanks and praises to my key Jesus Christ.

Thank you for sharing this with me . . . I must thank **many** people
who helped me:

My parents, Mary E. Shell, Charles Shell and James Lancaster Jr.

The mother of my children, Charita Thomas . . . "It's a mystery innit!"

My babies, Katryna and Krystin Thomas-Shell, and my foster son,
Desmond Smith, for allowing their daddy to be.

My families, the Shells, the Sanders, the Lancasters, the Thomases,
the Conroys, the Hewits and the Aymers.

My sisters and brothers (I have to mention them all by name or else
there'll be intense sibling drama), Brenda, Lisa, Craig, Dana,
Emanuel, Virginia and Gayle.

All my nieces and nephews, cousins, aunts and uncles, including
Aunt Donnie, Uncle Bobbie and Sister Harris.

Oscar Johnson and Lon Satton for kidnapping me from obscurity
and hijacking me to London.

My London family, including André de Shields (who lives in New York), Shezwae Powell, P. P. Arnold, Clarke Peters, Ulla Allen, Richard Welford, Carl McIntosh, Andy Lucas, Tony Barclay, Owen Thompson (my original Street Angel editor), C. E. and Elaine Smith, Milton Brown, Debra Lewis and Baba-Tunji Williams.

Andrew Lloyd Webber, Michael Crawford and Arlene Philips for asking me to tour America.

The cast and crew of the International Company of *The Music of Andrew Lloyd Webber*—September to June 1991–1992.

My London agents: Howard Pays, Jill Edwards and Dulcie Huston at CCA.

My New York agents: Rob Kolker and Robert Attermann of Abrams & Artists.

Ty Taylor, Tom Donoghue, Jimmy Lockett and Frank Porretta, who read the first twenty-four pages and told me to finish it.

Tony Fairweather and The Write Thing for arranging the acting job in *Disappearing Acts,* which led to my publishing deal . . . and Terry McMillan for writing me the part.

Mary Clemmey, my literary agent, for guidance, support and the multiplication of the miracle . . . thank you for introducing me to a different world.

My researchers who led me through the puzzle, Julius Carter, Jr., Nicky and Jane Husband, Darren Barnes, Aloha, aka Calvin, John Henderson, Orville "Chip" Clarke, Brenda Shell and Carl Boston.

Thanks to all the Corneliuses I talked to across America who helped me nail it down.

Michael Pietsch of Little, Brown & Co., Inc.

John Saddler of Transworld Publishers Ltd.

All at HarperCollins—my editor, Jonathan Warner, for pushing me
for more and letting me know that I picked right . . . Charlotte
Windsor, who made me fight for each word ("Is it lunch time
yet?!") . . . Mike Cheyne and Jane Thurlow for the marketing
muscle . . . Laura Jennings for shouting it to the world . . . Nick Castle
for the most amazing imagery.

Susanna Porter and all at Random House,
and Elaine Markson and all at the Elaine Markson
Literary Agency, New York.

Maya Angelou for the anointing.

Norman Brown, Ruth Shane, Mickie O'Keefe and Sue Sandeman for
guidance and support during my Street Angel years . . . Chris Bond,
Hugh Quarshie, Mark Haywood, Wayne Thompson and Street Angel
Productions for putting it together and keeping it there.

Mark Motyer and Anne Harrison for taking care of my expensive
business.

My students, all my Street Angels.

Muhammad Ali, Richard Wright, Amiri Baraka, James Baldwin,
Spike Lee, Eddie Murphy, Patti LaBelle, Aretha Franklin, Michael
King Jackson, Prince, Diana Ross, The Institutional Church of God in
Christ Radio Choir, Madonna, Shirley Caesar, Nikki Giovanni and all
my mirrors of inspiration.

Dr. Ralph Jackson, Arnold McCuller, Bob Camuto, Giano Caterine, Bob
Hale, Nicholas Matthews, George Epstein, Dean Carroll, Alan
Cooke, Mical Billups, Nike, Sian Martin, David Julian and Simeon,
Dean Hall and Abdul Idrissi for being my friends and showing me
the brightest lights of love.

Thank you all.

In memory . . . my spars gone on . . . we'll play again . . . Norman Carter, Michael Rhone, Carl Weaver, Chico Kasinoir, Michael Staniforth, Diane Burnett, Tom Jobe, Stanley Ramsay and Steven Hyman.

June 1993—My tower, London, England

RAY SHELL grew up in Brooklyn, studied acting and playwriting at Emerson College, and has been a professional actor and musician ever since. In 1978 he moved to London, where he has starred in a number of musicals, including *Starlight Express* and *Miss Saigon*, and made numerous film and TV appearances. *Iced* is his first novel.

ABOUT THE TYPE

The book was set in Futura, a typeface designed by Paul Renner for the Bauer Type Foundry in 1928. The type is simple in design. Futura has a geometric structure and a perfect uniformity of stroke.